PAST PERFECT
Vacation

DEBORAH CHANTSON

OMNIFIC PUBLISHING
LOS ANGELES

Omnific Publishing

2355 Westwood Blvd., Suite 506
Los Angeles, CA 90064

www.omnificpublishing.com

First Omnific eBook edition, February 2025
First Omnific trade paperback edition, February 2025

Library of Congress Cataloguing-in-Publication Data

Chantson, Deborah.
Past Perfect Vacation / Deborah Chantson – 1st ed. ISBN: 978-1-623422-78-3
1. Contemporary Romance — Fiction. 2. Time Slip — Fiction.
3. Marriage — Fiction. 4. College — Fiction. I. Title

10 9 8 7 6 5 4 3 2 1

Cover Design by Sweet 'n Spicy Designs
Interior Book Design by Sweet 'n Spicy Designs

Printed in the United States of America

To the maternal figures in my life:
Merry, Louise, May, Marie
otherwise known as
Mom, Ai-yee, Bor-bor, Aunty

Chapter 1:

IT CAN'T STAY LIKE THIS

I hate it when people aren't introduced directly, and you're forced to figure out what their name is when somebody calls out for them. And then maybe that person just mispronounces their name, and the original person just goes along with it because it's been so long that it was mispronounced, they just got tired of correcting it.

My name is Claudia Lee. It's pronounced the North American way. Claudia, like "claw-dee-a", and Lee, like Bruce Lee, no relation. I once met someone Polish, and while she probably pronounced her own name like mine, her mom called her "cloud-ee-a". My background is Chinese, although my family is Canadian, pretty through-and-through. I've lived in Toronto my whole life.

Me in a nutshell? I just turned 40 without any celebration. I'm pregnant with my third kid. I'm 6 months along with gestational diabetes, which means I'm making three or four different meals whenever we eat. I'm exhausted. I'll get a Caesarean section for this baby, so I'm asking for my Fallopian tubes to be removed at the same time. If, for some wacky reason, it's a natural birth, though a VBAC is highly discouraged, my husband Chad is going for a vasectomy.

Did I want another kid at 40? Not at first. But maternity leave in Canada is currently (up to) 18 months, and I could use that time to just take a break from work. It sounds stupid, I know. But having a baby girl after two boys is super exciting.

Is my husband excited? His initial reaction was shock. But then again, he who put off getting the vasectomy for so long until it was definitely too late must bear the consequences. And the ironic thing was that we weren't even having sex for the longest time. It was like a sympathy romp when he felt so sad about this project they lost at work. I thought a good feel up my boobs would make him feel better. One thing led to another and now we have Baby Girl (name TBD) arriving soon.

I'm like a whale. At 2 months, my belly just puffed out like a car air bag and that's when I thought to take a pregnancy test. (I totally thought the nausea was just food poisoning and stress.) And I've totally stopped caring what people think or say for this pregnancy. During my second pregnancy, when I was only 14 weeks or something, this woman at baby gym told me I looked like I was already at 8 months. But while she bragged that she had no stretch marks, this woman looked like her plastic surgery had been botched twice and she had way too much makeup to overcompensate. Plus, her child was kind of a little demon, so you know, it really didn't bother me.

It did bother me when people asked if I was having twins though. I really ripped the pharmacist a new one when he asked. Apparently, it had something to do with high blood sugar. I don't even remember.

My current daily routine is just a whole bunch of drop-offs and pickups while trying to cram in a full day at work. It doesn't stop until I finally lie down and fall asleep instantly.

My day starts at 6 a.m. Chad just sleeps through the first hour of the alarm, and I've given up trying to wake him because he's a night owl and won't change. We made the deal that to keep his night owl tendencies, I must wake up to an empty dishwasher, empty dish rack, and the coffee maker water jug full so that I can just pop in my pod and not feel that gauntlet. I am responsible for kid daycare drop-offs because the daycare is five minutes away from my work. Getting ready in the morning is an epic daily battle.

Sometimes I wonder what my life would be like if Chad was a completely different person. Taller. Something other than white. Handsome in a make-women-swoon kind of way. Logically minded for running a household more efficiently. A more experienced, pre-domestic skill charged model. Chad's last name is Parker, and he basically looks like a younger, chubby version of Colonel Sanders now that he's grown a beard. I did not sign up for the beard when marrying him.

Timothy is 4 and my golden child. Jeremy is 2 and just starting the stubborn age. Terrible twos are no joke. But they're just so … needy. Nobody wipes their own ass. Jeremy is struggling with potty training, and I think he'll just regress when the baby is born, so I figure I'll try when I'm on maternity leave.

They couldn't reach their own bowls, so one day I moved all their bowls to a lower drawer. Except that Chad keeps forgetting and putting them back high up so the kids can't reach them.

Timothy hates milk with his cereal, so I try to portion out dry cereal (which is in a bottom cupboard) into an easy open container the night before, and that way he can feed himself if he gets up early. Jeremy is … something else.

This morning is particularly hectic. Jeremy has taken Timothy's cereal and thrown it on the floor. He wants to get dressed lying down and Timothy is now crying because he needs new cereal.

Just as I'm cursing Chad for sleeping through all this, he waltzes through the living room.

I hear his footsteps down the stairs and I'm like a lion ready to pounce.

"Chad! Help get Jeremy dressed! Don't forget the moisturizer first." He always forgets.

The poor kid's skin dries up and leaves terrible rashes.

I gingerly step over the spilled cereal except my efforts are futile when I hear the familiar pop and crunch under my slippers. I get Timothy a new bowl then stuff blueberries and frittata into my mouth while I log them into my food app. I can't find frittata, so for logging purposes, it just becomes "cheese". Suddenly, I look up and Chad is going on about the cereal on the floor.

"Who made this mess and didn't clean it up?"

"It's Jeremy!" Timothy sputters out between chews.

"All right, Jerry, let's vacuum it up together. We have to be responsible for our actions." I watch as Chad walks away to get the vacuum and Jeremy plays with the mess like it's a sandbox. He tries to force Jeremy's hands as if to make him vacuum it up himself.

I snap at this charade. "Chad, can you just vacuum it up for him? We gotta go." I look at the clock – there's only 10 minutes before we need to leave.

"Oh shit, I'm late!" Chad screams, dropping everything. "Early morning meeting, sorry, bye!" And he dashes off. Literally runs to his car as I'm screaming out the front door, "Don't forget to pick up the kids from daycare tonight!" I'll have to text him later because I'm speaking at a university panel tonight. He has to get them.

I give a fruit pouch to Jeremy while I fall to the floor in a heap. Bending is really taxing on my body. I vacuum up the cereal and then it takes me a bit to get back up. Jeremy wants another pouch. I open two yogurt ones, then get dressed. I'll do my makeup in the car after they're at daycare. I brush teeth and scoop up all the winter gear to throw in the car. The saving grace is that I've managed to alpha female and park in our attached garage (also because Chad usually leaves first in the mornings – I know.) I throw both their coats into the middle seat and boost up Timothy. He lucks out and gets his seatbelt in on the first go. I wrestle Jeremy into his car seat while he noodles (goes limp) so it's basically impossible. He flops forward and suddenly I'm trying to lift and hold his bowling ball of a head with my wrist then maneuvering with both hands to get him strapped him and …

"OH MY GOD, STOP IT!" I scream so loudly that it stops both children in their tracks and then they both start crying. I open the garage and a neighbor is staring. I wave at her somewhat sarcastically when I'd like to turn my wave into a "flee now" kind of gesture before I tear it up down the driveway.

And just as we arrive at daycare, I hear Jeremy throwing up in the backseat.

Chapter 2:

NONSENSICAL MEETINGS WITHOUT FOOD SHOULD BE BANNED

*N*ormally you can't drop off a kid at daycare who has just thrown up, but today is a day where I NEED to be that asshole parent. I've got too many meetings, plus the event tonight.

Miraculously, he mostly threw up on the blanket I had over him so I didn't have to wrestle his coat on over top the harness, so I toss the blanket in the garbage (it was really on its last legs and threadbare) and with a quick wet wipe and minimal conversation with any grownup, I manage to drop off both kids and flee like the wind.

I'm still seething about Chad fleeing the house this morning like he did. Especially after sauntering downstairs in such a leisurely fashion. It's a common occurrence, and it totally makes me question whether I should prepare myself to be a single mom with three kids. As a member of the household who also eats and showers and uses copious amounts of electricity and toilet paper, and as the father to the offspring who also live there, I really don't understand how I let it happen that he does the bare minimum. And then again, I'm resentful that it boils down to this feeling of *I let it happen.*

It's to the point of wondering whether a divorce is worth it. But at this stage of my life, I can't financially swing it. Nor do I want to move houses or deal with a newborn by myself.

Every day, I tell myself to expect nothing of him, but that's impossible because he's an able-bodied grown-ass man who is awake at overlapping hours with the children. So, I've boiled down my expectations to this: keep his pay cheque flowing into the bank account. When I have my body back and can sleep for longer than two hours at a time, I'll figure out what my next move should be post-returning to work.

I don't see us being a long-term plan ... that ship sailed ages ago.

I pull into my office parking garage, quickly do my make-up (which will have to be redone later for the evening look), and rush in so I still keep up the "I got here before you so that's why I'm leaving before you" dance. The building is huge, so the lobby is very nondescript, but when you get up to our floor, it's quite a welcoming, functional space with big white leather couches and colorful throw pillows. Though they also use this space often for parties, so it's got a club vibe when you dim the lights.

My official title is Spot Producer in the commercials division at Global Spin Advertising, but it's such a vague title covering multiple jobs. At this place, it's supposed to mean I manage shooting commercials for our clients on a logistical front. I'm not supposed to deal with the concept and writing phases, I'm supposed to execute and get spots done when that's ready to go. What I really want is to work with the team that does all the pro bono stuff – cancer research fundraising, disabled foundation awareness ... the award-winners. Then I wouldn't mind being in from the ground up.

For now, I slog at this, and somehow, I make it home most nights to pick up the kids and go home for dinner. Only on shoot days does it get long and tiring, and then it's a whole thing of coordinating someone to pick up the kids from daycare and get them to bed on time. That's a whole other set of complicated issues.

Today we've got a meeting about a new commercial that shoots about two months from now. I'm the only person of color and most of the time it doesn't bother me, except that today it feels weird because the boardroom has 20 white people ... and me. One Asian female. There are usually four white women here – one sort of punk-like as if the look should have faded out in high school for her, and three others are pretty blondes (dyed) who honestly strike me as assistants from their lack of engagement in the conversation, but I can't fully tell.

I excel at most of this job ... I don't enjoy the people part of it but unfortunately that comes with the territory. My patience is short, I'm constantly exhausted, and quite frankly, I'd love to do most of this work at home, except that I fully admit that I would bugger off and take a most-of-the-day nap if left by myself in peace. After all, being pregnant and this gigantic means you want to stay put (and keel over) when you're not running off to the bathroom when this parasite-like mass (okay, child) within you is hammering on your bladder. And I do love sole access to my home bathroom.

I've done about a week's worth of work on this campaign in coordinating schedules and people and shoot days, blah blah blah. This particular team works best if there's a shoot day, and the hard, absolute deadline kicks their asses in gear. The only thing left is to find the talent that's available, but the client group has been going back and forth with the casting director over what they really want. The casting director is not at this meeting since she's working another job today and holding auditions. And the truth is that she doesn't need to be here – she's just waiting for them to articulate their wish list. But for some reason, the leader-like, or at least most vocal, white lady of this pack (who I've only met today and reminds me of a redheaded

Paula Deen) has some kind of vendetta against Cheryl. This lady also has a British accent that actually sounds kind of fake. Every once in a while, her "cahn't" and "shant" disappear and she sounds a little … New Jersey-like.

"Cheryl only needs you to figure out descriptions for the last two characters and then we're set," I say pragmatically, trying to bring it back to facts. I get up to the whiteboard, writing two checkboxes. "Character descriptions for casting." Checkbox 1. Checkbox 2.

Good grief. That sets off a whole different conversation. And this client has a weird non-hierarchical structure, so they must all creatively come to some consensus without a proper leader.

We go back and forth for an hour on what kind of person the scuba diver should be. It's such a ridiculous conversation that veers off into football, so I text Chad under the table.

Don't forget to pick up kids. Am speaking at UofT tonight for panel.

I'm really excited. It's the University of Toronto's Isabel Bader theatre where I've sat in so many lectures. Now I get to be on stage.

I usually give up on waiting for a response from him, but this feels like a big deal since it's been booked for months, and I've sent him dozens of Google Calendar reminders. Plus, I've got a really nice black dress hanging up in my cubicle that I'm going to change into before I go. Despite being pregnant, it hugs my figure and makes me feel elegant with my black boots since I can't wear stilettos like I'd like to. Some pregnant ladies can – not this one. Oh, if only that dress would look as good on my not pregnant body …

This stupid meeting conversation breaks my fashion daydream.

Most of the time it doesn't matter as much to me that I'm

the only person of color, but then some days … like apparently today … it all comes to a head.

"Claudia, what do you think if they're at an Indian restaurant?" says Boris, a tall blonde guy who I generally don't mind but today pisses me off with his constant veering off topic.

"I don't know, Boris, I'm not sure what an Indian restaurant would do when I thought it was decided they're scuba divers finding rare specimens underwater," I reply carefully.

What the fuck? Can you just let us go home already?

Boris clears his throat. "What I mean to say, is that they wouldn't have to be scuba divers. They could be … scientists! In an Indian restaurant. Would that be … okay? I mean, we'd check that diversity box, you know?"

Goddammit. Ugh.

I take a deep breath and try to answer as tactfully as possible when I want to smack this man pretty much half the time I see him. Or the times like now, when he just flips my ambivalent switch to rage mode.

"For starters, Boris, checking a diversity box for the sake of it is always overly obvious, especially in a case where the context makes zero sense. So, what I suggest might be a better approach is having the scuba divers be Black females."

Hunh. For once, everybody around the table is nodding in agreement.

I'm already gathering up my papers and that's the last checkmark off my list. Sweet relief! And they can all see that Boris is being absurd.

"Great! I'll ask Cheryl for two beautiful Black female scuba divers –"

"– wait, what if we make the scuba divers … dogs?"

What the royal fucking fuck, stupid ass Devin?

"I'm sorry?" I sputter.

"Yeah – people love dogs!" The two blonde assistants nod like bobbleheads. "I can totally get on board with a dog.

Can they be Pomeranians?"
I want to quit right now.
Nobody even notices me leaving the meeting rolling my eyes.

Chapter 3:

THE ADVICE YOU GIVE

*T*here's a new nonbinary intern named Lex who's been bugging me to give them more challenging work lately, so I head over to their cubicle. I don't know what they're doing here in advertising. From all our interactions, they hate people, they hate selling things, and they don't watch TV with ads. But they're a keen worker and I'll take that any day. Lex is some kind of other white mix (Italian-Ukrainian?) with thick black-framed rectangular glasses, multiple piercings, and rainbow hair. I hate throwing them in with that boardroom crowd, but the likelihood of heteronormative bullshit is far less so than microaggressions. I refuse to throw another person of color into that lion's den.

My shadow is already looming down the hall. Damn you, pregnancy waddle and shallow breath. Fuck it, I yell from where I am.

"Lex, I've got a job for you."

"I'm on it! What is it?" Lex replies quickly, bolting toward me.

"Do you have plans tonight?"

"Free and clear."

"Your task is to babysit that boardroom. They need to fill out the two blanks on the white board about the casting before they leave. If they're still here at 4:30, order dinner like you did last night. Don't forget to order an expensive dinner and dessert for yourself."

I get all wink, wink, nudge, nudge and Lex nods, getting it.

"If they can't come up with a decision by 7 p.m., threaten them with having to schedule a second shoot day 6 months from now because that's when that director they love so much is available again."

Lex is writing this all down. I love that. And I hate that Lex will be the best intern to up and leave us for greener pastures because they're awesome but completely ill-suited for this company.

"K, thanks, bye!" And I literally run-waddle away.

Before I set off to drive downtown, I text Chad again.

Haven't heard from you. Assume you are busy. Remember to pick up kids from daycare by 6!

I call Chad's office. I sweetly ask Amanda, Chad's department administrative assistant, to remind Chad to pick up the kids tonight, and she cheerfully says that when she sees him, "Will do!" Has she seen him at all today? "Yes, I saw him this morning."

I'm relying on Chad and super paranoid because our backup person is busy tonight. She's the person organizing the panel! Ciara (pronounced "kee-ra") Son is a gorgeous, brilliant professor in marketing and behavioral science – and my best friend since high school. She's two years older (42), but we met volunteering for the library homework helpers. Ciara is this superhuman triathlete, supermom of 10-year-old twins (boy Kent and girl Kelly), and super Asian fluent in Korean and Cantonese. Her neurosurgeon husband Jason is Japanese and she's learning to speak it better than him.

The event tonight is this panel about ethics in advertising, and as a commercial producer at Global Spin, I can talk about previous clients without feeling like I'm compromised on their products, so long as I don't mention the brand names. I can talk about better or worse campaigns, advertising spot strategy, aims, hits and misses. Like I said, my job entails far more than the title lets on.

Since Chad is picking up the kids, Ciara and I are going for dinner at this well, romantic (like dark and candlelit) steakhouse after the panel – I've already carb-counted my meal in anticipation. Steak, mushrooms, onions, cauliflower/turnip purée, with roasted asparagus and broccoli. All the vegetables I won't cook at home because my kids subsist on chicken nuggets, fried rice, and mac and cheese. I'm looking forward to a gestational diabetes-friendly meal, plus, it's one-on-one catch-up time with my bestie!

The panel starts at 5 p.m. I shouldn't be nervous but I try to wolf down a cold piece of frittata to keep up my blood sugar so I won't faint. The theatre is filling up – I didn't realize there would be so many attendees, but I can see this is half public, half student-oriented. Ciara also has a following of sorts because her lectures are fascinating and her students are always putting her sound bites on TikTok (that's how she regularly gets on the news too), so I'm unsurprised but wasn't totally psychologically prepared for a full house. I hope I sound smart. But if anything, I look freaking amazing in this dress. My baby bump is the cutest! And my hair is so shiny and full right now!

Ciara is the moderator, and there are four other people on this panel. From where I'm sitting, I don't know who they are and I can't see their nameplates. There's a woman on the end who reminds me of my free-spirited hippie art teacher aunt; a man from Chicago next to her who is surprisingly sexy despite a receding hairline; a woman in the middle who looks a lot like Ciara's mom but I know isn't; and the man beside me who looks like Ian Hanomansing meets Steve Jobs (for what he's wearing, including the glasses). Then me!

The first half-hour is taken up by experts discussing advertising to children – where and when is appropriate and how advertising online becomes both a reachability and liability

issue. I try to stay attentive as a mom, but somehow my blood
sugar is dropping as it gets further into the dinner window, and
I keep thinking how I'm glad I wore the incontinence underwear in case I couldn't make it to the bathroom in time. From
my university days and having used it before the panel, it's still
one of the nicest bathrooms on the downtown campus. Not a
matter of finding it, just a matter of getting there after a long
line at this rate. Ciara breaks my stupor by gently giving me a
heads-up pointer mouthing "Ready?" and I nod yes.

Ciara: "Claudia, can you tell us a bit about what
commercials for children are like in your experience?"

"Oh, it's hell," I say glibly. And the crowd roars with
laughter. Wonderful, I'm entertaining right off the bat and it's
the first thing I've said.

I say something intelligent about the aims of toy companies eventually calling the shots because children's cable TV
and streamer series are fundamentally built to sell toys, and I get
cut off by the male professor near the other end of the table
who astutely recognizes PBS and educational television's role
in edutainment. I concur and say something smart to save face.

Ciara brings it back to me. "It seems like you have an
interesting story about to surface. How does your experience
working with children differ from adults?"

As politely as I can, and without recriminating details,
I recall a story about working with a pair of siblings several years ago who have since gone on to be big stars in
Hollywood. The little one was a pre-reader, fine, but locked
herself in her mother's car for two hours and ran our schedule
into the ground. The older sibling kept messing up lines and
for the simple reason that he just couldn't read. Not from any
learning disability or dyslexia but was just lazy as fuck. He'd
coasted through "homeschooling" because his mother was
constantly taking him to auditions, but they'd auto-read their
scripts while driving to memorize lines because apparently, he
was a better audio-learner.

"I assume he learned to read by now, but this is the experience that makes me suggest puppets, stop-motion, animation – anything to avoid working with children in live-action settings."

Somehow, I manage to keep the crowd entertained with my stories of testing audiences; reshooting commercials based on feedback; and bringing it home … the ethics of advertising to children. Ciara is mouthing "wow" to my responses and I can tell she's so proud of herself for inviting me to this panel because I'm, apparently, hilarious.

We get to the Q&As, and a young Black woman in her 20s stands up to the mic. I expect she has a question for one of the real experts, but oh shit, it's for me!

"Claudia? Thank you so much for your fascinating insight."

Fascinating insight … well thank YOU.

"What advice could you give us young 20-year-olds getting into the business. Maybe we can avoid some pitfalls?"

I feel my chair buzzing, but I'm focused on the question.

Ah crap, the young advice question. Hmm … try to be inspirational, Claudia.

"I think being able to think creatively is really important in this business, so if that's not up your alley, then try something else. However, being able to relate to people is a huge part of any business, particularly this one. Advertising is about appealing to people's needs and desires. Dr. Son can tell you all about that. So, I'd say … meet everybody you can. Have long conversations. Get deep. Experience as much as you can, you know, safely. And for general advice being in your 20s: read. Travel. Learn. Indulge your passions! That's just me, talking as a woman pregnant with my third kid." I glance and see young women smiling and nodding.

"And in general, knowing who you are and setting healthy boundaries will do a lot for you in the long run."

My phone keeps buzzing repeatedly now. I rustle through

my purse as I vaguely hear the girl's appreciative thank you and see "KIDS DAYCARE" as the caller ID for the call I just missed. It's the 20th call. The last text message says:

No one has arrived to pick up your children! Please contact us ASAP!

It's already 6:15 p.m. and they charge $5 per minute that you're late past 6 p.m. per child.

Oh fuck.

Chapter 4:

YOU WILL FEEL MY WRATH ... EVENTUALLY

iara sees my face go white and immediately walks over to cover my mic.

"What happened?" she asks.

"Chad didn't pick up the kids ..." I stammer.

She immediately makes eye contact with Jason in the front row of the crowd and summons him. As I hear Ciara saying something about me having a family emergency to the crowd, Jason swiftly leads me offstage and outside, into a cab pulling over for us.

"Scoot in, I'm coming with you," he orders. I do as he says, and he tells the cab driver, a Cantonese woman in her 50s, that we're going to Joyful Daycare near Yonge and Eglinton and we need to get there as fast as possible and that her tip will be enormous.

"No problem," she quips back and floors it like I've never seen a cab driver even attempt.

I'm shaking and trying so hard not to cry.

I call the daycare. Sherry, my favorite teacher, answers. "Claudia?!" Her voice sounds frantic. "Are you okay?!"

I burst into tears and verbal diarrhea just spews out.

"I'm so sorry! I was a speaker at this big event and Chad was supposed to pick up the kids and I have no idea where he is!" I sob. "I'm at Bay and Bloor in a cab and I'll be there as soon as I can! I'm so sorry!"

"Okay ... I'm the only staff member here," she says slowly

… and I can tell it's a mixture of frustration and disappointment and probably anger. "You know about the late fee, right?"

"I do, I'm so sorry!" She hangs up without saying goodbye. And now I'm extra upset that now we're in her bad books.

My mind is racing at a million miles per minute.

Holy fuck, I want to scream. How do you forget your own fucking children?? Knowing him, I bet he forgot. You'd better be in a hospital, Chad William Parker. Oh my God, no, don't be in a hospital. What if something terrible has happened to you? What if I now have to take care of you too? But this is something you'd do. I shouldn't be surprised. You always think of yourself first. WHO FORGETS THEIR KIDS? Am I not allowed ONE night out? How am I having your third child? How did I have your first two?

I hold and watch my phone, constantly calculating how much I owe the daycare as the minutes tick by, clearing the daycare's multiple voicemails and missed calls and texts. I frantically search through my phone for any kind of message that I might have missed from Chad. Or any call or message from an unknown number. Nothing besides the daycare. And an email from Lex saying they've forwarded the casting descriptions to Cheryl the casting director.

It suddenly dawns on me that Jason is giving the cab driver directions which is why he's not talking to me.

"Take a left here, we can shortcut it through this alley," he hurriedly directs while somewhat following Waze directions on his phone.

"I know, I know!" the driver shouts back.

During peak rush hour, the drive from the theatre to the daycare might take around 30-45 minutes. Toronto traffic is like that. A GPS estimate often becomes double the time, especially in the rain. Miraculously, the two of them get us there in 9 minutes. And it's a clear night.

"Go, go!" Jason yells unnecessarily at me. I rush to the front door, sobbing as I see my kids in the front coatroom area.

Sherry is getting their stuff together and comes to unlock it as I stand there, tears streaming down my face as I hug both kids.

"BAD MOMMY!" Jeremy screams. "Time out for you! No i-cweam!"

"You forgot us!" Timothy wails and jabs his uncoordinated little fingers at me.

"I would never forget you! Daddy was supposed to come today!" I wail back.

Sherry doesn't even make eye contact with me. She's the most cheerful person ever and it kills me to see her this mad.

"The late fee will be automatically withdrawn from your bank account," she spits out.

"I'm so sorry for ruining your evening!" I wish this was Korea or another East Asian country where I could repeatedly bow to physically show how sorry I am.

"I was supposed to see a movie with my sister, but I won't get there in time now. And she pre-bought the tickets," Sherry says with a big sigh that makes my heart drop even more.

I quickly rummage through my purse for my wallet and pull out a $100 bill I keep for emergencies.

"Here! To cover the tickets!" I thrust the money into her hand.

She's a little taken aback, but it softens her.

"Thank you," she says quietly. "I hope your husband is okay."

"If he is, I'm going to kill him," I say exasperatedly as I recover between sobs.

"See you tomorrow," Sherry says while locking the door. She quickly disappears. I turn around and Jason is waiting patiently.

"Thank you so much, Jay - oh my God! My car!" I scream. "How do I take the kids home from here?!"

He doesn't really hear me because the kids have run into his arms.

"Uncle Jason!" they scream. It's a real treat seeing

Uncle Jason on a weeknight because they usually only see him on weekends and holidays.

"You guys are coming home with me for dinner while Mommy goes to see Aunty Ciara for dinner and gets her car!"

"What? Seriously?"

Jason smiles. "Totally. I'll walk them to our place from here. You get on the subway and meet Ciara. Just drop her off at home, 'k?"

"Oh my goodness, thank you so much." I'm overwhelmed with gratitude. I start crying again.

"Hey, hey! Come on now, it's okay." Jason hugs me tightly. "The cab! Sorry, here --" I reach for my wallet.

"Don't worry about it!" He physically puts my wallet back in my purse for me.

"Thanks so much. We'll get back quickly."

Again, he waves me off in that "no big deal" way about him.

I don't have a thing for any of my friends' husbands or significant others, and Jason is physically nothing of what I want in a guy, but at this very moment, I'm incredibly jealous of Ciara. I don't know if it was his idea or hers, but the fact that Jason was willing to execute the plan of taking my small kids home by himself, in fact carrying one and holding the other's hand as far as he can tolerate ... I can hardly believe my eyes.

I snap a photo with my phone.

And Jason often does super thoughtful things for Ciara. When he can, he attends big talks like the one tonight where his wife isn't even the main headline. He accompanies her to university events. He does this eye gaze flirting thing with her when they go to swanky hospital foundation dinners. I mean, he doesn't volunteer for the Parent/Teacher Association or manage the kids' daily school things, but he's a hell of a lot more present than Chad is and ever will be. And he's a freaking neurosurgeon! AND he plans their surprise date nights! Successfully!

The subway station is a bit of a hike from the daycare, but there are malls close by and I stop for the bathroom, because … pregnant. I check my phone and see Ciara's kind texts about meeting her at Bloor-Yonge station at street level. We'll grab a quick dinner then head back uptown together ASAP.

Not a peep from Chad. I text him before I get into the subway going southbound.

Cannot BELIEVE you did not pick up kids. Hope you are ok. Am waiting for explanation otherwise. Am FURIOUS. Kids w/ Jason. Going on subway downtown to get my car now.

I consider also texting, "sleep with one eye open" then delete it. I also delete the middle finger emoji. After all, what if he's lying in a hospital bed?

The ride from Eglinton to Bloor-Yonge has all the problems and delays that could possibly happen and make me even more grateful that Jason just got us both into a cab earlier on. I'm grateful for the cab driver, even though her driving is probably a public safety concern. I'm grateful for my friends, who have been like family to me for decades and totally come through for me on unprecedented occasions such as this.

And while my thoughts are spinning, it dawns on me that Jason can be so helpful and attentive because of their live-in nanny/housekeeper Mariana. Mariana is Brazilian and has been with them since Ciara was pregnant with the twins. Mariana used to be a pediatrician but fled Brazil when her abusive, gambling, alcoholic husband started getting tangled up with the neighborhood gang. Ciara and Jason lobbied so hard for Mariana's legal status in Canada that she feels indebted to stay with them, even though I've heard them encouraging her to get requalified in Canada. She won't. She feels like her name would become internet searchable and her life would again be in danger.

But I can also see why they don't push too hard. She runs

their household and keeps everything stocked. Tidy. Beautiful. She buys groceries and cooks for them. She'll probably be the one running downstairs to make my kids grilled cheese sandwiches when they arrive tonight.

My mind returns to stewing over Chad and the events of tonight. The train finally reaches Bloor-Yonge. I go up to street level and as I'm about to check my phone for her whereabouts, Ciara appears in front of me, ending a phone call.

"Let's go for steak," Ciara says soothingly while taking my arm. "You still fucking furious?"

"SO fucking furious," I steam. "Your husband is a saint by the way." I show her the picture and smile. I send it to her.

"Nah, he was in the dog box for something which I already worked out with my therapist and don't need to further sully our evening with, but going down on me still wasn't enough to smooth any of that over. He's trying for brownie points."

"Is it working?"

"Yeah ..." she shrugs. "You were amazing tonight, by the way. Before you had to run out."

"Thanks."

Wait a second ...

"How come no one is concerned that Chad might be in a ditch or hospital bed somewhere?"

"Oh honey," Ciara physically stops. "This is just a thing we expect of Chad. To forget his own children. Or pawn off the responsibility on someone else."

We enter our favorite steakhouse where Ciara is friendly with the hostess – apparently a student of hers. We sit down at the table and before we've even barely sat down, our food arrives – and the plate is exactly what I was dreaming of: the gestational diabetes-friendly steak, mushroom, onion, roasted vegetable medley. And a tall glass of icy water.

"What is this magic?!" I exclaim with pure joy.

"I called ahead," Ciara says nonchalantly. "When I got

you from the subway station. And this is what you messaged me yesterday. I could imagine you drooling while typing that."

I remember none of this, but I blame pregnancy brain. Which actually hasn't been that bad this time around. I've managed to maintain all kinds of details about that stupid commercial shoot – which I will only think about in the morning at this rate.

I don't realize I've gone silent and I'm just staring at my food until Ciara sneezes into her elbow.

"Oh, sorry," I say and continue with my food, which is delicious.

"Do you need to vent some more?"

I take a deep breath. "My brain hurts. I'll wait until there's new information."

"Can I talk about something entirely unrelated?"

"Sure."

"I'm thinking of cutting back on Mariana's hours with us," Ciara says quietly.

"WHAT?!" I don't recognize the volume of my voice until Ciara looks around and gestures for me to quiet down.

"She's like Mary Poppins and Geoffrey from *Fresh Prince* and Mr. Belvedere and Carson from *Downton Abbey* ..." those are all the outdated references to household managers I can think of.

"I know," Ciara says guiltily. "It's not like we're going to cut her salary or anything or even ask her to leave the house. I mean, she's family. But Kent and Kelly need to learn to be more independent. And when they're at extra-curriculars most days, we don't really need her to be around as much."

"Uh ... me, here – send her my way please." The words coming out of my mouth must be reflecting the what the fuck wavelength I have going on in my head.

"I didn't want to send her back down the nanny path, Clauds. I want her to move on from it."

"Please can I have your permission to ask her? I'll match

her salary per hour but I need Mariana or a Mariana-type person in my life."

Should I get on my knees to beg?

She slowly and thoughtfully relents. "Yeah … I'm sorry I didn't think of you sooner. Your husband might be a Senior Engineer for military-grade cyber information systems security… but he's got shit for brains, and you need help. But only if she agrees."

"Totally."

"And you have to give her a cooling off period to change her mind if she agrees."

"Absolutely."

"And if she's on the clock, she takes care of your kids at your house, not mine."

"Didn't even need to be said."

"Okay."

My eyes go wide. This opens a world of possibilities. I never thought of a nanny because in my mind, daycare was sufficient. But after tonight's ordeal, it won't just be a spiral toward the end of Chad and I, it'll be the end of me.

Ciara insists on treating for dinner tonight as thanks for participating in the panel, which she can write off as a business expense anyway, then drives us in my car back to her place with the reasoning that I might be too anxious. She also often prefers to be in the driver's seat as opposed to the passenger seat.

My body wins out over my mind this time. I wake up startled when we pull into her driveway.

"Did my phone go off? Chad?"

She shakes her head, resigned.

When we go in, all the kids are on Ciara and Jason's giant plushy sectional. Kent and Kelly are reading chapter books aloud in their pajamas, seemingly unaware that they've put my kids to sleep. Jason is asleep on the opposite end from the kids. He wakes up to Ciara's sweet, gentle kiss on his lips. I can't even remember the last time I kissed Chad like that. I get pangs of both jealousy and heartache.

Kent and Kelly give me lackluster hugs before heading upstairs. It's late. Time for bed.

Jason and Ciara put Timothy and Jeremy in their car seats while I use the bathroom one more time. I gratefully hug them goodbye, thanking them profusely for all their help.

When we get home, there's still no word from Chad. Part of me continues to worry, but my priority right now is getting these kids to bed.

I can't lift them, so it's lucky that they wake up with a second wind as if it's a sugar rush.

So I use the opportunity to do a proper bedtime routine with them. I get them to shower at the same time in the primary bathroom, quickly scrubbing and hosing them off. They get pajamas on and we read a bedtime story about a bear meeting bears of other colors and finding out how interesting their colors and experiences make them. Diversity in bears. But it's something, sigh.

I keep checking my phone, wondering now if I should call around to hospitals. The kids are finally asleep, and I figure I'll shower quickly now because who knows what the next hours could look like.

As I feel the hot water coming down, I'm a swirling tornado of emotions and the rage returns. Chad acknowledged my request to leave work early when we first talked about it and accepted the calendar invite with all the reminders. It's usual for him to ignore me and most of what I say. He completely expects that the kids will be my number one priority and that I should be the one to drop everything for them, including my career and social engagements. Like the 1950s.

I dry off and walk back into the bedroom. It's lit softly by both bedside lamps. DAMMIT, the kids are still awake!

Timothy rubs his eyes. "You have to fall asleep with us, Mommy."

"Yeah," agrees Jeremy, though sleepily.

"Okay!" I snuggle into bed with them.

"I wuv you, Mommy," says Jeremy as he puts his arms around my neck.

"Are we going to live with you forever?" Timothy asks.

"You can live with me as long you like, but you have to pay rent when you get a good job." I snuggle up and smother them both with kisses until they giggle.

"What's rent?" Timothy pipes up.

"Go to sleep!" I say with a laugh.

I send quick emails to say that we are all calling in sick both at work and at daycare (with profuse apologies once again). I watch as my sweet boys, all clean with that fresh baby smell, fall fast asleep with their long eyelashes clear against beautiful smooth cheeks. They breathe deeply and even their breathing is cute when they're asleep.

They take up so much of my energy when they're awake, but they are sleeping angels and I can't help but adore them and feel grateful that they are my boys.

I try to reassure myself that they were at a safe place tonight because if anything happened to them, I can't even fathom my devastation and heartbreak.

I kiss both boys on their cheeks, nuzzling them, which barely disturbs them so that they only roll over and away from me.

The sound of my buzzing phone on the nightstand wakes me up at 4 a.m.

It's Chad calling.

Chapter 5:

I JUST CAN'T WITH YOU

I grab the phone and tumble out of bed. I'm used to him working late and not telling me where he is, but 4 a.m. is extreme for calling when he'd usually just sneak in and go straight to bed.

"Hello?" My voice is raspy. I half expect someone else's voice to greet me, so I brace myself.

"Clauds? I'm so sorry."

It's him. And he sounds fine. My blood starts boiling and I amble down the hall so the kids won't hear me explode.

"You'd better have a fucking amazing explanation for fucking up tonight," I start.

"I know. I'm in Seattle right now."

"Seattle? Did someone kidnap you?"

"It feels like it. I can't say much, this is an unsecured line. I had to go to work early because they said a VIP was coming. As soon as I got there, a bunch of US army guys came into my office and said they needed three of us to get on a military jet. I was looking at my senior management the whole time, and they're nodding like, 'yeah, yeah just go.' I was a little suspicious, then I saw this guy we worked with last month in the lobby and he's briefing me the whole time on stuff that sounds familiar, so before we get on the jet, I ask this guy where we're going and he says, 'Ya have your passport on you?' I said, 'yeah, I got the card.' He says, 'Good, we're going to Washington, DC'. I said, 'Okay but I need to be back by 5 p.m. I got kids to pick up from daycare.' The pilot says, 'Roger that.' Then we take off.'"

I get that Chad is a Senior Engineer for Keeman Morleys in military-grade cyber information systems security, so he could be telling the truth. But he also does this thing where he embellishes his stories at parties, or when he knows he might have a captive audience in say, a family gathering of his, or airport lounge, and I can't tell whether this is one of those times or not.

It should also be noted that the only reason Chad has a US passport card at all is because I applied for it for him (and finagled the special appointment with a friend at an Acceptance Facility months ahead of when she could next book anyone else) as I apply for all types of important documentation in this household. I do that because he'll say things like, "I did it, but I haven't heard anything" but then when you ask him about application copies, records or tracking numbers, he has none, circling back to never having done it in the first place.

For the purposes of this "explanation," I give him the benefit of the doubt and let him carry on.

"I tried texting you just before we took off but everyone is like, 'Turn off your phone! Turn off your phone!' And when we land, I'm like, 'I need to call my wife right now!' This huge dude who makes The Rock look small gets in my face and says, 'This location is top secret. You are prohibited from disclosing any details'."

I'm tired. And this sounds more like Chad's brand of bullshit - when he gets the reenactment voices going.

"So why are you in Seattle now?" I sigh.

"It's the counterpart office. After we fixed the problems in DC, they flew us here."

"And you didn't think to say, 'This was a mistake, my kids come first, I can't go, I have to get back, or can someone else call my wife'?"

"They thought I was joking!"

I'm glad it's a regular phone call and not a video chat

because I roll my eyes and facepalm. If we were having this conversation in person, I might not have held back on slapping him.

"If they thought you were joking, that means they couldn't tell that that you were serious about getting to your children!" I scream.

"I tried! I really did! And then when my phone died, I just blanked on your number to dial it from a landline."

Holy shit, you are the stupidest man on the planet.

"If you were at a computer, you couldn't have Googled my office line? Emailed me? Started a social media account to DM me? Googled the daycare to get in touch with me? Googled Ciara? Or Jason?"

"Oh yeah … sorry. I thought about that, and then military people just kept barking orders at me!"

I heave a long, exasperated sigh not knowing what to say or do about this man as he continues to ramble on.

"I was waiting for them to bring me back but the jet took off without us for more important people. They're putting me up in a hotel room until they can fly me back on a regular flight. But there's thunderstorms and lightning happening here so all the flights are being cancelled until further notice."

"Yeah, okay. I'm gonna go now."

"Oh, yeah, you should get to bed, it's late."

"I was in bed. It's past 4 a.m."

"Really? Oh right, time zone. Sorry. Man, maybe it's the adrenaline pumping from the day! Oh no, my phone is down to 5% …"

I just hang up, because otherwise I will say regrettable things. I also don't want to waste my breath because it's a phone call and the only time I can ensure that Chad absolutely hears the words coming out of my mouth are when he nods and repeats them back to me, then answers a follow-up comprehension question.

WHY THE FUCK AM I HAVING THIS MAN'S

THIRD BABY?!

One great thing about this pregnancy is that while not pregnant, I might have stewed and brewed over the conversation and stayed awake and spun about wasting energy over a story that sounds faintly possible given his job and clearance, plus the fact that he didn't even ask what happened with the kids really pisses me off, but after I go to the bathroom, I snuggle into bed with my kids and fall fast asleep.

Everything can wait until I wake up.

Chapter 6:

IT'S ABOUT TO GET LOOPY

*M*iraculously, the kids let me sleep in until 9. Even more miraculously, Jeremy's diaper doesn't leak and with a dry diaper, I get him to the potty in time and we both feel victorious. I tell him I'm going to buy them ice cream later today! And then I remember that I can't have any because of stupid gestational diabetes. That's okay. I will get a small sample spoon and will have to be satisfied.

We have a lazy morning and I think about where to take these kids where we can park nicely, I can use the double stroller so I'm not at risk of having to carry anyone when they get cranky, and I can store a bunch of things without having to carry that either. I choose the Beaches which will be fine on a weekday morning.

While the kids play "petting zoo" with their zillions of stuffed animals all over the living room, I bake frittatas in muffin cups which makes it easier for me to call them "breakfast muffins" and then the kids will eat them. The exact same thing, in a casserole dish and then cut into squares, apparently does not constitute the exact same thing in a child's mind, so I carefully drop loads of cheese and bacon into cupcake liners in the muffin tin, add my egg mixture, and 30 minutes later, everyone is happy. I decide that these plus crackers are best done as a stroller lunch where all the crumbs and mess fall outside and not on my kitchen floor to bend and clean. I pack the whole lot into a container where the lid pops up for ventilation and then an insulated bag, and everybody's food will be the perfect consistency and temperature once we reach our destination. It works out gloriously with a beautiful, sunny day. No one needs a coat – even better.

I try not to think about being completely pissed off at Chad because that will ruin my happy day of an extended weekend since it's Friday, and if I go down that road, I will start to think of how this means it's not a day off where the kids should be at daycare and I can just sleep, but that it's an extra day of caring for children by myself while toting an enormous belly growing a currently parasitic but I'm sure very cute, small person inside of me.

We roll and stroll in relative silence. Everybody munches away at the plethora of breakfast items which I'm sure are landing more in their pocket bibs than their mouths. The boardwalk is long, the sunshine is warm, and when we get to the outdoor beachside café, a man has just picked up a coffee with no lineup.

"Are we ready for ice cream?" I ask my unusually sweet and well-behaved boys.

"PLEASE!" they both shout.

Timothy wants chocolate and Jeremy wants strawberry, and that is fine because both are available. I ask for samples of cappuccino and green tea and that's all I'm allowed before my blood sugar spikes and then I'll feel guilty about risking baby's health.

The gorgeous cashier has wild frizzy hair, a Brazilian accent, and a flawless complexion. She happily gives me my samples – maybe because then she's not bored – and I put in my orders for two kiddie cups and spoons.

"How much is it?" Timothy asks loudly as he receives his cup from my hands.

"SUPER expensive, so don't drop or spill it, okay?" He goes wide-eyed and nods. I pause in handing it over fully and he says sweetly, "Thank you, Mommy." These kids have been playing "ice cream shop" lately and charging a hundred dollars per scoop.

Jeremy gives me a kiss on the cheek when I hand him his. "Thank you, Mommy," he says in his baby way. "I wuv you." I kiss him all over his face.

I pay by credit card and take a seat at an outdoor table while the boys have their ice cream still in the stroller. There's a woman who looks a lot like Whoopi Goldberg but with sunglasses reading over the menu. Her voice surprises me – she has a Scottish accent!

"You used to have lovely breakfast options. Are they gone now or is it just too late in the day?" she says to the cashier.

The cashier looks at her apologetically. With her cute Brazilian Portuguese lilt, she tells the woman, "They're gone, sorry. The owner changed the hours to start later last month, and it was too late for breakfast."

"That's a shame," the Scottish lady replies. Then a long pause. "Is there any quiche today?"

"No, sorry!" my girl says sadly again.

"All right. I'll have a large cappuccino then please. And a large curry fries." The cashier nods and disappears into the back.

For some reason, I feel incredibly drawn to this woman. I unzip our lunch bag and see that I still have six breakfast muffins left.

"Here!" I cry out to her, startling the both of us. "I mean, I have six breakfast muffins if you'd like them. I made them this morning."

"Oh no, I can't take food from babes and a pregnant lady but thank you!" she says with a little laugh.

"I insist – they'll go cold on our walk back and I really prefer them straight from the oven anyway. It's basically cheese, bacon and egg. And a little bit of milk."

"That's extremely kind of you, I'll take one. I don't need this many! Thank you!"

"I have a Ziploc bag here so you can take them and keep them in your fridge for later. I make them all the time. Too often, in fact." I gesture to invite her to our table.

She uses hand sanitizer and joins us. I like her even more. She helps herself to one of the frittatas. Her face looks almost orgasmic.

"Mmmmmm … this is marvelous. I won't say no to the other five then. Thank you so much!"

"My pleasure!"

"I'm Mhairi – think of it like 'marry' as in have a wedding, but spelled M-H-A-I-R-I. It's a Scottish version."

"I'm Claudia, nice to meet you!"

"You sound tired of these delicious morsels. Too much of a good thing?"

I tell her about the gestational diabetes. That it's tiring to count carbs and do the insulin tests when you're not used to it. That worrying about baby and taking care of the kids while trying to handle it all is for the birds.

And then suddenly, as if she's a therapist, I'm telling her about Chad and how I'm still so pissed off.

"If he'd been available, would you have wanted him to come and see you doing the panel?"

I sigh. "If I'd asked him, I know exactly what he would have said: it won't be his thing and I should just go and have a good time. We haven't had a date night in ages because I don't think we enjoy spending time together. There's nothing about him that's attractive to me anymore."

"That's a pity," Mhairi says sympathetically. "It sounds like you need a holiday."

"It would only truly be a holiday if it was by myself," I say with a laugh. "When I can eat anything I want without worrying about what it would do to me or the baby." I sigh. "I miss my youth. Somebody asked me last night if I had any advice for somebody young like her, and I really wanted to say, 'You should eff everything you can before it all dries up'." Mhairi laughs at this.

"Mommy, I'm done!" Timothy squeals, holding out his

garbage for me to take.

"What about you?" I ask Jeremy. He drinks the last bit like a milkshake. I take both boys' garbage to the compost bin nearby.

"Was that a good treat?" Mhairi is asking the boys.

They both nod shyly. I wipe their mouths, etc. with wet wipes. Everything is just bound for the laundry, including the stroller insert.

"Well, I guess that's the end of our outing, boys?"

"I want to play!" says Jeremy.

"I didn't bring any sand toys, and we're probably close to nap time, buddy. But after nap, I'll let you watch TV while I make dinner," I offer. The boys think about it.

Timothy bargains. "What about before nap?"

"Only nature documentaries. About pandas."

Timothy loves pandas, and there's something about the narrator's voice that puts Jeremy to sleep, so it's a win-win.

"Deal," says Timothy.

Mhairi looks lovingly at the boys. "What little angels," she croons.

"It's an exceptionally good day," I reply with a relieved smile. "I'm so sorry I made you 'work' for your breakfast with my babbling. I'll leave you in peace."

"No, thank you, Claudia, it was lovely to meet you. Breakfast and the company were lovely. I'll return the favor sooner than expected."

"Oh," I say, a little confused. "Do you come down here a lot?"

"Often enough."

"It's not really our usual spot, but I'd love to run into you again. Have a wonderful day!"

"I will, Claudia."

She says my name pointedly … as if she knows me. But I don't feel creeped out, it's strangely comforting.

"Bye!" We all wave. Jeremy blows her a kiss all by himself

without prompting and you can see her heart melt a little.

So what if I just rambled on and on to a stranger? It's Toronto. I'll never see her again.

When we get home, the rest of the day is a blur. It turns out that there's a group email going back and forth on the casting decisions that the boardroom crew supposedly made last night and I've just been added. It's like cold feet on the commitment. I stay out of it but I'm grateful there's a written record of this madness and tonight, I'll just scroll up on the last response when it peters out. I confirm that their preferred director is only available six months from now so I'm not lying when I threaten the need for finality on the decision.

I tell the boys that the robot vacuum will eat all their toys because he's hungry, so they decently help tidy up the living room mess by putting the plushies away in their correct-ish places. I also want the couch cleared so the boys have a place to nap. I do what feels like a thousand loads of laundry. I order a cauliflower rice and salmon poke bowl and chicken katsu for the boys for dinner.

I haven't texted Chad because I'm still too upset to deal with him. He hasn't texted either. Maybe he just forgot about us and went straight to the office. I don't know but since I confirmed he's alive and well, I don't really care. If he gets home and needs food, there's oatmeal.

I get the boys to bed by 8 p.m. I quickly shower and fall asleep, snuggled into my covers in ultimate comfort.

I dream of Mhairi and bits of our conversation from today, except that instead of being at the Beaches, we're in my university residence cafeteria and Mhairi has gotten up to leave.

"I'm returning the favor," she says pleasantly and with a wink. "If you need me, find me at the Beach, except when it's raining." I hug her. Her hug back is warm and comforting.

I wake up to the sound of my alarm, and instinctively I hit the snooze button with my eyes still closed.

Wait.

It's not my usual phone alarm, it's my old clock radio alarm which I haven't used in more than a decade. That's weird. I still have the clock, but I only use it for the time.

I open my eyes.

Uh, this is my university dorm room … from when I was 20.

What … the … hell … ?

Chapter 7:

WHERE AM I?

I look around and study the room. It's also weird that I can see okay-ish without glasses. My vision is usually such that I can't function without them. My eyes don't feel dry, so I know I don't have contacts in.

Everything looks as it did when I was 20. On the nightstand, there's a framed photo of me from my 20th birthday dinner (the candles on the cake are 2 and 0) with friends I haven't talked to in decades now. My 21st birthday was a big family do, and I remember displaying that photo but not in this dorm.

The posters on the wall are the cool ads I remember liking for their colors and graphic design. The movie posters. The music groups. The old TV and TV stand I bought from an exchange student going home. My now ancient computer. My tiny flip phone that didn't text!

My hands go straight to my belly. It's flat. I'm not pregnant! Under the covers, I check out my lower half.

WHOA! No Caesarean section scars, no rippling skin, no stretch marks! My boobs are way smaller, but that's okay. I could confidently and appropriately wear a crop top with this body. I leap out of bed with amazing energy. If I'm in my university dorm, and I'm in my 20-year-old body ... this was when I was running every day and in peak physical condition. WHOA ... look at this butt! Look at these muscles!

I'm wearing my favorite old flannel pajama set and it's

like new! Hello, old comfortable friend. I open the closet to see myself in the full-length mirror behind the door. WOW. My hair is completely and naturally black without a whiff of grey or white. My eyes and face don't have the wrinkly laugh lines they usually do. I whip off my clothing and admire my body. Who cares if ghosts or cameras are watching – I look amazing compared to my age 40 body wrecked by pregnancy and childbirth.

Hanging up in the closet is all the thin, cheap clothing I used to wear but it fit me well in my slim years. There's a fuzzy purple sweater I could wear when I wasn't concerned about it accentuating my flab. Pencil skirts that zip! Skinny black pants! Ooh – and there's my dress that looks like an ombre sunset and makes my small boobs like so much bigger! I gave it away at one stage because I hadn't worn it for five years since we were done with weddings. I'm gonna wear it now with a pair of black knee-high boots. I have a cute lingerie set on because at this point, I didn't know that the world should burn underwire bras in hell.

This dorm room is in one of the (then-)newer residence buildings, so it's a suite with two separate bedrooms (with lockable doors), a shared kitchenette, and a shared bathroom. My roommate is Ciara! And if I remember correctly, she might have just started dating Jason, or maybe she's still stalking him around the medical buildings "pretending" to study and snack so she can "run into him" and share snacks while they "study" together.

I do my business, then check out all the toiletries I used to use. I put in a new pair of contact lenses since I don't know how long I've been using the last pair. I wasn't into makeup then, but I did own it for when we went clubbing at night and stuff. I do my makeup and look hot.

This is so weird.

So surreal. So scary. So thrilling.

I have no idea why I'm here. Or how I got here. At

the very least, I should be thankful. I am thankful. I have no idea how long this is going to last. But it *has* to do with my conversation with Mhairi yesterday. What is she? A spiritual magician? A wizard? A time traveling deity? I settle on "fairy godmother" until I find out otherwise.

I check the date on my tiny phone. It's Friday, April 29, 2005. I look at my exam checklist (on the front side of my bedroom door) that I was organized in pinning up so Ciara would also know not to disturb a cram session.

My last exam was yesterday! Ciara and I are both registered for summer session, which means that we don't have to move out of residence and into our apartment until the last week in August. Classes don't start until the second Monday in May. It's a week of freedom!

Ciara has a matching exam checklist on her door, and I see that her last exam is this morning. I check my planner (it is pre-smartphone and Google calendar days after all) - we have a late all-you-can-eat sushi lunch planned.

It's a holiday just like I said I wanted! When I can eat anything and I don't have to worry about Chad or the kids on this timeline, they aren't even in my life yet!

This is phenomenal.

My stomach growls. Oh yes, I'm on a residence meal plan, so I should get something from the cafeteria. I want to take my black bag that would go so nicely with my outfit, so I rummage through my drawers (there aren't that many). It's funny – my desk drawers have changed so much since university, but I see familiar trinkets that I still have to this day. Old printed out photos. Sunglasses I've since lost. The condoms I picked up from the health fair because they were free.

OH.

Right … this changes things a LOT.

Growing up, my Chinese/Christian/super conservative parents instilled a deep sense of guilt for any premarital sex. So Chad has pretty much been it. If I'd known that he'd be my only source of sex … I'd have fucked a mass of people in my twenties.

And to be honest, Chad has had great moments in the past, but now is not that great. He lacks stamina, has very limited skills, does not manscape, is clumsy around my parts so it hurts and he has not turned me on in any capacity for a number of years. He also does not care about my pleasure or orgasm. We do not cuddle or have intimate time post-sex. He is simply … there. And then not there.

Like I said, Baby Girl is a result of pity sex, not desire.

And right now, I'm horny as hell with the body of a goddess. Hungry first though.

I make my way down to the cafeteria and choose a breakfast sandwich, hash browns, and an iced coffee.

Wait – is this when I was lactose intolerant but didn't know it?

I cancel the iced coffee and make it a large iced tea. Why risk things on the first day?

I savor my breakfast and sip my iced tea as I stroll back to my dorm room. The hash browns are the best thing I've eaten in months. I want more! No wait, I'll have them tomorrow! Even though Ciara and I are small Asian women, we are deceptively very quantity enthusiastic sushi eaters at this stage of our lives. (We will later be more about the quality when we can afford it.) I will save room for that. And I need to buy Lactaid pills for the ice cream because my 20-year-old self will devour three scoops of green tea ice cream and suffer later, thinking it's the white fish and not the lactose-intolerance. Note to self.

I wish I'd had a step counter back in my twenties because having no access to a car of my own, I walked and took transit everywhere. My classes were on opposite sides of the campus, plus I ran because I enjoyed the route to Harbourfront and back to campus, listening to language textbook and showtune mp3s on my iPod. Wow, the days when my iPod was still working flawlessly.

This dorm has a security desk at the entrance and as residents, you physically need to come down to the lobby to sign your visitors in and out. Just as I'm about to pass the desk, I hear a male voice that sounds … familiar. But my heart fills with dread.

"Baby! It really is you!"

I spin around in dismay because now I confirm the voice … and the … person. My eyes go wide.

Oh shit.

"Damn! You look hot! I was calling you. How come you didn't answer?" He asks as if people still call instead of texting. Ha.

Oh, wait. They call because you can't text yet. Right. I look at my phone and see, "Conrad (1)."

Conrad.

Ugh.

My university boyfriend of two years, who has been a distant memory for decades and who I only check up on LinkedIn from time to time to see what became of him and what our then mutual friends are up to now. Whenever I think back to this time, it only stands out as a colossal waste of time and money. He was immature, made poor academic decisions, embarrassed me on countless occasions, and always pushed the idea of our future as a married couple. He would have made a terrible husband, forcing me to be the breadwinner and household manager. Or maybe he'd have been a stay-at-home-Dad but I'd still have to do the grocery shopping. We would have never combined finances because even then he made poor money choices, choosing CDs and junk food over things like textbooks and bus fares. But maybe he would have pushed me into law school if I'd had to strive for a career and money-oriented life.

I look at him and say, "Oh no," disgustedly. I don't mean for that to sound so harsh, but it just slips out of my mouth.

But oh no, you will NOT be ruining my holiday.

The truth just tumbles out. "Oh my God. I'm sorry, but

I have to break up with you right now."

Shocked, he replies, "But why? I love you! You're my whole world!"

"See, I don't love you. And this is an unhealthy attachment. Your friends always interrupt our time together, whether you ditch me for them or you make loud phone calls planning when to meet up with them. Your mother controls access to your own bank account and you're a grown-ass man who works part-time albeit for $10 an hour. You'll get over me just fine!"

I refuse to devote time from this holiday to do this whole back and forth thing with him begging me to stay (which he did when I originally dumped him), so I quickly mouth "help" to the security desk people and they knowingly move to remove Conrad from the premises.

Oh shit, wait.

I yell to him, "Conrad, don't go to Japan to teach English, choose Korea instead! It's gonna be more useful to you one day!"

And I run away, up the stairs and back to my dorm room where there's peace and quiet. I also block his number from my phone. For the record, Conrad and I experimented but never had full-on sex. I'm glad we didn't because it would have complicated our relationship and breakup that much more.

I catch a glimpse of myself in the mirror again and damn. I still cannot believe I'm in this body. And a little miffed at myself for how I didn't even appreciate it as much as I should have back then! Dammit twenties and still-forming personality!

As I'm just done touching up my makeup and figuring out what I should do for the next two hours, there's a knock at the door.

Oh no, did Conrad manage to sneak up? I hope not. I look through the peephole. It's the Cable Guy!

I remember this. This tall, hot, clean-shaven guy who looks like he belongs in a boy band came around to our dorm to change ports for our TV connections. I'd heard that beautiful, blonde Kate down the hall cheated on her boyfriend with this guy. I should have done that!

I flip my hair and open the door, striking my best "I'm posing-but-not-posing pose."

"Hi."

His jaw drops. This dress is fire. "Uh, hello. I'm … here to fix the … um, cable," he stammers.

"No problem," I say, and "accidentally" lead him by the hand into the bedroom.

I will never see this guy again in my lifetime and there are zero consequences, so I'm just going to go all out.

"Oops! It's like an instinct," I say, pretending to fan myself. "Sorry."

I hope I'm not striking out here and accidentally falling into a Southern Belle character.

"This'll just take a minute," the Cable Guy says. I watch him do the work because I'll still need the TV for the duration of my stay. I think he literally means a minute because it looks like he's done with the stuff in the wall. While he's changing out the panel and finishing up the last screw, I try to make idle but strategic conversation because again, I'm horny and I don't want to waste my time.

"I just broke up with my boyfriend."

He spins around with eyes wide. "Oh … I'm sorry to hear that." He says "sorry" in a way that is definitely not sorry and more like a question.

Shit, I'm going the cheesy soap opera route but I want what I want. Fine, play Southern Belle meets Jessica Rabbit.

"I'm not sorry at all. I was looking for a more manly man," I say suggestively as possible while sticking out my boobs. "Might you … know of one?"

"He's closer than you think," he says and steps toward me.

He kisses me with the most passion I've ever felt, gently holding my jawline so my face angles the right way to match his.

He expertly caresses my lips with his own and I feel like I'm melting. Floating. He also tastes like a cupcake.

"Oh, I know what you're thinking. It was a colleague's birthday, so we had cake at 7 this morning." His voice is deep and sexy. My stomach gets butterflies.

"Do you want to do more than just kiss?" he asks me between kisses and running his fingers through my hair and massaging my neck.

"Yes," I whisper breathlessly.

"I'll need to use your shower then," he says as he takes off his shirt and reveals a magnificent six pack of abs, powerful-looking arms, and smooth, hairless and evenly toned skin.

"Take me with you?" I put my arms around his neck. He undoes my dress while kissing my lips, my cheeks, my neck, my shoulders. He slows down the pace and kisses my back while I hear him unzipping his jeans. He pauses for a little bit and I know he's taking off the rest.

He puts his hands around my waist then extends his arms to hold me tighter. His hands start roaming up and down my body. I open the closet door so I can see his face behind me.

"Do you still want more?" he murmurs into my ear.

"Yes." I can hardly get the word out as I feel his smooth face caressing my back as he kisses my spine and sends warm shivers tingling through my whole body.

I unclasp my bra and wriggle out of underwear, tossing them into the bottom of my closet. I lead him into the bathroom and turn on the shower. It's not a big one by any means, but the size means we stay close while soaping each other with the body wash and our hands. When we're all rinsed off, he turns off the taps.

"That one on the left," I say, pointing to the towels hanging up. He kisses my lips again while using the towel to dry us both from top to bottom.

He puts the towel over his arm, then carries me to the bed. He kneels in front of me, parts my legs, then starts to feel between my thighs with his tongue. My body arches involuntarily. I can't even remember the last time Chad went down on me. Likely years ago. Cable Guy adds a finger to the rhythm and it's the most alive I've felt in ages. He's getting my G-spot and my clitoris at the same time with magic fingers. When he adds a finger, this is the most intense pleasure I've ever experienced – what have I been missing out on?! This guy needs to write the manual for Chad – not that Chad would make time to read it.

Cable Guy brings me to an orgasm that I feel through my whole body, and it lasts for a good while. And he keeps going with the motions that brought me there – he doesn't stop!

He carries on with his fingers but takes his mouth off to ask if I have condoms. He doesn't have them on him while he's supposed to be working, he admits mischievously. I point to the drawer I found them in this morning.

"Excuse me, my lady," he says while pausing to wipe his hands on the towel. "I apologize for the laundry," he says like a sexy knight.

He gets the condom package open and puts it on like a boss. It bothers me an iota that he has probably slept with countless people, but I'm here for the experience and his skills have obviously come from great practice. I'm more than happy to benefit as I close my eyes and relish the pleasure.

My orgasm is tapering off and he waits for the okay before tenderly pulling me up and propping me on all fours. He expertly resumes his finger action on my clitoris which makes my eyes go wide and leaves me gasping. He slides himself inside me but ever so slowly and gently. He angles himself rather than forcing me to move to accommodate him. "Is that okay?" He keeps checking with me until he's fully in and then he waits again for me to say that I'm comfortable and he can keep going. He slows down with his fingers on my clitoris as he angles himself slightly so that he's balanced and firmly footed. He picks up speed with his fingers as he moves in and out, and it's a deep pleasure that I've never even dreamed of. He speeds up even more on his fingers and as I start to climax (involuntarily noisily, who knew I had it in me?), he slows down with his fingers but goes faster in and out until reaching his own climax.

While we both recover and catch our breath, I see him out of the corner of my eye, disposing of the condom by wrapping it in tissues and carefully placing it in the garbage bin.

"Normally I would offer to cuddle you in a romantic way, but unfortunately I should probably get back to the job at hand," he says apologetically while quickly getting dressed. "I kind of owe someone for keeping my job as a summer contract and I'd hate to get fired."

"No worries!" I say cheerfully as I'm getting my own clothes back on.

"I'll take a raincheck though ... Claudia," he says while handing me a business card. I glance down quickly.

"Uh, that would be great ... Otis," I reply. "Wait, how did you know my name?"

"I knew it coming in because of the list, then I saw it on the door – the exam schedule."

"Oh ... that's clever," I admit sheepishly.

"I like to think I'm smart – I'm pre-med," Otis says, shrugging. "Um, it's Friday night, so I'm DJing at Up 'n Up tonight, if you want to come? I can put your name on the list so you don't pay cover and I'll score you some free drinks from the bar. Bring a friend so you're not alone on the floor."

What a day, an amazing fling and now I have a good plan for tonight.

"Okay, thanks. I'll call you if I can't make it," I tell him while walking him out.

"Great. Thanks for ... this." His voice has such a deep tone that I feel like it's a wavelength hovering around my heart. And lower.

"Thank you. See you later."

He grabs my waist and leans in for a last, longing kiss. I feel swept away. Then he opens the door and quietly leaves with a smile.

Oh damn – I gotta meet Ciara for lunch!

Bathroom first.

It kills the mood to say it but you need to use the bathroom within an hour after sex, otherwise you risk a Urinary Tract Infection (UTI) and while this holiday might be consequence-free, it might very well have consequences (that would be logical with what I just did). I do not want to waste my holiday time in the walk-in clinic, then the pharmacy, then remembering to take antibiotics.

Inner rambling aside, I check my makeup and wow, they really mean waterproof. The foundation washed away but the eye makeup has stayed intact. Incredible.

I fix my makeup (I can see why I only embraced it years later), change clothes to a more casual jeans and cute top outfit since I'm saving my *fuck me* dress for tonight so Otis will recognize me on the dance floor.

This holiday is going to be epic.

Chapter 8:

YOU SHOULD HAVE BEEN THE ONE

I arrive just in time to meet Ciara in front of the restaurant, and we join the line together. I love seeing 22-year-old Ciara. She's just as brilliant as she is at 42, but this is her pink and purple streaked hair phase and, oh yes, how could I forget that she's the one who got me into running because we would often go together. Until she and Jason started running with each other. And if I remember correctly, this is the day she tells me ...

"I finally talked to him!"

"Jason?"

"What? How did you know his name?"

"Lucky guess?"

"Super lucky guess!" She's too happy to notice my slip-up.

She tells me all about how she finished her exam, she's walking across campus with her hand all cramped up from writing, and she's so hungry that she can't wait for lunch and has to grab a hot dog. The only thing is that her hand is so cramped, she can't use her right hand to put on her toppings. Who just happens to be crossing paths near College and University? In desperation she asks him to do it for her and he happily obliges. Then they strike up a conversation.

Now I remember ... they had a hot dog cart at their wedding for the late-night crowd and this is why.

And it turns out, Jason noticed her as someone who was just around all the time; and to this day has no idea that she was "around" to meet a future doctor (parent pleasing safety net, long story) which later turned into a crush on him specifically.

Now they're going for their first date! If I remember correctly, the first date goes swimmingly, the second does not and there's a long pause before they sort out the misunderstanding and go on the third. I vaguely recall saying something about intervening with my big mouth in my speech at their wedding. It'll come to me at some point. Probably right before I'm about to fall asleep. Or maybe I'll get to relive it on my holiday and jumpstart their relationship again.

Ciara and I have an amazing lunch – just the two of us. The food is great and though the restaurant is busy, I plan on tipping generously on the pre-student discounted amount. We don't have any worries about spouses or children. We don't have to leave our phones on the table in case of emergency. We have the entire afternoon and night, plus we'll go back to the same dorm room. We also have each other's undivided attention. It dawns on me that I've been unknowingly wanting time like this with my best friend ever since her twins, Kent and Kelly, were born.

I tell her about breaking up with Conrad and her jaw drops in shock. I tell her that I'm not giving that a second thought and I'm already over it. Her brow furrows.

"Really? I mean, you guys seemed like you were on the path to marriage," she says in disbelief. "You must be feeling something."

"Oh, no, sweetie, I realized that was all him and the pressure. Anyway, that is to let you know why we won't be seeing him around anymore."

I pause before giving her the next set of news: Otis the Cable Guy and why we are going clubbing tonight specifically at the Up 'n Up.

"WHAT?!" she shrieks when I tell her about the sex. She lowers her voice when she notices everyone staring. "You didn't even do that with Conrad."

"I know, right?!"

She too has super conservative Asian Christian parents and right away, she asks about birth control, STI risk, and my state of mind.

I manage to calm her down, but she definitely knows something is up – after all, she's my best friend and a one-night (day) stand is completely out of character for 20-year-old me.

And then she asks quietly, "How did you know what to do?"

Oh.

Back in the day, Ciara and I only started talking about sex when Chad and I first started doing it – and it was long after she and Jason started doing it. She was always the more experienced one who could dish out the advice.

Right, she thinks today is my first time ever.

I tell her that I've been reading a lot of online magazine articles but that Otis was really a very considerate fling and far exceeded my expectations. In my mind, I also want to say that he must check out fine because Kate originally fucked him without a problem.

"But Clauds, you just met him! You fucked a stranger!"

"I know, right?! I've never had a wild moment in my entire life. Just think, Ci, when you're 40, you just have your husband. Unless you cheat on him or have an open relationship or decide together to be polyamorous, that's it. In a standard relationship, you fuck one person until you divorce or one of you dies. That's what you're supposed to do, anyway."

Ciara goes silent for a long time. She fiddles with her food and I realize it's half thinking and half her hand just being cramped from exams that it's hard to use chopsticks.

"I hope that I'm enough," she finally says.

"WHAT?!"

"I hope that I'm enough," she repeats. "For somebody to think that I'm the only person he's allowed to fuck for the rest of his life or until we divorce."

"Oh honey, you'll always be way hotter than Jason. I should remind him every week how lucky he is to have you as his wife." It just rolls off my tongue as I blather on but then catch myself. For the sake of not screwing up the space-time continuum and making huge ethical breaches, I instinctively know not to tell anyone their future. "Just … especially as you just started talking to him, you don't have to be exclusive right off the bat. I mean, play the field. Get some experience. For you and whoever you land up with."

Phew, think I saved that one.

Ciara goes very quiet again. I just let her think. In the meantime, I finish all the good tender beef while she's pensive, and write out my dessert order on the little slips of scrap paper.

"How do you prevent that from happening?" she asks.

"Prevent what?"

"That feeling of being trapped with one partner in the future," she says thoughtfully, measuring each word.

I have to think about this. And it's long enough that our server brings our ice cream and deep-fried banana. I tell Ciara I'm still thinking so she knows I'm not ignoring her.

"I guess …" I say after a very long while, "If you intend to grow old with that one person, you have to keep focusing on reasons as to why you feel happy and lucky to be with them … every day."

When the words leave my mouth, I know it should evoke some sentimental memory of Chad. Right now, it's a blank. The mama bear in me is still too angry.

And then I get this brainwave of a completely different sort. "Hey Ci, wanna be cultured this afternoon?"

"What?"

"Let's get cheap tickets – to anything. Ballet, symphony, musical, whatever."

"Yeah, okay!"

It turns out that we can score phenomenal tickets to *Coppélia* at the Four Seasons Centre for the Performing Arts at 7:30 tonight for just $20 each. And I'm thrilled. Because if Ciara and I wanted to go to the ballet in the present day, it would be a whole ordeal – for me, anyway.

Getting someone to take care of the kids, trying not to fall asleep as a huge and exhausted pregnant woman – all of that. Chad would never take me to the ballet. He'd tell me to go with Ciara. And now that I know he's capable of forgetting his own children, I'd have to arrange for a babysitter at $20-$25 an hour.

There's ample time to stroll back to the dorm room, change, share a banh mi (because who wants their stomach growling during the performance?), then stroll to the theatre. I'm wearing flats because as much as I love them, I don't know that I'm psychologically prepared to wear heels again when it'll involve so much walking.

We're on the orchestra level in the left section facing the stage. We have two seats together in row Q. In the present day, these seats go for about $125 each. The student price has jumped to $45!

"This is a great idea!" Ciara says while looking around. The lights dim and we're excited for the performance to start.

In a nutshell, *Coppélia* is a weird story about a small European town where basically, this dollmaker makes a doll that's so realistic that a dude falls in love with it, despite having a girlfriend. The dude's girlfriend finds her way into the doll-maker's shop, switches places with the doll and wins back her dude. And everybody lives happily ever after.

Like I said, it's weird. And wacky. But the dancers are talented, the choreography is inspiring and the costuming impeccable, so we just enjoy the ballet for being ballet and for me, knowingly without children or our spouses!

My mind can't help but wander as I watch though. What are some of the other things I'd like to do while I'm here? I should write a bucket list of sorts. There's one hard thing I should do, but I'll leave it for tomorrow. It's too late in the day now.

I wonder what my kids are doing. Are they in bed? Have we just paused time so we're all still asleep in the present?

I assume we are. So I try to lean into the moment and be present. Enjoy. This is a once in a lifetime gift. When I return to the present day, I'll find Mhairi to thank her.

When the performance finishes, we clap loudly. A standing ovation is gathering steam. Ciara leans over and cups her mouth to my ear.

"I feel like we'll be assholes if we don't join in."

I nod and we stand to clap. I enjoyed it but I didn't enjoy it that much.

We use the bathroom here because it'll be the nicest one we'll see all night. It's late enough that we have time for a burrito each before heading to the club. I am fully appreciating the eating whatever I want part of this holiday!

There's a lineup outside, but I approach the bouncer with a clipboard before joining it. "Hi. Otis said that I'd be on the list. My name is Claudia Lee?"

The bouncer is a hulking Black dude who reminds me of a cartoon character, but I can't remember which one. The character wears a suit like an FBI agent though.

This guy is cheerful and friendly and checks the list. "Oh yeah, Claudia Lee and guest(s)." He does this sort of knowing nod and once he checks our IDs, hands me four club branded tokens. "For drinks on the house," he says, looking us up and down. He apparently approves. "Have fun."

"Thanks!"

We both enter and I kind of knew but forgot exactly how loud clubs can be. And then I remember … I go digging through my purse and find exactly what I was looking for. A multi-pack of beige earplugs. I discreetly put them in, then hand Ciara a pair. She looks a little confused at first but then gives me that "you're a genius" look before putting them in too. I used to carry a pair of earplugs in my purse up until I had kids.

I spot Otis in the DJ booth. I have no idea how to get up there from the dance floor so I just wave and he waves back.

Ciara and I dance our asses off to so many of my favorite songs. Otis must have taken a quick gander at my CD collection which I keep on a shelf above my computer monitor. The last time I had a playlist this good was at my own wedding! Because I gave the DJ a list. He said he'd use it again in future, it was that good.

I don't know how bartenders can stave off hearing loss in a club as loud as this. Maybe they secretly wear earplugs when possible too. Ciara and I make our way to the bar. In the present day, if I'm ordering something with more than two items, I'll type it out on my phone in a note then hold it up to whoever's taking the order. I knew I couldn't do that here, so I hold up a piece of paper from my purse for the bartender.

Screwdriver and Shirley Temple (with juice) please

He gives me a quizzical look, but I mime driving and he nods. I hand him two drink tokens and a Toonie for tip.

Wait, I'm totally allowed to drink! There's nothing stopping me!

Nah, rather keep my wits about me, especially when Ciara's an extra lightweight.

A slew of more favorite songs come on, and Ciara and I get back to dancing, trying not to spill our drinks or be groped by nasty guys dancing too close. My mama bear comes out and I successfully get rid of one guy that shudders in fear and runs away.

And then across the dance floor, at the bar being handed a beer, it is unmistakably … him. My heart skips a beat and all the feelings I used to have come rushing back.

Jun Sung (pronounced like "June" with a short "oo" sound) is the gorgeous guy I had a crush on for most of high school and most of university until I finally gave up and settled for Conrad. I should have lasted out longer but, in my mind, Jun was unattainable being a little older and out of my league. He was already in university, and I hadn't even finished high school yet. He's Ciara's cousin so I couldn't really let on that I had a mad crush on him, but I loved being invited to her house for extended family dinners. We'd play board games with all the cousins together, and I'd fantasize that this could be my future, joining the family by marrying Jun. I wanted to be with him so much that I'd dream about us being a couple, then wake up extremely disappointed.

In the present day, even just a few days ago, I wondered if he was just hot to me at the time because I didn't know any better, but seeing him now, my teenaged self was right. Jun is a mix of my favorite Korean drama male leads – rolled into one person. His smile, hair, eyes, jawline, swagger – all of it – still makes my heart flutter. In his own words, Jun used to play at the fact that his name in Chinese means, "handsome, talented" or if you didn't care about the character or tone, "king."

And if he's single right now, I'm jumping at my chance to be with him.

Chapter 9:

CRUSH

As I'm staring at Jun, Ciara's slurring something at me but I can't hear her properly because of the earplugs. I carefully take them out and she yells, "It's JUN!"

She smiles and waves like she's seen a celebrity. She's also a bit drunk … oh, actually really drunk. She goes floppy onto my shoulder and Jun arrives just in time to catch her. She's half standing and then when she flops, it's like a dead weight.

"Oh boy," he quips. "Way to kill the night, Ci. Hey, Clauds." Because both our arms are full with Ciara, we can't hug, so he naturally kisses me on the cheek. It seems a very grown-up thing to do since last I saw him decades ago, and I strain to remember that at this point in time/history, he must have graduated and is now working full-time at something where he's less available for family dinners at Ciara's house but shows up often enough for me to keep crushing on him, and a little harder even because now he has a place of his own, unlike university guys who have at best, a grimy off-campus apartment with roommates.

"Do you have time to help me get her back to the dorm?" I yell over the music.

"For sure. My aunt would kill me if she knew I didn't help," he yells back.

As we're leaving, the song changes to another of my favorites and I realize that I didn't even wave goodbye to Otis. Out on the sidewalk, Jun is already hailing a cab.

"Whoops," I say out loud.

"What happened?" Jun whips his head back to look at me and accidentally puts down his arm. Ciara is still sleepy and very heavy between the two of us, but the cool night air is perking her up a tiny bit so at least she can walk. Sort of. Her eyes keep closing but she keeps her head upright. Sort of.

"Oh, I just remembered that I'm blowing off the DJ. I think he was angling for a second date but ... ah well," I say thoughtlessly. Man, I haven't forgotten how sex works, but damn, I've completely forgotten how dating works.

A cab pulls up and Jun gets the driver's attention. We get Ciara into the middle between us. I ask the driver to take us to our residence building and he knows exactly which one it is.

Once we're off, Jun turns to me and says, "Okay, say that again about the DJ? I didn't catch anything after that."

"Oh, just that I guess I don't know about a second date now." I should really have not said anything to start with because this is totally the last person I want to discuss any sort of dating life with, especially when it would be epic just to hook up on this holiday.

"Do you want a second date?" he asks.

"I actually don't care either way," I sigh and try to sound nonchalant. "It was a superficial connection."

Well, I mean, we did connect deeply. He was in me. Ha. But I wouldn't mind seeing him again.

"Are you dating a lot?" he asks carefully.

"I wasn't, but I broke up with my boyfriend today and a half hour later, this guy showed up."

"Damn, Clauds. You turned into a player," Jun laughs.

"YOLO," I say.

"What?"

"Oh ... you only live once."

"It's true."

It occurs to me that any time I get together with anyone in the present day, we schedule it with a Google calendar invite, but that doesn't exist here and I didn't even give this dude my phone number. He's waiting for my call. Hmm ... so the ball is in my court. I could have my crush plus a fuckboy if this holiday lasts for a few days. It could be over tomorrow for all I know.

Oh no. Please let it last longer than that.

At midnight, there's no traffic, so it hardly takes any time to get back to our dorm. Ciara is too floppy to walk, so Jun just carries her by himself while I open doors and sign him in as a guest.

"Now it'll be easier for you to come back and visit," I say half-jokingly. He gives a look that reads "not so sure about that."

Somehow, I get Ciara to go to the bathroom (it reminds me of the time I held her wedding dress so she could pee), wash her makeup off, half change her into pajamas and then I tuck her in and close the door. Jun is looking in our fridge.

"I've forgotten what it's like to be a student. There's nothing of sustenance in here."

"There's a meal plan," I scoff. "What would you expect students to keep?"

"Beer? Ice cream bars? What happens if the cafeteria is closed?"

My stomach growls. Dammit ... but then again, I have such love for my 20-year-old's metabolism.

"Like now!" he says, cracking up. "I'll order pizza. They'll deliver late."

"Let's go out," I say, a little defensively. "Plus, I don't want you thinking of me as a kid hanging out in a dorm room."

"Oh, there's no danger of that in *that* dress," he says offhandedly, then he looks as if he said something he shouldn't have.

Wow, this dress is magic.

He looks at me a little shyly, "Did you want to come back to my place? We could also catch up ... later?"

"Let's catch up now," I say directly, making full-on eye

contact. "Unless your girlfriend would mind us hanging out."

He meets my direct eye contact. "Nope, no girlfriend."

"I'm gonna need two minutes to get my stuff."

This is the 40-year-old me being prepared because 20-year-old me wouldn't have had the plan or foresight to bring things at all.

I close my door, grab a bigger purse, stuff it with socks, running shoes; the pretty form-fitting yoga outfit I quickly outgrew in my married days and gave away; condoms; the dental goodie bag from a recent dentist appointment; moisturizer, glasses, contact lens kit, and a clean lingerie set. I pop in my "clubbing" wristlet, which has my phone, the makeup touch-up stuff I need as well as the prerequisite ID, credit card and a $20 bill. I also grab my full wallet and my phone charger. I stuff my residence ID tag into the inside zip pocket.

As a mom with small children, I'm exceptional at packing quickly for a variety of other people's needs, and this is honestly a little weird to be packing for myself, for a very likely overnight fling WITH MY HIGH SCHOOL CRUSH.

I do a final look check in the closet door mirror. The bag is a little full but I could be someone who just came from the office heading to the gym after work – like a young professional. Good. I'm glad I chose not to use the backpack.

Whenever I've looked in the mirror lately, I've just been haggard with ruffled, frizzy hair and clothes that don't fit well because I only get time to buy them online.

I love what I see here.

Jun's look validates my thought. I quickly scrawl a note for Ciara.

Went with Jun. Hope you slept well. Love, Clauds.

Chapter 10:

I COULD FALL IN LOVE WITH
YOU OVER AND OVER

I wish I'd worn my sexiest stilettos because Jun is a gentleman and gets a cab for us back to his place. At this point, it's around midnight. I haven't turned into a pumpkin and been sent back yet, but maybe it's a thing where you only travel to and from when you go to sleep. So, I really don't want to go to sleep yet.

This is the first time that Jun and I have ever been alone together. We've always been around Ciara's family, or on campus where I just "happened" to be walking. It took ages to get downtown from my high school, so I always tried to walk there after field trips. Or I'd ask friends to go to the mall with me where he worked a part-time job at a kiosk. I once walked right into a tall cardboard shelf stand while waving hello. I don't know if he saw it, but my friend did and laughed for a long time.

Jun asks what I want to eat – am I still feeling up for pizza or do I mind leftovers that aren't pizza because that's what he'll have. I tell him that I don't mind leftovers. My stomach growls unforgivingly loudly and he laughs. I laugh too and tell him about our AYCE sushi lunch. And the burrito.

"I love both of those places," he laughs again. I tell him about the banh mi.

"Toronto classics."

It's a comfortable conversation that feels like chatting with an old friend, but as we pull up to his swanky building at King and

Bathurst, my high school/university feelings are bubbling up to the surface. It's the type of excitement I'd feel when I'd spot him working, or there playing with his cousins at Ciara's house, or not knowing if he'd show up to a dinner and then making this cool entrance. And plus, of all the twenty-something-year-old guys I've seen today, Jun always stayed away from horrible fashion trends – that's probably why I thought he seemed more "sophisticated" as an older guy.

I knew that Ciara comes from money – that's why Ciara was still in the dorm on a quiet floor and two years older than me (her parents liked the meal plan option and living with me), but I only vaguely knew about the money in Jun's family. I'd heard that he was in a condo and working downtown after graduation, and at the time, I thought it would just be a tiny studio.

"Welcome to my place," and he gestures for me to go in first.

As soon as we step in, I'm surprised at how large it is, given that I was expecting something shoebox-sized. There's a spacious 5x5 ft mat next to a coat closet for shoes and such at the entry.

I take off my boots and place them neatly to the far left on the shoe mat. I put my bag down neatly just beyond the carpet.

He has a grey sectional facing a big screen TV on the left wall. The kitchen is small but the outward-facing counter feels like a large island with a wide sink facing toward the TV. The island is big enough for four comfy bar stools, but there are only two spaced apart. His dining room table is one of those sleek tuck-in style ones, where the chairs get hidden away into the table, and then it just looks like a sculpture when not in use.

The view is decent. The city lights look pretty. He presses a button on a remote and the windows go frosty. I've only ever seen that at a science museum. I didn't know people had employed that technology for home use already –

and twenty years ago.

"Wow, it's so …"

"Clean?" he offers.

"Well … yeah, single guys don't normally live this neatly," I say.

"Thanks! I'm kind of a neat freak," he admits. "I just like things in their proper place."

"Do you have a roommate?" I ask.

"Nope, it's just me. Do you want a tour?"

"Yeah!"

Because I lived at home with my parents, I never had my own place before getting married, so I'm always curious as to what a single person's space looks like. I was already impressed that Jun has this large a living room, but his place has two enormous bedrooms. There's a three-piece bathroom as the "guest" bathroom, then his ensuite in the primary bedroom has a tub and shower.

"Do you have cleaners?" I ask.

"Nope," he answers instantly.

I half expect his second bedroom to be something other than a bedroom – like a home gym or something, but it's very pretty with a coordinated bed, desk, chest of drawers and TV just above.

"How often do you have guests over?"

"My parents stay here for a couple of weeks when they come to town every year. I home swap with an 'elite' few special cousins sometimes, but most of the time it's just me."

"So Ciara could have totally just lived with you during university!" I realize.

"No, no, we're not that close with family members that we'd want to live together. We're happy to go to hotels when we're in the same city at the same time."

I remember now that Jun's father is a big hotel chain executive and his mother is a nonfiction writer. I've forgotten which one it is, but Ciara's family always stays at the same chain because Jun's father gets them major discounts.

My stomach growls loudly. It's a little jarring to remember that I'm on this magical blast to the past but yet, I'm still human with physical needs. And although my 20-year-old body can go ages without the bathroom, I've reached the limit.

"I have to use your bathroom. Is this one okay?" I ask, pointing to the guest one.

"Sure," says Jun. "I'll just bring the leftovers out from the fridge and you can choose what you want to heat up."

When I come out of the bathroom, there's this huge spread of Persian food on the counter.

It looks amazing. There are two lamb shanks, potatoes, rice, kabobs, salmon, tahdig (crispy rice), hummus, two eggplant dishes and two soups.

"Wow, did you have a party yesterday or something?"

"I should have. It's a long story. This used to be … or well, is my favorite restaurant, and I got to know the owners really well. They were having a bad day with slow business, so I ordered all my favorites dishes. I told them I'd call some friends over, and I did, but they were busy." He shrugs. "I just ate by myself."

I help myself to a lamb shank and a little bit of everything else. Jun heats it up for me and I help him put everything back in the fridge once he's done dishing up for himself. His fridge has all these 1/2 cup containers stacked up neatly.

"It's rice pudding and chocolate mousse. We can have dessert."

I smile broadly. Several years ago, Ciara told me that Jun had opened up a rice pudding and chocolate mousse shop in Vancouver. I freaking love both those desserts! When I looked up his store online, I saw that there was always a rotating supply of limited-edition flavors.

Whenever I'm in Vancouver, I always want to go and try it but haven't felt comfortable seeing him in case of stirring up these feelings, especially after he got married. And eventually, so was I.

But Jun in his 20s hasn't even met his future wife yet, so he's mine, at least for tonight.

Wow, after all these years, I'm on a date with Jun Sung.

We enjoy our food at the dining room table. It's delicious. Even as leftovers.

I have to be careful about small talk because I don't want to slip up and talk about things that haven't even happened yet as far as Jun is concerned. Nor do I want to start talking about my kids. I feel a slight pang of longing for them as I realize I haven't seen them all day.

He startles me back into the conversation. "What are your plans for the summer?"

I have to remember that when he asks me questions like this, I need to answer as if I'm 20. And I'm having a hard time remembering what I'm supposed to be doing at this particular point in time in general.

Right, summer session.

"Summer session starts in a week and a half or so."

"What are you taking?"

Ah shit, think think …

"French!" I manage to say without straining too hard. But man, I must have looked a little stupid there. Also, I remember the summer French class, but why was I only taking one class? Or was it two? I can't remember the other one.

"And what are you planning to do until it starts?"

Ah, there's a reasonable question.

Hmm … it actually is a very good question which I haven't had time to process and think about until now. I basically woke up, realized I'd time-travelled, broke up with Conrad, had the best sex of my life, went to lunch, traipsed around downtown with Ciara, went to the ballet, got a burrito, went clubbing and now I'm here with my high school crush – who might very well be crushing on me.

It was a spectacular day so if I'm sent back tomorrow, I'll

feel a slight pang of regret but I know that for logistics it wasn't feasible to do the thing weighing on my mind. But if I'm here for a little while, I intend to get real sex and as often as possible in my very fit 20-year-old body; eat a lot of good things ... and then ...

"I should see this one friend and properly say goodbye before he moves to Singapore."

That's the one friend I sort of had a crush on for a while, overlapping with Conrad, but then I'm only ever going to see him three times more in my lifetime. I never wanted to ruin our friendship so I didn't make a move back then, but I wondered what it would have been like to hook up with him.

"Grab dinner with an acquaintance."

I met Conrad while his best friend was traveling and when we did finally meet, I was like DAMMIT, I should have met the best friend first! I'm gonna hook up with that guy too.

"Go to the symphony."

With my cheap student rate tickets ...

"Maybe take a quick trip somewhere."

I've never travelled outside of Canada, the US, and the Caribbean with Chad and I feel like we missed out on our chance to travel farther distances before we got married. Before having kids, we didn't have the money, and then after kids, because he couldn't get more time off work for vacation, and because he'd travelled internationally for work on his own, he had no desire to take babies traveling by plane to things they wouldn't remember.

"Do you have any upcoming trips?" I ask quickly, trying to put the focus on him.

"I'll probably be in Vancouver soon for work," he says, disappointedly.

"Why do you say it like that? Vancouver's awesome."

"I'll be stressed out. Working 16 hours a day. Traveling to clients means you don't get a work-life balance. They know you've flown in, you're living in a hotel room, and you're available to work all the time."

He takes a big pause before saying excitedly, "Wanna see what I really want to do with my life?"

"RICE PUDDING, CHOCOLATE MOUSSE SHOP OF YOUR OWN!" I cheer!

"YES!" he says, encouraged.

He brings out the containers of chocolate mousse and rice pudding, setting them up on his countertop. I take an eager seat in one of the bar stools.

Aw crap, I forgot to buy Lactaid pills. Do they even exist yet?

As if he heard me, or maybe saw my eyes in panic, he pipes up with, "Most are dairy-free and coconut cream-based," he says. "There are a surprisingly huge number of people who can't handle dairy."

Oh good, the last thing I want is to spend the night in your bathroom.

My favorite rice pudding flavor at Rice to Riches in New York City is "Man-Made Mascarpone." It's made with dried cherries, and I always take three Extra Strength Lactaid pills for the 8 oz. container.

I must be bold and responsible here.

"As much as I'd love to try the dairy ones, I'm going to go with the coconut cream base ones only please."

"Sure," he says without a second thought.

He puts them away, and he's still left an awesome selection.

I see now from the top angle that all the containers are labelled. It's like a private tour of his store offerings ... just for me.

He brings out a massive container of clean, tiny spoons, his dishwasher cutlery basket with a paper towel underneath it, then Post-It notes and pens. Then he pulls out a binder with a chart.

"I'm trying to perfect the recipes," he tells me. "So your feedback is actually going somewhere."

"I'm more than up for the task!" I say eagerly.

We each take a heaping spoonful of the sample at hand. He writes down what I tasted, then I can give him feedback.

I can see him furiously taking notes in a chart with columns for Rice Pudding / Chocolate Mousse, Flavor, Notes, Date Tested, and Date Retested. He's got a real system for feedback!

I tell him things like, "pretzels in peanut butter chocolate pretzel rice pudding need to be smaller." "Try dehydrated blueberries for summer berry so squishy blueberries aren't the same texture as rice." I devour the entire passionfruit sample. Same with the mocha. I tell him that people can fight me for Monkey Lovin', the one with bananas blended in.

I give him notes about using some canned ingredients in case of supply shortages and rising costs for fresh fruit which he appreciates.

"I think that's the most valuable and honest feedback I'll ever get," he tells me.

"Why? Is everybody else just enamored with a free treat and too polite?"

"I think so. And they're probably afraid they'll hurt my feelings. Plus, at this stage, they don't think it's a viable business."

"Oh, incredibly viable," I say encouragingly. "Just offer 2 or 4 oz. portions as combo deals so people don't get saddled with one HUGE container. You want them to come back and recommend a bunch to other people!"

"That's a fantastic idea," he says excitedly, writing it down.

This is my problem with Rice to Riches in New York – 8 oz. is just too much. And I don't want to stand there asking for a billion samples and then just commit to one. I don't say this out loud because I don't know if it even exists yet.

I wonder if I should email present day Jun with more of my ideas. "And calling something 'limited edition' is probably good for enticing people to give their repeat business before their favorite flavor goes away. But then you'll have to bring it back every so often if you're not going to add it permanently to the menu."

"Noted," he says, writing it down.

Jun has been cleaning up as we do each sample, so all he has to do is put the last sample in the fridge and the cutlery basket in the dishwasher. Oh wait – I ate it all, so he puts the empty glass container in the dishwasher.

I'm so happy. And full.

40-year-old me would have gone straight to bed at this point, but it's 2:30 a.m. and 20-year-old me doesn't feel the least bit tired or food coma prone; also because I probably only woke up at 11 this morning. That almost never happens with the kids!

"I saw a guitar in your bedroom as we were doing the tour," I say inquiringly. "Do you play often?"

"Yeah," he says excitedly. "I'm pretty good, too. Wanna hear?"

"Won't your neighbors be bothered this late at night?"

"Nah, both sides of me are out this week for work travel." And the soundproofing is great in this building anyway."

"Yeah, okay!"

Jun grabs a three-ring binder out of the TV stand and gives it to me while he gets the guitar. It's all sheet music in alphabetical order.

"Choose a song you want to hear."

I ask him to play "Everything I Do (I Do It For You)" by Bryan Adams. He sings and plays beautifully. Wow, he was already swoonworthy and I'm legitimately falling in love all over again.

"Can you sing?" he asks.

"I'm not bad," I say.

"Pick a song, let's do it together," he says with a smile.

I flip through the binder and choose "Islands in the Stream" by Dolly Parton and Kenny Rogers.

He pats the seat beside him.

"We should be on the same side so we can read the music together."

"Right," I say.

He starts his part, and I come in at the right time. Man, my voice sounds amazing. Is it the acoustics in here or something? Is it our harmonizing together?

I remind myself to be careful and not ask for something that doesn't exist yet. Otherwise, I'd ask to do Taylor Swift's "Exile" or Lady Gaga and Bradley Cooper's "Shallow". Those would be my karaoke jams!

Just pick from the binder, Claudia!

We do Queen and David Bowie's "Under Pressure" and we're a karaoke dream team.

I always want to do karaoke with Chad but he never wants to go with me. We did it once and it was so much fun!

Chad doesn't play any musical instruments. Or speak any other languages. Or cook. Or clean that well.

Jun is just so much more interesting to be with.

We do Elton John's "Don't Go Breaking My Heart", and we would for sure kick ass at a competition if there was one right now!

When he finishes the song, he looks at me with his amazing smile. He sets the guitar aside on the couch, then reaches for my face to pull me in for a kiss.

I spent so many years wishing for this to happen and now it's real!

I kiss him back with all the passion my teenaged self built up. I make the first move and start unbuttoning his shirt. I love the feeling of his smooth and built upper body. I start undoing his jeans, and he helps me the rest of the way. He stands up to take off his pants and socks in one smooth motion, but he leaves his boxer briefs on.

He looks like an underwear model!

"Is it okay to take off your dress?" he asks me in between kisses.

"Yes," I say quickly.

He takes it off carefully and tosses it on the couch.

"Do you want to take a bath with me?" he says, and boy, is he ever so sexy.

"Yes."

He takes my hand and leads me into his bedroom. He holds me and keeps kissing me as we wait for the water in the tub to fill.

Being with Jun is better than I could have ever imagined. He's comfortable, but at the same time, he makes my heart flutter. It's like a thrill ride with only the good parts.

Even though I hope this holiday lasts more than just for today, I'm grateful for every hour, every touch, every kiss, every lick, every caress.

Chapter 11:

BREAKFAST AT JUN'S

As he's kissing me, I still have my 40-year-old's brain working overtime.

I am not keen on Jun seeing me without my make-up, even if the lights are dimmed.

I don't like baths, especially when there's no glass wall to contain the water when you have to rinse yourself off.

I have sensitive skin and is that a bath bomb he put in? Am I gonna break out in a rash?

Because nothing about that is attractive.

Okay, so it has nothing to do with age. It's just my personality. And then I look over and see the clock.

"WHAT THE FUCK, it's 4 a.m.?!"

"Oh damn!" he says, also shocked.

It's as if my eyes are fighting magnets to stay open. Super sleepy, I'm turning into a pumpkin. There was not enough caffeine in the delicious mocha chocolate mousse to keep me awake.

I snuggle into his body which, to be honest, smells a little sweaty up this close so we'd have needed the bath, and look into his eyes.

"I'm so sorry, I didn't realize it was this late. Do you mind if we take a raincheck on this please?"

He's a little stunned, but says, "Actually that's totally fine because I didn't want to do an all-nighter and burn tomorrow."

He kisses my lips. "But that doesn't mean I want to cut

my time short with you." He kisses me again. "Would you like to sleep in the guest room, or should I take you home?"

"Guest room please?" I sleepily smile.

He kisses me again. "Good, because I wanted to make you breakfast."

"Mmm … thank you."

I have just enough energy to take my makeup off and wash my face so I don't mess up his bed linens when I roll around in my sleep. Someone did that to me once and it absolutely pissed me off when they wouldn't replace the set.

I floss and brush my teeth because dental bills are expensive. I spend my life telling my children this.

I like to shower at night because I think you sleep better when you're clean, but I don't have the energy at the moment. I fall asleep as soon as my head hits the pillow.

I'm not used to sleeping in such a brightly lit room, so the light is what wakes me up. It takes me a second to realize where I am.

Hey! This is Jun's place! And that means there are things I have to do today in case this holiday ends abruptly.

I can hear Jun banging around in the kitchen.

I also don't want him to see me having just woken up.

I manage to duck to the bathroom with the bag of stuff I packed.

He's left me an assortment of towels as a matching set – a bath sheet, face cloth, regular bath towel and bathmat. This says something about a single man who knows how to entertain guests.

I do need to shower after yesterday.

I take a quick look at what products he has on his shower shelf – and yay, he has sensitive skin stuff, which is good because I forgot all that.

I use it quickly, do my makeup. Then I get dressed in the yoga outfit that fits me amazingly well. It accentuates all my good curves and shows off a flat stomach. Hello, flat stomach! Haven't seen you since … well, my 20s.

I'm all for being comfortable in your own skin for anyone else but having known what my own body looked like prior to having had two children plus being pregnant with a third child just … makes me sad. My body is just not, nor will ever be, the same again with stretch marks, scarring, and the like. I wouldn't trade the experience because I love my kids, but damn … my body was in awesome shape back then.

I miss my kids. I don't even have my phone to see pictures of them, and it feels weird to be apart. I haven't ever spent more than three days away.

I'll get back to them soon. Enjoy the break!

My stomach growls. Loudly. Geez, my 40-year-old stomach doesn't growl like this.

Maybe because it has the fat reserves to live off of.

After I've put the wet towels in the washing machine and cleaned up any loose hair off the floor, I make the bed. As part of being a good houseguest, I'd strip the bed, but I actually hope he'll invite me back soon.

I walk to the kitchen, and we kiss just after he's flipped a pancake. "Good morning," we say simultaneously.

"I hope you like pancakes and breakfast sausages," he says.

"Ooh … I really do. Especially homemade by someone else."

"Maple syrup, fresh fruit assortment, and your cutlery, mademoiselle," he says cheekily while presenting me with a knife and fork.

"Why thank you, kind sir," I say as I take a bar stool seat.

I try a piece of pancake. "Mmm … delicious. You really know how to cook."

"I try my best. So, are you free tonight? Can I see you again?"

"It's gonna be pretty late …"

He looks disappointed. "You can just tell me no."

"That's not it. I want to see you again. But I'm not available today."

"I'm flying to Vancouver on Monday," he says. "Can I see you tomorrow?"

I nod eagerly. We agree on Sunday afternoon. He'll pick me up from the dorm.

Okay, so this will be a fling because there's no way this is carrying into a long-term relationship. I suspect that this is the point in time when he makes the move to Vancouver and decides he's moving there permanently. And again, who knows how long this holiday is going to last. I don't even ask when he'll be back. I'll happily take the fling.

I take my plate to the dishwasher but purposely brush up against him and linger. "Thank you. That was delicious." And we exchange maple syrupy kisses.

"I'll drive you back to the dorm. Unless you want to hang out here?" he asks hopefully.

"I'd love to hang out but I really gotta go, sorry."

We head down to the parking garage where his car is parked. It's a silver Audi A6. It looks new and old at the same time.

"Before I start driving, give me your phone so I can add my number," he says.

I hand him my phone. "Me too," and we exchange. Goddamn, these old phone interfaces were so clunky for everything.

I'm trying to add my last name and he says quickly, "You're the only Claudia in my life, Claudia Lee."

"Really? I know like 10 Juns," I quip back.

"Really?"

"Nah," I giggle. But I text faster than he does, even on the retro phone, and in goes "Jun Sung."

I've had the same number for decades now, and I get this pang of annoyance that Chad couldn't remember my phone number and boarded a plane before making arrangements or alerting me about picking up our children from daycare.

Try not to think about it … just enjoy the gorgeous man standing in front of me.

And while he's here …

"Um … could I ask a favor please?"

Chapter 12:

THE THING I HAVE TO DO

*I*t's about 9:30 a.m. when Jun drops me off, so I pretty much have the rest of the day.

Ciara has left me a note.

What did you and Jun do that you didn't come home?!! :-) Tell me ALMOST everything. Are we going to be real family now? Hahahahaha

Went home to sleep for the weekend. See you Monday.

As soon as I'm dressed in an elegant white sundress with big printed flowers and a black sash, black shrug, and practical ballet flats with straps, I sit at my desk and take a deep breath.

Now is my chance to spend time with my Mom.

Yesterday was Friday, which meant that it was a normal workday, and she would have turned me down being at work. But today is Saturday and my parents never plan anything big. If they do, they tell my brother and me long in advance with an email of all the important contact numbers for where they're going.

If we'd had that kind of ideal mother-daughter-as-best-friends relationship, my Mom would have been the first person to call yesterday. But we didn't and, to be honest, getting a life reboot/refresh (from Chad, my gigantically pregnant body, my sugar/carb-free diet, my kids, and my job) was the thing I need-ed first. Like putting your oxygen mask on first before helping anyone else.

I dial the number and try not to cry.

For the 40-year-old me, my Mom died a few years ago, before the kids were born. She answers after the second ring. "Claudia, are you okay?"

The tears stream down my face. I haven't heard her voice in so long. I try to talk normally but I'm so happy and crying at the same time.

"Hi, Mama. I'm fine." I pull the phone away from my face for a breather. "I happened to run into a friend who could do me a favor. Can I see you today for an early Mother's Day surprise?"

"Really?"

"Why, are you doing anything besides cleaning today?"

"Dad and I just came back from grocery shopping. We were going to go to Edwards Gardens later this afternoon."

"Tell Dad I'm stealing you for today. Can you come to the King Henry hotel for 11 o'clock?"

"What's the time now … okay!"

"Wear something nice. We're going to the restaurant there."

"Ooh, I'm excited. Thanks, sweetie."

"Good!"

"Okay, love you!"

"Love you too. See you soon."

As soon as we hang up, I cry and just let it out. See you soon.

My Mom and I fought constantly while I was growing up, and things got much better when I moved out, but we didn't share secrets or talk about crushes, or anything of major substance for that matter. In fact, I don't think my Mom ever took my career path seriously. Maybe because she couldn't ever explain what I did in one simple word, like "doctor" or "accountant" or "lawyer." Now she could sum it up as "makes commercials" but it was a long winding path to get there.

But I dropped everything and rushed home when I heard that she had days and weeks, not months to live. I was part of the rotation of people keeping vigil at her bedside for fear of leaving her alone when she passed. And though I struggled to write her eulogy, because even my cards were generic and not as thoughtful as they should have been, I know that there was more love between us than anything else and led with that.

One of my favorite memories of my younger days was getting a Groupon for afternoon tea at this swanky Toronto hotel. I took my Mom for one day, and a friend who was like a second mother on another day. I say this because looking back, I probably sought out missing pieces of a mother-daughter relationship where I could, and it framed my real mother-daughter relationship in terms of expectations and disappointments.

I don't remember anything about the day with the friend (who I probably subconsciously lost touch with on purpose as my relationship with my Mom improved), but I do remember how happy my Mom was on our day together. She was smiling broadly and gave me a collapsible purse hook – it's to hold your purse under the table so it doesn't touch the floor. I still have it but haven't used it – my purses are always too massive for such a dainty hook. Maybe one day when I'm not carrying a thousand things with me for me and three to four other family members.

That day, I think she appreciated being treated to a fancy occasion. She wouldn't have enjoyed a spa day but loved anything to do with afternoon tea.

Since Jun's dad is a hotel group executive, I asked Jun to get me in for an afternoon tea sitting at one of the nicer places because I knew that they'd be booked for months in advance. Jun thought of the King Henry Hotel himself. He was very polite on the phone, but when he introduced himself as his father's son, they must have thought Jun meant "hop to it" because it sounded like the person at the other end was saying,

"Right away, sir."

When I arrive at the King Henry, my Mom isn't there yet, so I wait in the lobby, kind of steeling myself up. When I last saw her, she was dying in a hospital bed. I managed to get her last smile, but she was frail and mostly incoherent, then later unable to talk or even open her eyes. She just snored and then peacefully slipped away.

I do a double-take when she walks through the door. It's her, dressed in a navy skirt I salvaged from her closet as we sorted through her belongings, and a light blue floral blouse. My Mom doesn't have the greatest fashion sense but this is a nice outfit. On her arm she has a giant black purse which I can only assume holds a book and her running shoes, since she's wearing those low-heeled pumps I always thought were uncomfortable for her but couldn't figure out what to otherwise suggest.

I'm so overwhelmed and happy to see her that tears stream down my face. I run to hug her as tightly as I can. It feels the same as it always did to hug her and I don't let go for the longest time. She just hugs me in return and rubs my back, telling me it's okay.

When I finally let go just to see her smiling face, my own crumples as I say, "I've missed you a lot." Fresh tears feel like a waterfall on my cheeks.

"I missed you too!" she says and wipes my tears with a tissue ready from her massive purse. "Have you been having a hard time?"

I just nod. And she wipes more tears away.

I take her hand and we go to the hostess. "Hi, Jun Sung made a reservation for me – I'm Claudia Lee and this is my Mom, Jovie."

The hostess's eyes widen and she nods, as if in alarm. "Yes, right this way please."

It's a little weird when she takes us past the dining room, up an elevator, but then we arrive at this beautiful, private, glass-enclosed, flower-filled solarium overlooking the city.

"There is no one booked for this room until much later this afternoon, so please, take your time and enjoy," she says graciously. "Here is the tea menu."

"Claudia, this must be so expensive!" my Mom says, freaking out a little.

"Mom, don't worry about it," I say. And I'm legitimately not worried. As long as the bill doesn't max out my student credit card with a $2500 limit, I'm okay. Plus, I expect this holiday to have no future consequences whatsoever. I haven't even checked my bank account. Maybe I'll check it if I've been here for a few days. Just in case.

A server appears and tells us that his name is Jean-Marc and he'll be taking care of us today. Jean-Marc reminds me of this handsome producer I once worked with, even if it's just because of his brown hair, pronounced jawline with stubble, and thick Québecois accent.

Jean-Marc asks if we have any dietary restrictions right as my Mom is lining up all her pre-eating pills.

"Yes," I say. "We are both lactose-intolerant if that can be accommodated, please?"

"Absolutely," he says with certainty. "I would be delighted to take care of that for you. Have you chosen a tea?"

My Mom chooses an oolong. I choose a cream of Earl Grey.

"Excellent," says Jean-Marc, taking the menus.

His accent is so pronounced that I instinctively break into French. *"Merci beaucoup,"* I say flawlessly with an appreciative smile.

"Vous êtes bilingues, mademoiselle!" he says surprised.

"Oui, mais j'ai oublié, désolée, s'il vous plaît parlez en anglais pour ma mère."

"D'accord. Il était très gentil de parler français avec moi. I will be back shortly."

Putting away her pills, my Mom says, "I didn't understand anything, but your French is nice. He understood you. Good to get some practice."

My Mom smiles and admires the view. I admire her. She's healthy, and I wish she would have lived longer like this.

DON'T cry, DON'T cry.

When he disappears, my Mom leans forward as if she's just remembered. "Who is this Jun Sung who made the reservation?"

"Um, well, I don't know what to call him … I guess you could say – oh well, he's Ciara's cousin."

I was never able to lie to my parents and still cannot, so I do the thing I've always done – which is to omit information.

"Oh," she says nodding. "Make sure you call him later to thank him."

"I will."

"What happened to Conrad?"

"I dumped him!"

"What?!" my mother says, shocked.

"Yeah. There's nothing much to say about that."

"Are you all right?" she asks with great concern in her face.

I realize I have to fudge this a little because otherwise she'll think I'm a psychopath, devoid of feelings since at the time, I did take some time to recover from the breakup, even though I did the dumping back then too.

"I was upset about it when it happened. I'm totally fine now."

"When did you break up?"

"A while ago?" I say, feigning forgetfulness because I can't say "yesterday."

"Really, I'm fine now," I say quickly.

Her face changes – softens even, like relief.

"Did you not like him, Mom?"

"It's not that I didn't like him. And you can choose who-ever you want. But I think an Asian man might understand you better. And you need someone more mature than Conrad or most guys of your age in general."

"Why?"

"Because even though you are 20 and think you know yourself, you are still trying to figure out who you are. Only when you know yourself will you know what you want in a partner."

Damn, my mother has never sounded so wise. I wish she'd given me this advice when I was actually 20 - when I need- ed it. Like how I needed the advice in *high school* about avoiding sugar, because with our genes, sugar exacerbated acne. Instead, she told me this as a married adult, long after I'd done rounds of Accutane as a teenager.

She asks how classes are, and I keep it light in my response, because I honestly don't remember how they were. But I tell her about my favorite professors (only because I've emailed them in recent years, and they were so gracious in their replies).

I want to tell her so badly about my boys, and that I'm pregnant with a daughter. That I think she would love seeing their faces as they enjoyed her food. How Timothy would love to play board games with her. How Jeremy would cozy up to her and fall asleep.

I stifle my impending tears with a cough. And just in time because the food arrives.

Jean-Marc brings a tiered serving platter and explains the menu. "Usually, there is a choice of items, but I understand Mr. Sung is a personal friend of yours, so we have included all the items. If you have not finished everything, we would be happy to package the remaining food for you to take home."

He puts the tiered serving platter on what looks like a metal cutting board, and I learn it's like a cold plate to keep your food cold.

The selection includes:

Sandwiches

-- egg salad
-- smoked salmon with lactose-free cream cheese and capers
-- Manchego cheese and fig jam
-- curry chicken salad with cranberries
-- ham and lactose-free brie with sundried tomatoes and roasted eggplant

4 Texas cupcake-sized lactose-free quiches
-- bacon, mushroom, asparagus and leek
-- lobster, scallion and artichoke

Lactose-free scones
-- blueberry
-- peach
-- cheese

An assortment of pineapple, mango, apricot and strawberry jam and lactose-free whipped cream

Tiny lactose-free desserts
-- crème brulée
-- macarons
-- macaroons
-- brigadeiros
-- carrot cake
-- chocolate lava cake

Jean-Marc then brings out a hot plate for each of our teapots to keep them warm.

"Let me know if you would like a refill or different tea," he says while giving us a tray of lactose-free milk, sugar, various sweeteners, and a teaspoon, cup, and saucer each.

I wish I had my real phone so I could take pictures of all of it, but I remembered to bring my dinky digital camera. I take an awesome selfie of us two, the food, and then separately, I take a beautiful portrait of my Mom. I wonder if I'll get to keep the photos at all or whether it all gets wiped when I go back to being 40.

The food is phenomenal and that it's all lactose-free is even more incredible. Jun must have called them back and secretly given them a heads up.

We talk about books. I explain the plots of the latest Korean dramas I've watched. I tell her about seeing *Coppélia* last night and ask if she'd like to go with me to another ballet. She would.

I ask her what it was like to be a stay-at-home mom and she tells me all about cloth diapers and how I wouldn't sleep as a baby. How in those days, I would just sit on the floor and play with toys by myself so she could do all the chores at home, but my brother had to be watched like a hawk.

I ask her about her university days and she doesn't remember a lot. Just that she studied hard and didn't have a lot of money.

I remember now that my Mom doesn't have much to say when talking about herself. I can't resist. I tell her that in the future, I can see myself having two boys.

"I think I'll name them Timothy and Jeremy."

She nods and smiles. "Those are beautiful names."

"I haven't thought about a girl's name yet." I'm honest about that. I haven't.

"Ah, you still have lots of time before that happens," she says laughing. Then her face goes serious. "You're not pregnant, are you?"

"Not at the moment, Mom!" I say laughing. "I'm pretty sure all the parts work though." My face turns red. "Let's change the subject! Here, have a macaron."

We chat idly about how it's cute that they have both macarons and macaroons in the same menu.

"Maybe someone got confused and then they said, 'we should just have both so no one feels like they missed out on what they really wanted but didn't know the difference'."

We both giggle.

Before we know it, several hours have passed. Neither of us needs to say we're full. My Mom starts to shift uncomfortably in her seat.

"Mom, it's okay, you go to the bathroom first. I'll take care of the rest. And don't do that thing where you sneak off to pay the bill."

"I won't. I had a whole pot of tea so I can't hold it long enough to do that." And she disappears to the bathroom.

Jean-Marc appears as if by magic. We've finished a good portion but there's still quite a bit left over. "I will take care of this for you," he says while swiftly clearing the table.

"And I'll take care of the bill, thank you."

He nods. "*D'accord.*"

He disappears but the hostess returns in his place shortly after.

"Miss Lee, your dining experience is compliments of Mr. Jun Sung."

WHOA!

Stunned, I squeak out, "Oh, thank you so much. I'd like to leave the gratuity."

She smiles graciously. "He has taken care of that as well, and very generously, so there is no need."

"Wow, thank you. Everything was amazing."

"Our pleasure."

My Mom returns just as the hostess is leaving. Jean-Marc shows up with this beautiful box of our leftovers. It's heavy when he hands it over.

"Oh my!" I say, surprised.

"It's heavier because each tier has a reusable ice pack on the bottom. Our chef is very concerned about food safety."

SWANKY. This must have cost a fortune!

"Thank you so much, Jean-Marc."

"It has been a pleasure, ladies. Have a wonderful day."

He nods and disappears. I debate leaving a cash tip but

then decide against it because I don't want them to think I didn't believe Jun was generous with them.

"How much was it?" my Mom asks.

"Mom, you can't ask that when it's a gift!"

"Okay. Thank you. I loved this." She holds up the leftovers like a prize. "And your father will love this too!"

I know not to bring up that Jun paid because that will lead to all kinds of questions and in my consequence-free holiday, I'm just going to let her assume that I treated. I will definitely call him when I get back. It's a bit weird that I can't just text or video call him upon finding out about his generosity.

I quickly use the fancy hotel bathroom before heading out because I too have had a pot of tea. I prompt my Mom to change into her running shoes, which she does. On the way to the subway, I show my Mom my favorite hangout spots, mostly because they have nice bathrooms or delicious food at student-budget prices.

We ride the TTC together and my Dad meets us at Edwards Gardens for the walk like they originally planned. It's good to see the younger version of my Dad.

Mom and I are still stuffed but he makes a picnic of our leftovers and enjoys every bit.

And "bit" is accurate, because during the meal, we cut everything in halves or quarters, so we'd try it all before filling up.

My Mom admires the budding flowers and sunset. It's a perfect time as I stroll along the paths and bridges with my parents. I savor the time with them. Watch their faces. Watch them holding hands.

It's getting darker so my Dad offers to drive me back to the dorm. I know he'll feel better, and my Mom will too, so I accept. I ask to sit in the back with my Mom – me in the middle and her on the right-hand side so she can still see my Dad. My Mom must have whispered to him that I was having a hard time, so nobody questions it. I weave my arm around hers and hold her hand the whole ride back.

I'm sad it's ending, yet satisfied that this whole day with her went as perfectly as I could have hoped for. If I get sent back tomorrow to the present, I will be okay.

When we get to the dorm, my Dad pulls up to the curb. There's a line of cars and it feels a little like an airport drop-off. I kiss my Dad on the cheek and thank him for the ride.

"Love you," he calls out.

"Love you too," I reply.

Being on the right-hand side and blocking my exit, my Mom gets out of the car first and walks me to the door for a last hug.

"Thanks for being my Mom." I squeeze her tightly and don't let go until she says with a laugh, "Okay, it's cold and I'll have to find a bathroom soon."

She smiles so widely. "I had a beautiful day with my beautiful daughter. I love you. Goodnight!"

"I love you!" I yell. And I give her one last hug.

As she closes the car door, she quickly rolls down the window. I run to her.

She says thoughtfully, "I think because my name Jovie means happy and cheerful, it's almost like it helped shape my personality and how people saw me. If you have a daughter, what do you think of the name, 'Joy'?"

"That sounds great, Mom."

They drive off and I stand waving goodbye with tears that feel like they won't stop.

Chapter 13:

I CHOOSE DESSERT

I think it was half Toronto and half people just knowing to give me space, but people just leave me alone to cry.

When I've finally stopped, I head upstairs to the dorm room. It's a good end to the day because if I'd slept over at my parents' place, it would have been awkward without my stuff, and I wouldn't have wanted to cuddle with them to sleep. They only have a double bed and my Mom snores way too loudly.

Once in my dorm room, I collapse onto my own bed and call Ciara.

"Hey!" she says. "How's it going?"

"It's okay ..." I start. I vaguely tell her about the day with my Mom, and my parents. "It was really perfect," I manage to squeak out without crying.

"Aww ... that's lovely. Okay, enough about that. What's going on with Jun?!"

"Well ... so I'm calling because ... what does ... um ... Jun's dad is an executive at Hoitview Group, right?"

I know Ciara's proud of me for pronouncing it "hwa view" like the secret "view of the flowers" Chinese-French play on pronunciations it is.

"No ... Jun's family *owns* Hoitview Group. That's why we stay at their hotels when we travel. We just leave generous tips and pay for everything at cost."

"Ohh ... that totally explains a lot of things," I say. And it dawns on me why his apartment is not as lavish as one would expect for that kind of money because it's probably one of several rental units that he just lives in. Their main residence would be palatial.

I tell her about how well Jun treated us for afternoon tea.

"That's super sweet," she says, surprised. "I didn't know he had that in him. So what did you guys do after I passed out on Friday?"

"We didn't sleep together if that's what you're getting at!"

"Really? I thought you'd be all into hooking up after, you know, Cable Guy." She's genuinely shocked. "And you didn't come home!"

"I know, we were just chilling and then it got too late that I fell asleep there. In the other bedroom!"

"What does chilling mean?" she asks.

Oh right, we don't say chilling yet.

"Hanging out."

I tell her about the guitar, and the Persian food, and the chocolate mousse.

"He makes chocolate mousse?"

Oh right, it's probably still his secret talent.

"Yeah, it was amazing. So I'm gonna call him to thank him. Are you cool if I keep hanging out with him alone? Does it weird you out?"

"I thought about it … and I can't stop two consenting adults. So it doesn't really matter what I think. But keep in mind that it's going to make things super awkward if you break up." She says the last part with a little bit of doom in her voice.

"Okay … got it. I will not sully our friendship and will not tell you any details that will gross you out," I say as reassuringly as possible.

"I give you my blessing," she announces as if bestowing a royal honor. "Gotta go, bye!" We hang up quickly.

Damn …

20-year-old me would have been quite intimidated with

this new information. I probably would have thought something along the lines of never being able to get in with his family, not measuring up, not being able to break into that circle of money and I'm sure the hidden upper echelon of society that would just be out of my wheelhouse.

Not 40-year-old me. 40-year-old me is excited about that prospect because in the next 24 to 36 hours, there might be something else amazing happening like finding this extra secret tea room in Toronto to enjoy with my Mom. These are exciting highlights of my holiday and that's about it.

At this point in time, I'm pretty sure Jun goes to Vancouver, and I'll never see or hear from him again. I hear *of* him, that he gets married, opens the chocolate mousse and rice pudding shop, but he doesn't come back to Toronto. I'll never run into him. I have no reason to contact him. Even for Ciara's wedding, something happens where he's not able to make it.

For a fling, this is fine! Absolutely fine. And then I get to live out my dream of getting together with my high school crush, then I will move on to the other two guys. Or three! Either way, this holiday is gonna have some excellent sex. Or at least different from Chad. I can blow off steam before returning to reality.

There, I gave it decent thought before proceeding. I call Jun.

"Hey," he answers kind of excitedly.

"Hey! Thank you so much for a beautiful experience. My Mom and I loved everything about it."

"My pleasure, my pleasure. Did you get Jean-Marc? I asked for him."

"Yeah – he was the best! The food was amazing. You should add your rice pudding and chocolate mousse to the afternoon tea menu!"

"Nah, my Dad doesn't think it's sophisticated enough for that setting."

"What?! Just put it in a fancy goblet or something and

it would be amazing." His silence is a little telling. "Just think about it," and I say no more.

Maybe this eventually comes to fruition. I should check the current menu when I get back to 40.

"Thanks for the vote of confidence. I appreciate it."

"Oh – and thank you so much – did you give them a heads up about the dairy?"

"I just said you might prefer lactose-free or dairy-free items so they were prepared for both."

"They totally were – my Mom was dazzled. We were both dazzled!"

"Good, good. I'm so glad to hear that."

There's a bit of a pause. I'm waiting for his invitation. And then he says, "What are you up to now?"

"I just got back to my room, I haven't thought about where I'm going next." There's a slight pause there.

He clears his throat. "Do you ... want to come over?"

"YES!" I exclaim.

He tries to play it cool but I kind of sense excitement on his end. "Take a cab here. I'll meet you at the front door."

Damn, I'll need stuff. I could end up staying over for two nights if he's flying out on Monday. I feel no shame in taking the backpack because we didn't define what we were going to do.

As I'm packing, I'm still kind of reeling from the beautiful day with my Mom, but grief goes in waves. I don't want to overthink it because I'll start nitpicking and suddenly it becomes less than perfect. I just want to treasure the time and think fondly of the exquisite memory because really, this is the last time I can say I saw my Mom, not saying goodbye in a hospital room. I cry again and take a breather to sit on the bed.

And then I'm okay.

My student closet is not nearly as big as my current home closet and there's not much thought needed. Before the kids, I travelled a lot for work and, as if old habits die hard, I go into autopilot packing as if I were going on a work trip. Comfortable clothes (for being on set), one dressy outfit (in case of a client meeting), and nice workout clothes because you never know when you'll run into the client at the hotel gym. But in this case, I pack the condoms, my second-best lingerie (he's seen the first), a complete toiletries bag, and my glasses. I use the big purse from today that's ready to go and then carry my stilettos separately. Maybe naïve 20-year-old me would have done that thing where you show up in lingerie under a coat, not even carrying tissues, phone or wallet, but nah, 40-year-old me has been through too much to see where that could go wrong.

The cab ride to Jun's place takes almost no time at all, again because it's Saturday night. I keep all my belongings in the back seat beside me so that I don't forget anything in the trunk.

And then goddamn, now I remember what a pain it was to text on these old phones, pressing the same button 4 times to cycle through to one character, and why it was so cool to get the next type of phone that had a keyboard for easier messaging. I text Jun "in cab" as a courtesy but then by the time I'm done, we're two blocks away.

When I arrive at his building, Jun is standing at the front door. I wave and as soon as the cab driver stops, Jun opens the passenger side door to give the driver cash. WOW.

I pull out my stuff as gracefully as possible, but then Jun grabs my hand and helps me out. He takes my backpack, sliding the strap over his shoulder, and then he takes his change, grabbing some and handing it back for a tip. I quickly check that I haven't left anything behind. With my purse over my shoulder and stilettos in one hand, I have a hand free to hold his.

"Thank you," I say, reaching for a kiss. "Mmm …"

"It's chocolate," he says. "I was going to experiment with crêpes. I've never made them."

"Ooh," and my eyes go wide. "And?"

"I got all the stuff together to fill the crêpes, just didn't get the crêpe part going. Maybe in the morning." He adjusts the backpack to wearing it with both straps. "You moving in?" he says with a mischievous smile. He lifts my hand with the stilettos.

"Well, I thought I'd rather be prepared for whatever you might want to do. Or maybe what *I* want to do." I give an equally coy smile and he blushes a little, which is ultra cute.

We quietly make small talk as we walk through the lobby, go up the elevator, through the hallway, and to his condo. He opens the door and ushers me in first. I put my stuff down, take my shoes off, wait for him to do the same.

All the food is covered with clear plastic wrap, but it's totally a feast for the eyes. He has all the fixings for fruit and chocolate fondue. He even has sliced starfruit! And pineapple! Last time I saw a fruit assortment this pretty was at a buffet restaurant with a chocolate fountain. But as demon children do, I watched in horror as one put in his fingers, then his face, trying to catch the chocolate pouring down. I recall this story for Jun and he recoils in disgust.

"What a food tragedy," he says, shaking his head.

"I can help with crêpes if you still want to make them, Jun," I tell him while washing my hands at his kitchen sink. He wraps his arms around me, puts his hands on top of mine, soaping ours together. He kisses me on the cheek, grabs a hand towel for us, then spins me around to kiss me on the lips. I kiss him back and linger. It's comfortable with him. And it feels like I've known him my entire life – which is kind of the truth – high school does seem forever ago.

"Are you hungry?" he asks.

I'm not sure if he wants me to say yes or no.

"Well, that depends … who did you make this for?" I gamble.

"It started off as a project for inspiration …" he admits. "And then it just …"

"Got out of hand?" I joke.

He smiles a genuinely handsome, sheepish smile. "But look who just arrived that can share it with me."

I fully expected to walk in the door, pin him to the wall and get right into his pants, but I don't have gestational diabetes in this magical world. 40-year-old me says fuck that, sex can wait. Especially if my 20-year-old body will not suffer the consequences of said dessert.

Some might say you could combine this sexy scene and drizzle chocolate over each other as you sex it up – but nah, fuck that too. That is how you get yeast infections. And ruin perfectly good bed linens. And possibly the mattress.

He offers me tea (I decline), then water (which I accept) and when he opens his cup cupboard, there's a whole alphabet of personalized Scrabble mugs.

"Scrabble fan?!" I say excitedly.

"I am, but I'm not a fanatic that I bought these myself. A friend bought me the whole set because they went on an awesome clearance sale." He hands me the C mug.

"Can we play Scrabble while eating?" I ask, raising my eyebrows daringly, like, *Are you up for the challenge, Jun Sung?*

"Yeah," he says, with his eyebrows being like, *You're on, Claudia Lee,* and he goes to the other cabinet of the TV stand, opposite to where he keeps his sheet music binder, and shows me the assortment of board games, including Scrabble.

Without us even saying anything, he arranges food, and I set up the game on his table. He has a small bowl of chocolate for each of us (so you can multi-dip to your heart's content), two small plates, and the fruit platter with tiny tongs. We each get a pair of chopsticks which I think is super cute and functional because we're both Asian, but also chopsticks can be multipurpose for fondue as in lifting, stabbing, and skewering one's fruit. He puts down some fancy napkins which is a little reminder that though he's very down-to-earth, his family does own a huge network of hotels. He's like a Chinese Hilton, but you wouldn't know that just by looking at him.

Well ... I mean ... he does have great hair, so there's no way he's doing $18 haircuts in Chinatown. And his clothing does fit him exceptionally well ... so I don't think he shops at standard department stores.

He starts the game with the word "helpful" and uses all 7 letters. Goddamn, I'm playing with a champion.

Every bite of fruit is delightfully sweet. The chocolate is a dark bittersweet mix, so it's the perfect balance.

I counter his Scrabble play with the word "quick", but I miss out on maxing out the points because of where I have to place it.

He keeps score with a pen and notepad from the Hoitview Group. It's good that we eat and play Scrabble, because I don't really feel like talking. I have questions, but I don't want to pry. And I don't want to get too deep into conversation because I also want this to be a light and fluffy fling. I also have to avoid talking about my work, current events, kids, school (which I can't even remember), and the latest memes. That's like ... everything. Oh, we could talk about ... oh wait, we cannot talk about how I used to create situations to run into him – not even in a joking way. I can't get too familiar. I don't want to fall too much for him when I know it won't last long.

He's actually killing it with this Scrabble game, and I'm impressed. I played Scrabble with some engineers who went to the University of Waterloo and damn, they were brilliant – like Jun right now.

I get stuck with some weird letters and to buy time, I tell him we should put the dirty dishes in the dishwasher. It catches him a little off guard with my timing, but he joins me instantly.

I stack the dishwasher while he puts the rest of the fruit into a freezer bag. He catches me looking in horror.

"All that work when you cut everything so nicely!"

"I'm gonna make us dairy-free smoothies in the morning!" he says, reassuringly. I'm touched by his sweet and considerate plan. And now I'm gonna jump his bones.

Chapter 14:

GETTING WHAT I WANT

*M*y face must have lit up nicely because he leans in to kiss me. I kiss him back, keeping it to just lips, no tongue. I only really have Chad to compare with from recent years and while Chad used to be a great kisser way back in the day when he took the time to shave, I don't want any more than a peck on the lips from him now because he has a scratchy and prickly beard I despise.

Jun has zero facial hair and gets rewarded for it. I want to ask, "How are you single?" but at the same time, I feel his hands roaming over my body.

No, no, the question is how am *I* single?

Of course, I wished this would happen when I was a teenager but now that it is happening, I hope I haven't overhyped this up in my head. But because we'll never see each other again, I'm also not afraid to demand what I want and take the lead to make this go my way.

"I don't like baths. I want to take a shower with you," I say while unbuttoning his shirt.

"Yes ma'am," he says as I take his shirt off. I don't know how many hours a day he's working out to counter the desserts he makes but whatever he's doing, it works and his topless, athletic body takes my breath away.

Damn, what would have happened if we'd hooked up when I was actually 20? What would my life have been like?

It's not 4 a.m. like last time and I am wide awake. I take

his hand and we go to the guest bathroom shower I used last time. He has two sets of towels waiting for me.

"How thoughtful," I say, surprised. "Thank you."

He smiles at me and runs his fingers through my hair while he kisses me. "I figured you'd stay a little longer this time."

"Take off my dress," I tell him. He unzips and while I expect him to let it drop to the floor and leave it there, he hangs it up neatly.

I get my fingers on his jeans zipper. I can see he's hard already. "Are you ready?" I ask while strategically grazing my hand over his crotch.

He nods, his eyes already rolling up in pleasure. He's already so expressive – I'll think about giving him a blowjob because it's fun to see his face like this knowing I did it to him.

"Take this all off," I say, pointing at his lower half. He does what I say. I smile when I see his junk. He manscaped nicely – I almost think he went for a wax.

"I like what I see. Excellent work," and I manhandle him to the point where he's visibly unsteady on his feet.

"Start the water and I'll keep going." He nods as I reach around him from behind.

He puts his hand in to feel the temperature. "It's ready," he manages to gasp out.

"You go first," I say, letting go, only to get my own lingerie off. I strike a voilà pose for him and he smiles eagerly as I join him. The shower is more than big enough for two people so nobody's getting pinned against a wall unless they want to be. In fact, it's actually big enough that there's a built-in bench.

"Can you switch to the handheld part please? I don't want to get my face wet," I tell him firmly. I know the foundation and powder will steam off but I love how I did my eye make-up so I don't want it to run. In the mount, he aims the handheld part away from me, then takes my hand and guides me into the shower. I rub up against him and he holds me as if we were to slow dance. I reach behind him for the handheld nozzle, running the water down over his shoulders and down between us.

"Hold this." I swap him the handheld nozzle for free hands to get body wash. He runs the water over my shoulders. I lather up the body wash and go straight for his penis and a hand job. I take back the nozzle and run the water over the rest of his body and mine.

"How many times in a night can you come?" I ask sexily.

"I don't know," he tries to reply.

"Let's find out," I say coyly. And with my mouth I go down on him, watching his face as he groans in ecstasy. Maybe it's my skill or being able to read him really easily, but I know just the point at which to take my mouth off and change to my hand so he spurts at the wall, and I hose it off with the hand-held nozzle. He slides down to sit on the bench, recovering.

"Thank you," he says breathlessly. Clearly it was a good time.

"Feel me," I tell him as I hand him the body wash. While I run the water over us, he obediently lathers me up, running his hands over my breasts, then my waist, back up to my shoulders. He spins me around and down slowly so that I'm sitting between his legs. He reaches between my legs and fingers my clitoris. He refills on the body wash and with soapy fingers, he stands me up then bends me over a little to run his other hand between my buttocks. It makes me squeal excitedly.

He pulls me gently back toward him. "Just in case you wanted to do something there," he murmurs into my ear.

"You should do the same for yourself. You never know." His eyes go wide, and he stands up while I rinse myself off. I reach for the toggle to change to the overhead showerhead, but I realize I don't know which one it is. He reaches his beautifully toned arm around me for it. I take a giant step from the shower to the counter, laying down a bathmat for us overtop my little puddle, wrapping a bath sheet around myself. The towel is warm! I hand him the other bath sheet as he turns off the shower and steps out.

He pulls me close and helps dry me off. I do the same for him. He kisses me, then along my shoulders and collarbone. When he takes the towel off, I see he's hard again, but it's my turn to climax so he'll have to wait.

"Oh," I look around at the floor disappointedly.

"What's wrong?" he asks with genuine concern.

"I hate having bare feet on a cold floor," I say. "I forgot my slippers."

Effortlessly, he picks me up so that my legs are around his waist.

"Better now?"

"Yes," I nod.

"Where should we go now then?"

"Choose a bed," I reply.

"Good," he says, and carries me to his own bed. "My bed's the biggest."

We get under the covers to warm up while he kisses me and then he turns on the heater with a remote. Jun definitely gets bonus points for snuggling. And I feel like I fit comfortably in his arms, contoured against the shape of his body.

We stay like that for a little while until he says, "Are you ready for your turn?"

"Yes," I say excitedly.

"So …" he nervously starts. "I can't go down on you because I've got a TMJ disorder from playing sports as a kid. Just … getting hit in the face and head too much."

"Oh," my face must be contorted in sympathetic pain.

"I'm fine most of the time! And I can kiss you, but sticking out my tongue for any prolonged period of time will just fuck me up for a whole day. But we'll see how this goes, and I know it's not a substitute, but I will … pleasure you in other ways."

I'm a little confused as to what he means, but he pulls out a paper gift bag from a drawer. "I bought this for you! Today!"

and he shows me just the date on the receipt with today's date – April 30 2005.

"Wow, so you were *expecting* to sleep with me!" I say teasingly.

"Very much *hoping*," he corrects. He pulls out several boxes of condoms (including ribbed, non-latex, and ultra-thin), a packaged vibrator, and a packaged vibrating cock ring.

"HOW MUCH SEX WERE YOU HOPING FOR?" I near-scream.

"It's just options! You can take it all home with you!" he says apologetically.

I make dead serious eye contact as I say, "Well, until you fly out on Monday, I was expecting a lot of sex." And he looks so relieved as I grab the packaged vibrator and rip it open. My ninja mom skills have trained me in the art of inserting batteries as quickly as possible into a new toy, so it's ready in seconds. He takes it from my hand, spoons me from behind and instantly finds my clit with the vibrator.

Ooh, talented.

I let out audible moans and he heightens the mood by murmuring in my ear, "Baby, you are so sexy right now, but I want to see you." Still holding the vibrator, he gently edges me up upright so I'm facing his closet mirror door on my knees, but my legs spread apart. I instantly understand why Olympic athletes are notoriously promiscuous at the Games. If you have superhumans all gathered in one place, then why the fuck would you not have one epic sexcapade after another?!

I see the two of us in the mirror.

Wow, his whole body is ripped, and this was soooooo worth it. And look at me … I could be a porn star if I wanted!

He kisses my shoulder and my neck, and his voice sounds so hot when he says, "I'm gonna add your G-spot." I nod okay, and he inserts two fingers into my vagina and starts a stroking motion outward – and oh does he find it.

Is he secretly a gynecologist?!

With the combination of the action on my clitoris and my G-spot, and seeing what's going on in the mirror, I get the lead up to and orgasm of my dreams. My whole body convulses in pleasure for ages, and just as I'm coming down from it, he asks, "Any preference for condom type?" I shake my head no. He chooses one quickly and puts it on, with the cock ring on top.

"Am I okay to go in?" he asks, and my answer is just to pull him in myself. He slides in easily because I'm that wet, and it feels so good. Even better when I turn my head to the mirror and see him thrusting in and out of me, that it only takes a little bit to lead up to another orgasm for me. He keeps it going and comes soon after.

He disappears to his ensuite to clean up, but I'm still riding my orgasm after-shocks, wanting another one. He comes out wearing clean boxer-briefs (again, looking like a gorgeous underwear model). He sees this and smiles, then resumes his position behind me with the vibrator and his other hand, and I orgasm twice more like this.

I catch my breath, and he kisses me from behind.

"I'll get us some water," he laughs and rolls out and away. I watch him walk away. He is so hot.

He's back in no time with two Scrabble mugs, different letters this time. His sheets feel luxurious against my skin as I sit up to take a sip.

I check the clock – it's only 11 p.m. and we have hours to do this again.

Chapter 15:

THE MOST PERFECT SUNDAY - PART 1

For the next hour, we recover, watch late night TV, fuck again twice, and then debate going to a club but then rule it out because our dancing will lead to getting hot and heavy, and the bed is right there. Plus, he has all the fixings for a cocktail if I want one, and if we want to get drunk, we can do it that here too without risk of spraining an ankle in my stilettos. But he does promise to take me out to dinner tomorrow so that I can wear my fancy dress with them.

And he did find me slippers – they're soft slip-ons with an adjustable strap, a quality bottom, and Hoitview Group logos embroidered on the tops by the toes. He hands me a matching robe which I wear over my naked body, and when it comes undone at the top, I don't really bother to do it up which he enjoys. I enjoy watching him walk around in just his boxers, although he "admits" that he's getting cold and needs to snuggle me to warm up.

I start yawning and realize that it's probably a good time to go to bed. It's been an incredible day. I thought that the time with my Mom was already more than I could ask for but topped with hooking up with Jun and getting multiple orgasms, it's chef 's kiss perfect.

I kiss him, then say bluntly, "Thank you. I'm going to bed. I don't want you to see me without my makeup, so I'm sleeping in the other room." He pretends to be wounded then says we should say goodnight properly. He starts kissing me then whispers, "My hands are cold, can I warm them up under your robe?" And we both start laughing.

"Let me show you something," he says quickly, and opens the closet in the second bedroom. There's an assortment of guest towels and Hoitview Group hotel brand toiletries. I snag a disposable eye makeup remover wipe because I like those.

"You're a perfect host, Jun," I tell him appreciatively. And he is.

He kisses me goodnight and then says ever-so-sexily, "If you want to come and wake me up in the morning, you know where to find me. Clothes optional."

I just beam back, but I turn my back to him and lower the robe ever so seductively. "To keep you excited…"

"Whoo," he replies. "Are you sure you don't want me to stay?"

"Yes. I'm not ready for you to see me bare faced."

"Well guess what, I've already seen you without makeup!"

"That was kid Claudia, this is *grown-up* Claudia," I say in my sexiest voice and batting my eyelashes.

He gets the message about respecting my boundaries and kisses me goodnight.

"You know where to find me if you need anything. Sleep well."

"Thanks. Goodnight," I say, as he turns to leave.

I do my stuff in the bathroom, take another shower because I just want one by myself, and when my makeup is off, my face is washed and I've brushed my teeth, I feel happy and clean. I didn't bring pajamas, so my nice lingerie and workout clothing is what I wear to bed. I starfish under the covers and fall asleep.

I wake up at 7 a.m. but feel recharged and well-rested. This holiday is the perfect antidote for refocusing and living a better life when I go back. I'm not sure how I'm going to do that, but I feel more ready for tackling the problems in my job, marriage, diet, and family life, not necessarily in that order. I think it's that I've found me again, and physically/psychologically getting the sex and intimacy I needed. I don't know how it'll work out to go back to the once-every-six-months pattern we have going but I certainly don't want to change too much in my life with a newborn coming along. I probably won't need sex since I'll be breastfeeding and bleeding for at least 6 weeks. That will be the last thing on my mind once my Baby Girl is here. But because my hormones have been raging and everything in my lower half is just swollen, I've been wanting sex all the time while pregnant. And now I get it with my super young pre-pregnancy body. YEAH! I'll have vivid memories to live off of in combination with a vibrator.

I do my thing in the bathroom, getting in my contact lenses and applying my eye makeup just the way I like it – little less than yesterday, but my eyeliner comes out perfectly. Not like the way my 40-year-old creases cause lines to go wonky unless I use foundation as a base. And even then, there's the time needed to correct the mistaken smudging.

Jun's hospitality supply in the closet is fascinating to me so I have another look. And then I spot a PlayStation 2 box with the original *God of War* game, unopened.

"Oh man, I've always wondered what that looked like," I say absentmindedly.

"What do you mean always? *God of War* came out last month," I left the door open and Jun startles me as he walks in. He's dressed as if he could go for a run or something – athletic pants, and a sleeveless t-shirt that shows off his incredibly muscular arms and hints at his chiseled torso. *Hot.*

"Oh, um … I mean, I've been seeing … ads for it …" I think this is a smooth enough cover, because I played the 2018 release of *God of War* (things you can do while breastfeeding) and now *God of War: Ragnarök* is something I haven't been able to play because, well, kids and a need for sleep.

AND THEN I SPOT IT: *Dance Dance Revolution* with a dance mat! "WHAT?!" my eyes light up and my voice goes totally shrill. "OH MY GOD! AAAAAAAHHHH!"

I fucking love this game and I am SO good at it.

I realize I didn't even ask him to play, I just started pulling it out. "Oops, please can we play?" I ask out of politeness but not really expecting a "no."

He laughs. "Yeah ... eat breakfast first ..."

"Okay ..." I jokingly make a sad puppy dog face – which turns into an excited face immediately after because I see that Jun has done the crêpes, cut up more fruit, made more chocolate sauce, and has the fruit in the blender all ready to go.

"WOW, yes, *Dance Dance Revolution* can definitely wait," I say just before he turns on the blender and drowns out any kind of conversation. He hands me my smoothie in a tall beer glass with a bubble tea straw.

"Thank you," I take it in exchange for a kiss.

He makes me a crêpe with chocolate and fresh blueberries, strawberries, and bananas. It's heavenly.

"How long do I have you for?" I ask him in between bites.

He puts down his cutlery and gives me his full attention. "I should leave here at 4:30 for a 7 a.m. flight, so I'll drop you off after dinner. Nah ... dessert."

"Don't you have to pack?"

"It'll take five minutes."

I finish my food and don't realize I'm staring at him.

"What?" he says, finishing his last bite. "Is there something on my face?"

"No," and I check. "No."

"What then?"

"I just think it's cool to be here with you. It's totally surreal."

He smiles back at me. "Yeah ... same."

There's a pang of sadness that this is just for a weekend. It's partly that I've finally managed to hook up with my high school crush and it won't last, but it's also that there's nothing to worry about here and I know that's temporary. If I were actually 20, I'd maybe be worrying about what I was doing here, and where we expected the relationship to go, but knowing that this is just a break from my life, I'm only concerned about my next meal and if I should really go ahead and try to find those two guys to see what it would be like to hook up. There's *zero* mental load here. I don't care about grocery shopping, or how much toilet bowl cleaner is left, or when it's a themed day at daycare. Or whether my colleagues have sorted out the issue that's waiting for me on Monday. I'm not worried about anyone else's next meal, or who will eat what because if I don't plan, then somebody small inevitably complains about the meal I've set in front of them.

And when I go back, then *poof,* this all goes away, and I go back to expecting Baby Girl and being the house servant – neither in control of my body nor my life.

I let out an audible sigh and it kind of jolts Jun, who was probably in screensaver mode. I hate how guys can do that. They can literally just think of *nothing.* But then I realize he was probably watching me.

"Are you okay?" he asks, concerned.

"I'm taking in the moment." I smile. I don't know what it's like to be on a date anymore, but I also don't know how to hold back in a casual (i.e. non-professional) setting and not be myself.

"Are you thinking of *Dance Dance Revolution?*" he laughs.

I had actually forgotten about it, and it must show in my face. Jun kisses me. "Maybe it's a good thing to take your mind off things. I'll clean up," he offers. "Do you know how to set up the game?"

"Yeah, I'm sure I can figure it out," I say with half-confidence. Is this pre-HDMI cable time? I can't remember.

It's not that hard to set up the system, game, and dance pad. In fact, I have my Player 1 turn while Jun is still busy. It's a track I don't recognize, but it's Easy, and the rhythm isn't bad, so I breeze my way stomping on the arrows as they come up on screen in time. I replace Jun's high score with little effort. I wonder why none of the game seems familiar and then I realize that it's *Dance Dance Revolution SuperNova* that I got good at, but it hasn't been released at this point in time yet. Same with *Guitar Hero* and *Rock Band*. Ah, I think our whole day would be blown if I'd found those in Jun's closet.

Jun joins me just in time for his turn with two glasses of water he leaves on coasters on the TV stand. He chooses a song, and I see now why I was able to beat his high score so easily. He's kind of ... terrible. He stomps at the wrong time and misses arrows.

"I'm better at the arcade! Where you can hold on to the bars!" he yells above the music, and that just makes it worse because he can't multitask. The song finishes and obviously he fails. He facepalms. "Okay ... I'll make you a bet. First one to lose gets naked first."

It makes me burst out laughing. "Go get towels unless you like sitting naked and sweaty on your couch!" With a mischievous smile, he does what I say but not before kissing me and pulling me closer by my waist. It leaves me a little dizzy.

"Hold on, hold on!" he calls out from the bedroom. "I choose the song."

"Fine," I say, thinking I'll win at whatever he chooses.

"No, this one," and I see that the song he's chosen has a high score on it with his initials, but it can't be his. I wonder who else he's played with. I'm pretty good at *Just Dance* on the Switch which uses your whole body and not just your feet, so I feel okay as I start the song. I've got this.

I do the dance and it's fine, but then all of a sudden, there are some really diabolical combos. Stomp right, back, left+right, front+back, left left, left right left right … I almost fall down in the middle but I make it through the song. Barely.

Jun slowly claps for me while laughing. "I could watch you bounce all day," and he kisses me on the lips, gently grabbing my ass with both hands.

"Meh, at least I tried it. Can't wait to see you naked," I taunt.

He starts up the song and then … *kills* it. My jaw drops. Where did this super coordinated man come from? It's a fascinating sight. I wish I could video record it and put it on YouTube. He finishes and enters his initials for the high score.

"That was my old high score," he says, a little out of breath.

I'm playfully horrified. "Were you secretly in *Riverdance* or something? What was that?!"

"You know they only take white people! This is skillz, baby!" He holds up his arms like a victory pose and I *love* that he has no armpit hair because I hate seeing that on basketball players. "Okay, I win my bet." And he points to me like, "Pay up."

"You fleeced me!" I say incredulously. "Do you do this to all the girls?"

"Only you, baby." He grabs my hands and pulls me up off the couch to kiss me.

"Ack, sweaty!" I say, making an X with my fingers and ducking out of the way. He pulls off my shirt and says, "Let's hit the shower then." It's like a marathon but I'm happy to spend the next several hours in bed with him. Well, bed … other bed … couch … wall … rug … chair … table. We try all kinds of positions I've never tried with Chad. It's not disappointing at all that he can't use his tongue for oral sex, because Jun continues to make up for it with stamina, strength, and general expertise on female anatomy. And he's imaginative with positions by himself – he doesn't just leave it to me or settle on lazy positions where I have to do all the work. He doesn't crush me when he's on top of me for missionary and he changes position, so he won't drip sweat on me (but he doesn't do that anyway, because unlike *Dance Dance Revolution*, he doesn't really sweat during sex). I hate when Chad drips sweat on me during missionary – which is one of the only, maybe, three positions we can regularly do because he's gained so much weight. I'm a little miffed to be thinking about Chad when I've got a gorgeous man inside me, and it makes me want to fuck Jun even harder. So I do.

As I'm recovering, Jun turns to me and says timidly, "Baby, I think I have to take a break to eat." My stomach growls and we both laugh. I suddenly have a craving for a lamb shank and potatoes, Greek style. Ooh, and if this is 2005, then the Mr. Greek is still at the Eaton Centre – before the renovations that took away my beloved food court.

"Do you want to run to the Eaton Centre with me?" I tell him about the thing I'm craving.

"Ah, that's close by to the Marché! Damn, they make a good salmon and potato rösti meal!"

My face goes all OH. "I WANT THAT TOO!"

He laughs. "So get them both."

"I think I will."

We put on our workout clothes from earlier. I grab my wristlet and he puts his phone, ID, and two credit cards in his pants zip pocket. I notice his top credit card is a black Amex – the kind you only get with an invitation.

Yeah … this romance is definitely a weekend thing only. I'm not cut out for marrying into a family with a hotel empire kind of money. I think you have to be brought up with private schools and excessive wealth to smoothly transition into that. Well, I don't know what to ask for that would be of a luxury level, so if he's agreeable to food court food, that's cool. Because for me, it's really a hit of nostalgia.

I suggest that we run to the Eaton Centre (because I kind

of want to test out my body for its current athleticism), and maybe because he doesn't want to seem lazy, Jun agrees to it. We go up Bathurst and turn on to Queen. On the way, I see tons of girls checking out Jun while we run, but at the same time, I see tons of guys checking *me* out. We pass by Dufflet Pastries and I make a mental note to order from there for the next kid's birthday, even though it'll be expensive because I won't want to decide on just one, so I'll choose a few. We pass by a dress shop where I got a bridesmaid's dress for a friend's wedding. The shop closed a few years ago. We pass by sushi restaurants that I remember going to on countless occasions with friends. There's one where a friend once forgot his wallet, so I treated him to lunch. He offered to buy me my next meal and just by coincidence and getting caught up in our separate lives, I don't think I've seen him since.

We pass a high-end menswear shop and Jun says, "Uh, I just have to stop in here and check on an order." I nod and tell him I'll wait outside to catch my breath. He disappears into the store, and then there across the street, I see my fairy godmother, Mhairi, getting into a cab.

"Mhairi!" I yell.

She looks up and points at me in recognition. She beckons me over, "Quickly, quickly!" she yells.

I check for cars then dash across the street. When I reach the other side, I'm about to thank her, but she says hurriedly, "I can't talk now. Find me at the spot where we met tomorrow morning." She gets in and slams the door prompting the cab driver to pull away.

I yell, "What time?!" and she holds up her fingers through the back window for 10. I hold thumbs up.

I've got nothing better to do at that time. Jun will be long gone on a plane.

I cross the street back to where Jun went into the store. He steps out just in time.

"Ready?" he asks.

"Yeah, let's go."

We arrive at the Eaton Centre and there's my glorious food court still open. I order my lamb shank with extra potatoes instead of rice and an iced tea, then as I'm fiddling with my wristlet to get out my credit card, Jun swoops in and pays for it using the black card.

"Sorry, sir. We don't take Amex," the man says at the cash register.

"It's okay, I got —" I say, feeling a little bad for his failed gentlemanly gesture.

"Can you try this one instead?" and Jun produces his top-of-the-line Air Canada/Aeroplan Visa card — another one of those with a super high limit.

The transaction goes through, and I say, "Thank you!" to both Jun and the man behind the counter, loudly, because the food court is noisy.

Jun smiles at me. "You're easy to please."

I smile and nod.

We get his food from the Marché. It's such a blast from the past. I used to love this restaurant too. Jun gets two portions of rösti potato and smoked salmon, one with sour cream and one without.

"This is a lot of food," I say.

"Don't worry about it," he replies and successfully pays with the black card.

He grabs an extra set of cutlery and napkins to throw into his food bag, and then as we're walking toward an open table, he grabs my hand. Like we're a couple. In public!

Wow, it's one thing to be a weekend fling but people can see us here.

And then I see he was just pulling me back toward a table behind us while I was gunning for a table straight ahead. Jun opens his food containers, and I open mine. I put some of my food into the lid of his.

"Thanks!" he says, kind of surprised. "I did kind of want

to try, but you know, never want to get in the way of a girl and her food."

I shoot him a look.

"Whoa," he pretends to cower behind the food bag. "It's true! I've seen girls get really vicious and protective over their food!"

"I admit to this," I reply honestly. And then I dig in. My food is just as good as I remember it. Ah yes, the last time was at a different mall but the same chain. With another friend I no longer keep in touch with. Such is life.

Jun finishes his rösti potato and salmon pretty quickly, so I give him some more of the potatoes from my food.

"Thanks," he says.

"I don't want you to eat both röstis!" I say in mock pre-protest, sliding the other container toward me.

"There! That's the viciousness!" he jokingly says while pointing his fork at me. I smile and mock a "my precious" Gollum look.

"You're too pretty to pull off that impression," and he winks at me. "We can get other food later, you know."

"I know. I'm just hitting up all my favorites while the opportunity is here," I tell him while gathering up my first forkful.

Mmmmm … this is definitely the stuff of my memories. The rösti is crispy in just the perfect way.

I don't want to talk about our current lives because I don't want to slip up and ask about his shop, or his wife. Just as I've mustered the courage to ask about Jun's current day job, there's a very unfortunate-looking guy asking for money or food. Jun has just finished eating.

"You know what, dude? Let's go to the Marché and I'll buy you whatever you want to eat," he says while getting up to go with the guy. He turns to me, "I'll come back and clean this up, okay, babe?"

Awww. What a guy. And he called me "babe" in public.

I finish my food and start to clean up. As I look up, Jun

is paying for a *huge* bag of food. As they leave, the guy is visibly appreciative and says repeatedly, "Thanks, man. Thanks, man!"

Jun says, "No problem. Have a nice day."

"Wow, how come you bought him so much?" I ask.

Jun shrugs. "I figure he has friends out on the street and maybe he can rack up some favors for a cold night down the road."

Man, this guy just got even sexier.

"Whoa, you ate all that?" he points at the table, all cleared off, no evidence left behind.

I get playfully indignant. And then I whisper in his ear, "I'm gonna burn the calories while fucking you some more."

"Let's go," he replies immediately.

Chapter 16:

THE MOST PERFECT SUNDAY - PART 2

As soon as we get back to Jun's place, I make good on my promise, and we resume our sexy marathon. Time seems to fly by. You'd think we'd get bored, but I have a string of mind- blowing orgasms and I'm pretty sure so does Jun.

We cuddle in bed together and in my mind, I psych myself up for what I think should be the last time. I hint at him that we should wrap it up by asking if we should make dinner reservations somewhere.

"Yeah … I want a late-night dinner place though. I'm not done with you yet," he says half smiling while looking up a number on his laptop perched on the nightstand closest to him.

He dials the number and switches to Cantonese when the other person picks up the phone. He talks so quickly and then there must be a different person that comes on because he switches to Mandarin. I recognize "8 p.m.," "lobster," "Peking duck," and "two people." Being multilingual must run in the family. Ciara is just as talented switching between the East Asian languages.

I wonder where we're going because most restaurants in Chinatown except for Asian Legend close around 8 on a Sunday. Asian Legend doesn't have Peking duck or lobster as far as I know, so I don't think we're going there.

He hangs up the phone and says, "Yes! Nice. We're going to my special occasion place. I feel like this is a special occasion." He kisses me and picks me up so I'm sitting in his lap. I put my arms around his neck and kiss him. He strokes my back. We start up again and it's a great last time.

My bag is in the other room, so I get dressed there. I pack up all my things, careful not to leave anything because I know this will be the last time I get to be in this condo. I smash all my stuff into the backpack so that all that's left is the wristlet, my stilettos, and my very sexy black dress, which I change into. I didn't pack a sweater, but I figure there's nothing I can do about that now. I think I look pretty good when I'm dressed for dinner and I've touched up my makeup. Jun whistles when he sees me. Yeah, this dress does make me look gorgeous – I feel it too. But wow, he looks hot. He's dressed in a blue collared shirt, black dress pants and a black tailored suit jacket.

Oh, how my life would have been different if you'd fallen for me sooner. Or I'd been bolder to approach you with my feelings.

I silently say goodbye to each room in the condo as I do a final sweep for my things, and we go down to the parking garage in the elevator. Jun seems to be lost in his own thoughts. We ride down quietly. When the doors open, he pulls me in to hold me for a minute.

Jun looks even cooler driving when he's dressed up and he has a super nice watch on his left arm. My dress hem slips off my knee, showing my thigh, and Jun makes a "whoo" face. Jun turns on to Lake Shore and then I notice we're on Queens Quay West. I love this area. He pulls into the parking garage underneath Harbourfront Centre. I can't remember which restaurants are down here, but soon enough, we're at Pearl Chinese Cuisine.

Damn ... I came here once when I was a kid, and it was swanky even then.

Jun seems to know the two people who greet him in Cantonese. He smiles brightly while talking to them and introduces me as Claudia. I wave hello and smile. Another lady comes out to greet him and he hugs her like an aunty. He switches to Mandarin. I understand enough to know that she asks if I'm his girlfriend, and he says, "not yet." She says I'm so pretty, congratulations.

We're seated at a table by the window and it's a beautiful setting. I can see why Jun calls this his special occasion place. There are just a few boats as we overlook the water. It's super peaceful and if I had my choice of residence anywhere, I would definitely choose a waterfront place with boats and twinkling lights. I wonder how many waterfront places Jun's family owns, and I dangerously drift into daydreaming about where we could travel together.

Stop that, this isn't lasting past tonight.

I take a look at the menu but it's all in Chinese. I assume the prices are steep, but for a guy who had a food court lunch, he's certainly not a food snob.

He puts down his menu and leans forward toward me. "I hope you don't mind. I gave them a heads up on the phone, so there's a lot of food coming already,"

"Okay!" And I slide the menu toward the end of the table. Sure enough, several servers come out with a whole Peking duck and:

-- braised lobster with ginger and green onions
-- eggplant with spicy garlic sauce
-- sweet and sour pork
-- beef short ribs with honey black pepper sauce
-- gai lan (Chinese broccoli) in garlic sauce
-- steamed white rice

-- stir-fried broccoli with crab meat

-- deep-fried spicy soft shell crab

-- steamed scallops with tofu in black bean sauce

There's enough food for 15 people. It's nuts!

"Jun ... are other people joining us?"

"Nope," he says while digging into the lobster. He dishes up some of the lobster into my bowl and pours my tea.

"Do you always just go to a restaurant and order all your favorites by yourself?"

Instinctively, I tap the table when he's done pouring tea.

"You're welcome," he says without missing a beat. "I'm not ordering for myself tonight," he says flatly. He washes his hands in the little finger bowls provided and starts preparing a Peking duck pancake.

"You know you're flying out tomorrow, right?" I say with wide eyes.

"Yeah, I'm sending this all home with you. You and Ciara can share it. There's tons of room in your empty fridge. Your freezer is probably empty too!"

I laugh. "Thank you," I say, which is well-timed because he swaps the Peking duck pancake with my empty plate.

"What do you think of the food?" he asks while I take a bite.

Oh my goodness ... it's almost my orgasm face. I smile. "It's so good! I'm going to be craving this in the middle of the night in the future. Damn you, Jun Sung!"

He laughs between bites.

I ask how he knows the staff so well, and he tells me how his parents used to bring them most weekends for family dim sum. Sometimes they'd bring Ciara's family and as they got busier and the kids got older, it was up to Jun and his sisters to go to Ciara's house for homecooked meals when their parents were traveling.

Ah, so that's why I don't really remember Jun's parents all that well.

Jun tells me about how he's such a good host because his Dad made the kids help clean hotel rooms as teenagers. He'd pair them with the staff cleaners, but it wasn't an easy ride, he'd hear about it from the cleaners if they slacked off. It was to teach them about what it was like to run a hotel from the bottom up, and to think about anticipating guests' needs.

"That's clever," I say between bites. "You probably didn't think that at the time though."

"Yeah … I thought it was the worst thing ever when my friends were off enjoying their weekends. But then I got sick and almost died. That's why I can't stick out my tongue – sports contributed but it's definitely that illness. My parents are just grateful I'm alive, so they don't push me as hard to take over the family business. They still think of me as a sickly kid."

He says "family business" as if it's a convenience store.

We talk about Vancouver and things he's looking forward to out that way. I just listen. It's nice hearing him talk and open up to me. I also like hearing his deep voice. And the way he asks the staffers to pack everything up in both Cantonese and Mandarin. He pays the bill with his black card. I don't even make gestures to pay, it's like he bought a Chinese New Year feast just for the two of us.

"Thank you very much for dinner," I say.

"My pleasure," he replies. "Thank you for your pleasure … and my pleasure," he says winking with the innuendos. I just laugh. I will miss how easily he seems to make me laugh.

Everything fits in one gigantic bag with thick handles, and they've packed it so nicely with good takeout containers and plastic bags in case things leak. I put it on the backseat floor of Jun's car, and it fits snugly so it won't rock around.

We kind of ride in silence to the dorm, having run out of things to say. I know I won't see him again, so I alternate between staring at him to enjoy the moment when he's not looking (or maybe pretending not to notice) and staring out the window trying not to cry. How can I not cry after spending an extraordinary time with this man, my high school crush, and living out the dream of actually having him as my boyfriend, if only for less than a weekend.

When we get there, I'm glad no one else is around, because I get to say what I want to say. He helps me get my backpack and the leftover food out. And then he gives me a long kiss.

"I had so much fun with you, grown-up Claudia. Thank you."

Tears slowly stream down my face, and he looks into my eyes, wiping my tears. "Why are you crying?" he asks with that concerned look.

"Thank you for an amazing weekend, Jun. I had the best time with you." I wipe away a tear. "I don't expect to ever hear from you again, so I want you to know that I think you're a dream come true. I used to think about you all the time in high school and university and wish you'd be my boyfriend. I never knew you'd turn out to be this kind, or generous, or thoughtful, or caring. Or this great at sex. I wish you the best future you could possibly have."

"Claudia, I'll be back as soon as I can," he says, puzzled. "I'll call you from Vancouver."

I smile and feel a little silly hearing that, but I know he won't come back. I wipe another tear. "That would be great. But I won't hold you to it. Thank you for everything."

And with that, I turn and walk straight in without looking back. I can't. I know I'd run back and not let go. I'd never want to go back to 40. And I can't do that to my kids.

Chapter 17:

MHAIRI CALLS ME FRITTATA

ecause Mhairi said today to see her at 10 a.m. tomorrow, I don't have to worry that I'll suddenly be transported back to 40. So I make plans for the next day. Ciara might not be back for the whole week. At this age, it wasn't unlike her to say that she was going to stay longer at home when she had originally planned to come back downtown. But maybe I'll text – no, wait, call her – to say that Jun has these scrumptious leftovers for us.

Since losing my Mom, I feel like I've become exceptional at compartmentalizing grief. I cry to let out my feelings about Jun, then I get on with a list because being a mom yourself means you still function. You have to. And you get stuff done in an allotted amount of time because you're a multitasking boss.

10 a.m. is a decent meeting time, but it'll still take an hour to get there by transit tomorrow, so it's better if I do stuff now in preparation. I don't want to be late now that I know Mhairi possesses superpowers. I get laundry started and set a timer. I make up a container for Mhairi because if she liked my frittata, she'll love the Chinese food from Pearl even more. I label it so I don't forget, with a note to grab a frozen bottle of water as an ice pack. I dish up my own breakfast for tomorrow so it's one less thing to do. I don't want the food to go to waste, nor do I want to waste my time going down to the cafeteria and risk making small talk with people like Conrad. I run down to put my clothes in the dryer, but most of it has to be hung up (like

my dresses and my workout clothes and the lingerie) so it'll be a quick dry for what's left.

I look up Canadian Opera Company Under 30 tickets and I snag two for tomorrow night at 7:30 for *Tosca*. I message my friend Kyle, the one who will go to Singapore for the rest of our lives. He instantly responds and is totally up for going to the opera with me as a last hurrah. He'll take me to an all-you-can-eat Korean barbecue at the Korean Grill House for dinner since it's so close by. YEAH! I haven't been there in ages because 1) I'd have to take the family, 2) I can't really fit/sit comfortably as a giant pregnant woman, 3) I'm always afraid the kids will jump up and accidentally burn themselves on the grill, and 4) I have to do the work of barbecuing because Chad feigns incompetence and says he'll just burn the meat, so it's like I'm still making dinner for everyone ... in a different place.

This will be fun. Kyle is good at grilling, and he'll do it all.

While talking to him about arranging times and what else we might want to do tomorrow, I load up Shockwave Games and play my all-time favorite games that no longer work because Adobe Flash stopped running at the end of 2020. It's 2005, baby! There's a game where you stand at the top of a building and drop eggs on pedestrians' heads for points and their funny reactions. There's a mini golf game I used to love during high school. It perks up my mood – but I mean, how much can it really perk you up to go from the ultimate sex marathon to ... Flash games? I should turn on the TV and watch something no longer running or available on a streaming service. The timer goes off for my laundry and I run to retrieve it. Even though it never happened to me, I'm scared someone will go throw it outside or something. I'm used to doing laundry late at night (like the goddamn laundry fairy) but not in a communal setting.

Hanging up and folding and putting away my own clothes takes almost no time at all. It makes me a little grateful that I'm not having to deal with three other people's clothing as well. But it also makes me miss my kids. I'm not ready to go back yet, but I'm glad I'm seeing Mhairi tomorrow so that she can at least tell me when the holiday is over. I like to plan. It wasn't by choice, but I like that I had scheduled Caesarean sections, so I knew when to expect my children's births.

Just as I've finished putting everything away, I get an email from my Mom.

Dear Claudia,

Sorry this isn't a handwritten card, but it will take too long to get to you if I mail it. Thank you for a lovely and special time yesterday for afternoon tea. I loved spending time with you, my gorgeous daughter, in such a beautiful place. I'm sure you have, but please pass on my thanks to your friend for the favor.

Dad and I are going on our two-week European cruise tomorrow so I'm packing. He's gone to sleep already.

Love you lots,
Mom

Ah yes, this is my Mom's style – to write a thank you. I tear up, but I don't want to call her because then I'll wake up my Dad. I also don't want her to hear me crying on the phone before her trip. I write back:

Dear Mom,

It was my absolute pleasure to take you to the King Henry. I love you so much. Thanks for being my Mom! Have a wonderful trip. I know you will enjoy the food a LOT. Try to walk or do something to balance it out. Haha.

Love,
Claudia

When I'm ready for bed, I read her email again and cry

myself to sleep. For her, for Jun, for missing my babies.

I guess I needn't have done all those things last night because I wake up at 7. Jun should be getting on his flight now. No message or call from him. Rightly so, because there were no "do not disturb" features on phones then, I mean, now. No email either because we didn't exchange email addresses.

I go for a run because I figure it's fun to see the city as it's waking up, plus I think this is how my 20-year-old body maintained a figure. I must have walked or ran at least 10 kilometers every day going between classes and that would have kept up a fast metabolism. It's also easy to go for a run on a weekday – there's no need for childcare and I'm not going to work. I clock a good route running through Yorkville, past the RoyalOntario Museum, down Queen's Park, then College up through Hart House Circle, through Trinity College and then past Robarts library and back to residence. I shower and hand wash my workout clothes at the same time since I don't want to do laundry again. When I'm done, I replace the dry clothes on the rack in my room with the wrung-out ones. I get dressed in skinny jeans and a cute aquamarine v-neck sweater and a spring trench coat I'm so happy to see again. I do my makeup, then head out with Mhairi's food and a bottle of water for us both. I wear runners because I know it'll be a lot of walking until I see Kyle, and that's when I'll wear boots and a skirt because he once said he really liked that look.

I take transit down to the Beaches and it takes ages. On the way, I feel a pang of sadness that I didn't take any photos with me and Jun, especially when we looked so good together for going out to Pearl. I brought my camera with me today though. Kyle and I have photos from each time he visited from Singapore, but almost none from our university days. I guess because I didn't have my own digital camera back then. It was only during my postgrad diploma days that I invested in one of my own. But I look at the photos of my Mom and me at tea, and it makes me both happy and teary. Even if the photos disappear as I go back, I'll have them to look at while I'm still here.

I get to the beach café at 9:55 a.m. and take a spot at the table where Mhairi and I first met. The café is closed – I see from the sign it's open Tuesday through Sunday. It's a sunny day and there's somebody flying a kite on the sand. It's still too cold to swim. I see Mhairi walking up the pedestrian path and I wave to her. She waves back. I still stand by my description of her as Whoopi Goldberg-esque with a Scottish accent. I zoom in and snap a picture of her.

When she comes closer, I mean to hug her, but she looks at me with a sort of vague recognition, so I don't. Then she snaps her fingers and says, "Ah, Frittata. How are you?"

"I hope my nickname doesn't get replaced with Chinese food because that's what I brought you today." Her eyes light up. "There's lobster and duck in there," I say while handing her the package and the bottle of water.

"Magnificent, thank you," she takes it gratefully and sits down with me.

"Thank you, Mhairi. This holiday has been phenomenal. I'm getting to do all the things I wanted to do."

"That's good to hear. Though here's the thing ..."

"Oh no, you're sending me back today," my face drops.

She shakes her head. "You've got until Monday, which I think the gods have given you quite generously. Usually, you get a free pass to whatever you want, no consequences ..."

I knew it!

" ... but not with you."

"Shit."

"Something you did over the weekend changed your life

trajectory. And if you don't change it back, your kids won't … exist."

I gasp in shock, my hands to my mouth. "Like *Back To the Future?*"

"I haven't followed pop culture for a thousand years, so I don't know what that is," she says flatly.

"It's a movie. Only the first one of three parts was good. The main character gets sent back to the past and has to make his parents fall in love or else he and his siblings will disappear."

"Ehm … well, okay. You're the parent here. I don't have much information other than that you'll be sent back Monday morning."

"Dammit, just in time for work," I say reflexively and regret instantly when Mhairi shoots me a look. "Which is fine!" I try to cover. "Do you know what I did?"

"No. What did you do?"

In my head, I try to recap the weekend in a nutshell. I did a lot of stuff. "Was it breaking up with Conrad?"

"I'm not getting a sense it was that …"

"Was it fucking the Cable Guy?"

"No …"

"Was it fucking Jun?"

"Oh my, you had a good weekend."

"Was it seeing my dead-but-now-alive Mom?"

"Definitely not that … the gods would not be so cruel."

I'm stumped.

"Are there rules here, Mhairi? Likes ones where I should be told explicitly that make this not a holiday and change the space-time-continuum?"

She seems lost in thought, but I give her a bit to think. "Well, you should probably not tell people when or how they're going to die or talk too much about the future."

Phew, I'm safe there. I've watched enough TV to know that instinctively.

She continues, "But the gods are powerful enough to

wipe people's memories. So, I don't think it's that."

I'm getting a bit frustrated. "How do you know what you know about my kids then?"

"Look, every time I meet someone, it's like I have a sense of their lifeline. If I meet an elderly person, I can feel when they die and I can visualize their face at that moment even if we're miles away. I've met your children, but this is a different feeling. I can visualize their faces, but I don't have that same sense of presence. And it might be because their existence is in jeopardy. They need to be conceived in order to be born. That might be your first clue."

"What if I meet someone else? Can't my kids still be born with a different dad?"

"I think biology could tell you the answer to that, sweets."

I'm super frustrated now. "So when I leave here, I have to figure out what I did that would alter my timeline to prevent my kids from being born."

"Right. I have to go, I'm sorry I can't help more."

"If I need your help, Mhairi, how do I contact you? Can I call you?"

"I don't have a phone, love."

"Email?"

"Nope. I won't get a phone until I have to get an app to order food, but that's not for another 20 years."

"So I'll find you around this area?"

"Aye."

"Oh man. If you need to find me, I have plans for the Korean Grill House and the opera tonight. Can you take my phone number just in case please? I'll give you quarters for a pay phone."

"You can try. I suppose I should take some care of you since I did bring you back here." I'm glad she says this and not me. I'm grateful for the holiday and the experiences, but not at the cost of losing my kids.

I give her my phone number and "Claudia Lee" written

on a napkin with high hopes she won't just use the napkin and lose it. And then I dig through my wallet for quarters.

"I have to know ... why did you choose me, Mhairi?"

"Because you were kind to me. You looked like you needed a break, and your world was falling apart. And if you're set up for postpartum depression, it's awful for the wee ones too. Oh, and I only do this for people who give me delicious food, by the way. I don't remember anyone's name. I just remember what they gave me."

I take the napkin back and write "Frittata" next to my name.

"Thanks, love," she says it like she'll try to memorize the number but I'm pretty sure she won't. "I'm hungry again, so I'm going to go heat this up soon. You take care."

"Mhairi, will I just go back to my time when I sleep?"

"Aye, lass," she says as she walks away.

"Thank you," I call out.

She waves. "You'll figure it out, don't worry!"

Well, what if I don't?

Shit.

I rack my brain because if fucking someone doesn't change anything, then what did? I've passed countless people now in random encounters. Passing them on the street while running. I don't meet Chad for at least another year at this point, so this has nothing to do with him.

I guess I'm okay to hook up with Kyle later if things work out because he wasn't even part of the equation when Mhairi told me the news.

Feeling totally alone, I call Ciara. She picks up. "Hey! How's it going?"

"I'm ... uh ... are you coming back to the dorm today?"

"Oh, no, sorry, I decided to catch a last-minute trip to New York City. I was just about to call you. Wanna come?"

Hunh, that is an option, but I should probably figure this thing out. "Uh, I have plans tonight, sorry. I'm going out with

Kyle."

"KYLE! Aww. Say hi for me. I'll probably call him up for lunch in Singapore."

And she will. He'll send back a baby gift for Timothy. "When will you be back?"

"You know, I'll probably only come back for my Tuesday class."

"Ah, okay. Yeah, now I remember. Your classes are only Tuesday and Thursday for the summer session."

I vaguely remember that Ciara stacks a full course load into the Tuesday and Thursday and picks up an amazing internship somewhere for Wednesday and Friday, but I can't remember where for the life of me.

"Bummer, 'cause Jun got all this food for us from Pearl."

"REALLY?! Oh damn, I meant to call you to find out how things were going, but I gotta get going, sorry."

"No worries, we'll talk when you get back," I say. I'm kind of glad not to have to talk about Jun. Because then I'll start needlessly pining for him.

I don't feel like I should grab any kind of opportunity with Ciara because I see her all the time at 40. I just have to arrange to see her when the kids are in daycare if we want decent conversation, and her schedule is flexible enough, so it'll be fine.

But what the hell do I do about my kids right now?! Maybe I have to find Chad?

I dunno. I think at this point in time, Chad is in Texas or somewhere. I can't remember! I've never had to concern myself with anything in his life outside of the time I've known him.

My phone rings just then – it's Kyle.

"Hey," he says, and I'm so excited to hear his voice. He was a good friend to me during our university days and we did hang out all the time. Until I met Conrad. And Kyle and I didn't really have classes together anymore, so it was more effort to get together.

"Hi! How are you?!"

"I'm great! Hey, I just realized that there's this new Degas exhibit at the AGO and I got two free member preview tickets. You wanna go with me?"

"Oh, yeah! Thanks for thinking of me! But hey, I have all these leftovers from Pearl. Wanna have lunch with me at the dorm first?"

"Uh … yeah, thanks!"

All the way back, I'm still racking my brain as to what the problem is. But I can't really … run the problem by anyone. I really do have to figure this out on my own. Zero solutions are coming to my brain so I'm going to change into a nicer outfit and enjoy the day with Kyle.

Goddammit, Harry Potter gets handed the solutions to all his problems.

Chapter 18:

KYLE

I choose a tight blue dress with an off-the-shoulder asymmetric neckline, black knee-high boots, and a navy blue blazer with embroidered flowers. I don't know if I've achieved the whole "look what you could have fucked if we had more time look", but I open the door to Kyle and his jaw drops. I guess mission accomplished.

"Whoa. Hey," he says, carrying some groceries. "I dunno why I bought so many canned coffees but I can't take them with me so you guys can have them."

"Thanks! I love these!" And I genuinely do love them. This brand gets discontinued in Canada and I have to go buy them in the States seven years from now.

Kyle is an astronaut kid. His parents birthed him and his brother in Canada, raised them in Hong Kong, sent him and his brother to boarding school and university in Canada, after which they've spent the rest of their lives in east Asia.

It's good to see my friend in person.

I lay out all the leftovers and hand him a plate to microwave what he wants. Together, we make a big dent in the food. I know Kyle will want a second helping, so I just leave everything uncovered and ready on our mini counter. As I start heating up his plate in the microwave, he waves his hand around inquisitively at the food.

"Did you miss Chinese New Year or something? Where did all this come from?" He mock gasps and says, "Did you have a party and not invite me?"

I tell him about Jun taking me to Pearl.

"That sounds like a date. What happened to Conrad?"

"Dumped him." I shrug.

He has a look of relief on his face. What, did everyone hate him and not tell me? But wait, leave it to Kyle to be totally honest. Which is kind of why I wonder why we never hooked up – he would have honestly told me if he'd had feelings for me, wouldn't he?

"Good riddance. I fucking hated that guy," Kyle says while trying the duck. "Oh my God, this is awesome."

"You hated him? Why?" And I put my plate in the microwave.

"He's such a loser. He failed a year of school because he was just fucking around. And in his second year, I'd see him all the time just hanging around and it was like, 'When the hell are you actually going to class?' And he's got a weird face. And I always thought you were just way smarter than him. Like shit, what does she see in him, he's so gross."

"Well, no, please don't hold back," I say sarcastically with a laugh.

"You're so much better than that, Clauds," he says, taking another bite.

"Thanks! I know now."

I suppose this would be a good moment for me to get all seductive and stuff, but I feel ... nothing. Maybe it's that I know Kyle doesn't have as built a body as Jun, or that Kyle's smile doesn't do the thing to my insides that Jun's does. Hunh. I mean, I haven't seen Kyle in forever and the last time I did see him, his wife was with him. This is fine. It's kind of perfect it's just us as friends.

Kyle does go for a second helping of food and so do I. Between the two of us, we clear out a whole bunch of containers. There's enough left for maybe two more meals, down from ... say, eight, so I'm glad Kyle was able to share with me.

He helps me wash the containers and dishes and I put away the food. Then we take a slow walk to the AGO sipping a canned coffee each. He tells me about his moving plans and his brother, his new place in Singapore, which aunts he can stay with in Canada when he comes back to visit. Right – one time I pick him up from a building in Scarborough, but another time he meets me downtown for lunch when he's in town.

He gets us the member preview tickets and we stroll through the gallery. I love going to art galleries without kids – they always whine, and need snacks, or sometimes you're not allowed to take a stroller in and then you can't see the exhibit you really wanted to see. The best is when they're babies and you just push the stroller while they're asleep, but then you're looking for change table facilities in anticipation of the inevitable. Kyle comments on Degas capturing the movement in the ballet dancer sculptures and I smile. It reminds me of a time when I was sporting a way bigger crush on him, and I wonder why I didn't make the move. Maybe because I was scared of losing this – an easy ability to hang out and call each other up to get together if we were available. A relationship would have certainly taken that away if we'd broken up.

But I also wonder if Kyle ever had a thing for me and if he did, how come he never acted on it.

Or maybe it's just that thing where it's out of sight, out of mind. We didn't see each other regularly throughout the last year and maybe he was dating other girls. I don't remember and at 40, I wouldn't feel comfortable texting him to ask what his dating life was like during university.

We stroll through the galleries and I manage to see most of what I wanted – mainly the giant plushie hamburger. The red wall room. Things from the Renaissance. Kyle and I walk together, then not. We separate and flow back together.

I think about what Mhairi said. It's something I did. What did I do?!

Ah … I've got it. I think I'm so hung up on Jun now that

I'm back to comparing everyone else to him. And then Chad will pale in comparison so I'm less likely to want to date him. So I'll be single forever! Oh no.

But wait a minute … in my normal timeline, I did get over Jun. And then I met Chad. So what gives?

Kyle must see me doing this inner monologue because he comes over and quietly says, "You know, you look like you have an imaginary friend over here."

"Oh … sorry." I find a bench and sit down. He joins me. "Someone told me something I did is totally fucking up my future and it's really messing with my head. And I can't really talk about the problem because it's so complicated and I don't think anyone would believe me anyway."

"What could you possibly do to fuck up your future this early on? What? Is it like your grades, so you won't go to law school?"

"Nah, nothing like that."

"Is it Conrad? Did he say something like leaving him would curse your life forever?"

"Nah, I haven't heard from that guy since I dumped him. Plus, I blocked his number."

"Really? Didn't he at least try to grovel for his place back?"

"Maybe he did. I've been too busy this weekend, so even if he tried, I wasn't really answering messages or anything. And I wasn't even at the dorm."

Wow, remember those days? When you couldn't check email or messages because you'd have to check it on a desktop?

Since we're not really going to be in each other's lives, I ask him point blank. "Do you think we could have dated in the past, Kyle?"

"Sure. I mean, we have a lot in common. We both like art, good food, good conversation, we care about international politics." He kind of wavers … it looks like he's wondering if he should add more to the list.

"So how come we never got together?"

"I dunno. Timing? What? Were you interested?"

"At one point. But I can't say when."

"Dang. I should have made a move then. But then you were with Conrad!"

"I would have left him for you."

"Really? Shit ..."

"Ah well." We both laugh.

We spend the rest of the afternoon talking about Singapore, Hong Kong, his childhood, his boarding school. We compare our university experience and his fraternity versus the dorm.

When it's time for dinner, the Queen West Korean Grill House totally brings back great memories. Even with Conrad, this place has been an awesome center for a lot of fun times with friends, birthday dinners, and dates. It's only fitting that I have a last hurrah dinner with my good friend, Kyle. To start, we order beef short ribs, pork belly, and salmon. As I expected, Kyle does all the grilling.

As we eat, we talk about our future plans. I try to stay tight-lipped, but it comes out that I see myself working in some kind of commercial producing but for causes and non-profits. He thinks that's cool. He talks about how he doesn't know if he'd be a good dad given that his parents have been quite absent the past few years of his life. I say it doesn't matter and that he'd be a great dad, just remember to put your children's car seat buckles at underarm level. (I say this because his wife posts too many Facebook photos of the buckle all wrong.) He says he probably wants to go to law school at some point, and I say I think he'd be very good at that and hope he gets good use out of his law degree. (He won't.)

I'm happy to listen and eat. Kyle grills. We order more food. We have a good time and before we know it, it's time for the opera.

As the performance is about to start, my phone buzzes.

It's Jun. Hunh. I turn the phone off because if he calls back, I don't want it buzzing. He can just leave me a voicemail.

But I'm kind of excited. Does he want to see me again? Or did I just leave something at his place that I should collect? Or is it that he can't stop thinking about me because I kind of can't stop thinking about him?

I can't. I have to get over you, Jun!

I'm glad these tickets are discounted because seriously, my mind wanders all over the place. If anyone asks me what *Tosca* is about, I'm going to have no idea. Luckily Kyle is super smart and catches me up during intermission.

Ah … wait, this is why I didn't think to date him. Because sometimes I just feel really stupid around him. And not for lack of reading or actually being any less intelligent, or that he purposely makes me feel that way, but I just do. Like I'm getting schooled. I'm perfectly capable of reading the program or looking up whatever it is he explains but it's just this feeling I get when I'm with him. Not all the time, just sometimes. Now I remember.

I still love him as a friend though.

I try to pay more attention during the second act but I'm actually kind of losing my patience so in the second intermission, I go looking for a signal to check my voicemail. There is one waiting.

"Claudia, it's Jun. I … hope you can call me back when you get this message. Thanks. Bye."

Uh … okay.

I go back to my seat and Kyle is leafing through the program again. "What was that?"

"Oh, just a voicemail from the guy who bought all the food."

"What did he say?"

I shrug. "To call him back when I get the message. Does he not leave voicemails on a regular basis? That sounds pretty … basic. Well, I'm busy right now, so he's just going to have to wait."

He sighs. "Okay, you know what your problem is? You're oblivious to all the signals. Every guy who's tried to date you, you probably shut them down, not even aware you did it. I don't know how that asshole Conrad broke through your force field but kudos to him for that."

I strain to remember. "I think he just said out loud that he liked me. And then … I guess we just started seeing each other more? I dunno, I don't respond to subtle."

Kyle laughs and facepalms.

The lights go down and I strain my brain to think of my first date with Conrad. Or Chad. Can't remember at all. I remember the non-date dates that Chad and I went on. The dinners we went to as friends but not yet as a couple. Kyle is definitely right about missing signals … I mean, one time a guy was hitting on me at church and my Dad had to point it out for me.

After the opera, we go for late night bubble tea and condensed milk toast. Kyle can't get drunk because he's got so much to do before leaving the country permanently, so he doesn't want to get hungover. I'm going to have to watch *Tosca* on YouTube or something at some point. I hardly remember any of it. But Kyle gives me enough of his opinion on stuff that I can repeat that if anyone ever asks me about it.

I assume correctly that Kyle will walk me to my dorm building so I don't have to go in the dark by myself. It's the last time we really get to hang out in person locally and I like that I'm getting a second chance to treasure the moment.

"Thanks for being my friend, Kyle," I say while taking his arm. "I'm not hitting on you, I'm just afraid of spraining an ankle in the dark."

He laughs and shakes his head. "You're a character, Clauds. Are you gonna call that guy back?"

"Which guy?" I say cheekily, and I give a half a thought to Otis the DJ/Cable Guy who I could ring for a booty call since

I should probably get more sex before my Monday deadline.

"Which guy?! Clauds, you player," Kyle says playfully.

We get to the front door of my dorm building and I give him an extra-long goodbye hug. "Have a safe flight. And call me any time you know we're going to be in the same city, okay?"

"Will do," he says.

I watch him walk off. I heave a sigh and turn to go inside.

"Claudia!"

I spin around. OH DAMN.

It's Jun.

"What are you doing here? You're supposed to be in Vancouver."

"I said I'd come back as soon as I could."

"What? That means you've been on a plane for 11 hours today!"

He nods. "I didn't get to say what I wanted to last night. You are ... unforgettable. I've been thinking about you all day. Were you trying to break up with me? Because you can't. Being with you just feels like it's meant to be."

I'm about to kiss him like it's some 1940s movie but as I get close to him, I think of my kids and my instinct kicks in and I back away.

"No! I can't be with you!" I cry out.

"Why not?!" he yells back.

It all comes tumbling out of my mouth. "Because you're supposed to go to Vancouver and meet your wife and get married and open a rice pudding and chocolate mousse shop while I go off and marry Chad," I say with tears streaming down my face. "And Fàn Times is a really fucking clever name."

"Thank you! There are so few people who get that rice is "fun" and fun times - wait ... how do you know about the shop?" he says with a puzzled look.

"Because you opened it the year that Timothy was born."

And then we both look at each other. "What ... " we say at the same time.

Chapter 19:

ACROSS THE COUNTRY JUST FOR ME

I remember that Ciara went to Vancouver to celebrate the opening of Jun's shop, but she also didn't want to miss Timothy's birth. Luckily, it turned out to be a planned Caesarean, so she was able to make it back with two days to spare. Jun's family had a lukewarm reception to Fàn Times, but with Ciara's connections, he got some news coverage, and apparently a lineup had formed down and around the block the day after.

I give him major side-eye. "How do *you* know about your shop?"

"Oh," he coughs. "Because I've been planning it for years. How did you know what the name is?"

I want to run away, yet my feet aren't moving. "Because … I'm … a …" I say "witch" at the same time that Jun hisses "time traveler" and I feel my eyes widen in shock.

Now my feet lift. I turn to run but he grabs my hand just in time. "No wait," he says tenderly. And then he hugs me.

"It's okay," he says reassuringly. It's comforting. And not having to carry around this secret by myself is a relief.

Wait, what the hell?

"Why aren't you scared?" I say, moving so I can see his face for the full answer. He's super relaxed, maybe even relieved too.

"It's that … uh …" He stumbles for words.

I push him away, then dig in my purse for my camera. I

flip to the picture of Mhairi and zoom in, showing it to Jun.

"Do you know this woman?" I demand.

He doesn't even have to say anything, I know right away from his guilty face. "Oh no," I say reflexively, stepping back from him.

Is it an "oh no"? Oh my God … my kids.

He steps toward me and kisses me. "You're the reason I'm here. I get a reboot … with you. It's a whole new path together."

I put up my hand to stop him from coming closer. "Oh no, dude, this is just a holiday from my life. I've got too much to get back to."

"Really?" he says. Like he sees right through me. "You're with the love of your life? You're working a dream job?"

"It's none of your business!"

"It could be my business," and he gives me a look. "What do you think about that?" He suddenly wobbles on his feet and looks like he's going to pass out.

"Oh shit," and I lunge forward to catch him just in time. We slowly sink to the ground together and land sitting with me holding him.

"Sorry … I didn't really get a chance to eat today," he says slowly.

"What was the last thing you ate?" I say incredulously.

"A granola bar for breakfast."

"Drink this," I thrust the bottle of water from my purse at him.

I really wasn't intending to see him anymore but damn you, hospitable Asian genes. "Come upstairs and you can have left-overs …" I start to say begrudgingly but end with "… which you bought." I hear the words come out of my mouth and instantly regret them.

"My carry-on is over there," he says, pointing to a bench around the corner. It's a really nice one too – I've got one but a later model and a darker blue than this light blue.

That's why I didn't see him at the front door.

"How long were you waiting for me?"

"I called just before takeoff from Vancouver. You didn't answer, so I was worried. I took a cab straight from Pearson."

I can't help but kiss him. I feel heartsore. This man. On an airplane all day across the country and then back, because he wants to be with me.

Life is so unfair. How can I not be with this man?

We get upstairs and I warm up leftovers for Jun. I figure he can just have the rest. I'll go to Pearl with Ciara when I'm back to 40 and the baby is born. Jun eats as expected for a built man who works out and hasn't eaten the whole day. It's the first time I've just watched him eat (without eating simultaneously) and there's nothing about his table manners that annoys me. Chad has this thing where he forgets to chew with his mouth closed. And he gets food stuck in his beard which grosses me out.

Rather than stare at this beautiful man and debate fucking him, I stand up and say, "I'm gonna take a shower while you eat."

"Oh ... wait for me," he suggests and reaches for my hand. I avoid contact.

"No, no ... you eat. We're not doing that tonight. I'm getting into very unsexy pajamas," I declare. "And I'm taking off my makeup," I add for extra unsexy measure.

To try and fend off temptation, I put a robe over my pajamas. My makeup comes off as promised and I'm wearing glasses and bunny slippers. There's hardly anyone in the dorm because of this week between the spring and summer sessions. Plus, there are a lot of people wearing pajamas in the building around this hour, so it won't matter when I walk Jun out through the lobby looking like this.

As I open the door, Jun has washed the dishes and opened his carry-on. He smiles when he sees me. "You look like a cute librarian I'd want at my slumber party."

So many thoughts are running through my head. I want you, yet I shouldn't want you. I have a bad feeling about this. Will you go home tonight? I hope you stay. No wait don't stay. Stay until I fall asleep …

I'm obviously bad at poker faces. He sees my bewildered look and says, "Uh, sorry, I figure I should freshen up after … you know, today. Is it okay if I use your shower?"

All I can do is nod. And hand him fresh towels.

I putter around in my bedroom while he showers. I try hard not to imagine him in there. I try hard not to join him having seen what I've seen. Suddenly self-conscious, I turn off the ceiling light and turn on a dim lamp.

Ugh, idiot. Why did I bring him upstairs? Well, I mean, if I was fainting in front of his place, I'd totally expect him to be polite and feed me leftovers from the expensive meal I bought yesterday too.

He comes out wearing a well-fitting t-shirt and sweat-pants, and he still looks hot. In all honesty, Jun could come out wearing a paper bag and would look even hotter.

"Is Ciara coming back tonight?" he asks with his wet towel in his hands.

I shake my head. "She's in New York."

"Ah, that would make sense, if we're not using it," he says nonchalantly. I can only guess that he means a place. It's probably swanky. Like a brownstone on the Upper West Side full of expensive get-dusty-and-have-the-butler-dust-them chandeliers.

"Should I put the towel in the hamper or hang it up over the shower rail?" I point to the shower rail. When he raises his arms to put it up there, his arms look so good. Damn.

I take off my glasses. I just have this urge to feel him. I snuggle into him, and he snuggles me back. He smells so good after a shower. He kisses my forehead and my cheek.

STOP IT, you can't be with this guy!

I step back. "Tell me why you're here," I ask.

"With you?"

"No, in 2005," I clarify.

"I'm not telling you because I don't want you to think you're some kind of rebound."

"I'll tell you my story," I bargain.

"Can I hear it lying down?" I'm about to suggest he sleep in Ciara's bed and then I realize that at this point in time (it changes as she gets older), Ciara likes to work out and then collapse into bed sweaty, so her bed must smell kind of gross.

Before I know it, he's sliding into my bed and pulling up the covers. As I open my mouth to protest, his eyes are closed and he's breathing deeply within seconds – he's already asleep. He looks really peaceful and agonizingly cute. He doesn't snore. So, I let him sleep. I take a picture of him because even if it's just until I go back to 40, I have something to remember him by.

I have 6 more days. I'll fix things starting tomorrow.

Chapter 20:

HAVE YOUR CAKE AND EAT IT TOO

I dream about my kids. They're soundly asleep with me, just as I left them before I woke up in 2005. They're so adorable in their pajamas. I readjust my huge pregnant body, and it makes them roll into each other and hold hands, just like they do on airplanes when it's time to descend. Their other hands clutch plushies – Jeremy with a teddy bear and Timothy with a dog. I watch their beautiful faces with their long eyelashes on flawless, kissable cheeks. Then they wake up smiling. They shout, "I love you, Mommy! You're the bestest! When are you coming home?"

I wake up missing my babies like crazy. If I'm still pregnant and everyone is fine in my dream, it probably means I'm still on track to get back to my life. Right? Right.

Holidayyyyyyyy … false alarm!

Jun rolls over to face me. His shirt has risen up in his sleep and aside from a little sleep residue around his eyes, he still looks gorgeous.

Uhh … yes please. I will have the cake and eat it too. This man who wants to be with me, thinks I'm all that, and gives great (and multiple) orgasms ... why would I say no?

It's 7 a.m., so I get dressed and made up ever so quietly with a good lingerie set, a really pretty white dress with pockets, big flowers and a black sash. I don a dark green sweater, and I look super cute, like I'm ready for a garden party ... or a baby shower. And my boobs look fantastic!

I had intended to sit on the bed with a sexy pose and wake up Jun with my hand but my stomach growls and there's only canned coffees in the fridge. I leave a note, then sneak out of the suite, trying to remember that I can't let the door slam because that will for sure wake up Jun.

And he kind of does need to sleep after traveling all day yesterday ... for me.

In preparation for the summer session when the residence gets rented out for tourist season, the cafeteria should be serving all sorts of yummy things just like a hotel breakfast bar.

But oh no ... there's a sign ... the cafeteria staff are on strike? Dammit.

That's okay ... cheap student breakfast is easy to find in downtown Toronto. I go to a place around the corner for breakfast sandwiches and muffins. There's a sign in the window that says, "Now serving Montreal-style bagels" and my heart leaps. I love Montreal-style bagels and anyone can fight me when I say they top the global standard of bagels. But then again, I've never had, say, a Japanese or Norwegian bagel, so I guess I only have New York and Montreal bagels to compare.

I pick up six because who knows how the day will go, and then I get two breakfast sandwiches with bacon, egg, and cheese, because who doesn't have gestational diabetes? This gal! I ask for butter and ketchup because seriously, my dorm room now has no food.

With my big, delicious-smelling bag, I walk back to the dorm, almost skipping because I'm that happy. Just as I get up to my floor, I'm startled to open the door and see Otis in his cable guy uniform.

"Claudia!" he says excitedly.

"Otis! How are you?"

He props an arm up against the wall. "Better after seeing you," and leans in to kiss me. I don't duck away in time and oh my, he reminds me that he is a very skilled kisser that leaves me weak-kneed. "I didn't even see you leave on Friday."

"Sorry about that. My friend got kind of drunk, so I had to bring her home."

"How come you haven't called?"

"Oh, um, things have come up," I say awkwardly. In my head, it's a bullet train of thoughts like I spent an awesome weekend fucking Jun nonstop. I wonder what it would be like to have them both at the same time.

"I can take a break now, if you're free?" He leans in and I get a slight brush of his boner through his coveralls. He whispers, "You are so fucking hot. I wanna do really naughty things to you."

It makes me blush and I have to catch my breath. But right at that moment, Jun walks out of the dorm room looking like a model with his collared shirt and dress pants. Otis was already looking like a 10/10 but Jun's possessive face just shot him up to a 15.

He grabs my waist like he's scooping me away. "She's not free," he tells Otis with his dead serious face. I'm kind of stunned as he rushes me back into the dorm room, I mouth, "sorry" at a very surprised Otis.

I don't like being thought of as property but Jun getting jealous is such a turn-on.

When we get in and close the door, there's no conversation, he just takes the bag, puts it on the kitchenette counter, then kisses me passionately. We kick off our shoes, and even though he probably just got dressed, he starts unbuttoning his shirt. I help with the rest of the buttons. He takes off my sweater so putting my arms around his neck and feeling the muscles in his back with my bare arms is so enticing. I run my fingers through his hair as he kisses me more, then he kneels down to take off my panties. He picks me up to sit me on the table, then resumes kissing me but gently starts to finger my clitoris. His urgency stirs the pit of my stomach, and I want him just as much.

"Here or bed?"

"Bed," I say quickly.

He helps me off the table and we both shed the rest of our clothes. He grabs his towel from last night and lays it on the bed just before gently pushing me down onto it. I point him to the desk drawer where I keep condoms and my vibrator. He puts the condom on.

"Just so I'm ready, but it's your turn first," he assures me.

He expertly holds the vibrator against my clitoris and adjusts while watching my face. He adds a finger inside, then gradually another, all the while watching my cues for when I want more. Admittedly, it takes a while for me to get fully wet and ready, but I don't feel rushed. I wonder if Jun works out with exercises specifically to build sex stamina.

He pulls me closer to the edge of the bed so we're perpendicular. Still holding the vibrator, Jun crouches down so our angle is good, then lets out such a satisfying groan as he enters me that it kicks it up a notch toward my climaxing. He starts slow then speeds up, all the while watching my face and paying attention to my breathing. Eventually I get there, and he sees my whole body reacting with a ripple. He only stops pumping when I tell him to. When it seems like I'm okay, he picks me up and carries me to the wall, still inside me. I wrap my legs around his waist. Ooh, I don't think I've ever done it against a wall like this.

Jun makes me feel weightless as he lifts and drops me onto his dick. That our heights match up for this is super thrilling. I point my toes using a random Cosmopolitan magazine tip and it works wonders because Jun's face just lights up, then it doesn't take him long to finish. It's so satisfying to watch him climax. I slowly drop my legs to stand.

"Thank you," he says after relaxing.

He kisses me, then hugs me tightly. He pulls out and ties the end of the condom, then wraps it in tissues and throws it in the garbage. He cleans himself off with the towel, places it in my hamper, then holds my vibrator with his wrists.

"Here, I'll wash this for you since I'm going that way anyway," he says kindly. Wow, super considerate. If I'd known in my real 20s, and fucked around this often, I would have totally judged the whole cleaning up act as a marker for potential marriage material.

I want the cuddle time but now I'm practically starving so I put on my lingerie, then throw a robe on. When I turn around, Jun has his underwear on.

"Stay that way … unless you're cold," I say sexily.

"I'm a little cold," he says with a cute face. And he undoes the robe to wrap it around the both of us. He kisses my neck and nuzzles me up to my ear.

"Food first!" I laugh. "But I want that later."

We managed the morning without talking, but now I want some answers.

Chapter 21:

PRE-BLISS

*I*t is a bit chilly in my dorm room, so Jun gets dressed in what he was wearing before. I watch and daydream about what it would be like if we had gotten together in my actual 20s.

Maybe our daily life would be a lot like this. He catches me watching him and smiles back at me. While I'm getting out the canned coffees and plates for our breakfast sandwiches, I wonder what he looks like in the present. Has he just aged slightly with a little grey hair? Or has he given up working out and has a dad bod? Did he stop manscaping? Does he have kids? I'm too afraid to ask.

I want to avoid spilling messy food on my dress, so I eat with just my robe on. It slips open and I sort of fix it, but generally leave it. Jun totally notices and it's fun to distract him while he eats. He's just as excited as I am about Montreal-style bagels so he's already happy. After his breakfast sandwich, he goes in for a plain bagel with butter. He offers to butter one for me and I say, "yes please", but I want to take a walk with him and eat it outside in a bit, so I tell him so. He wraps it up for me in the breakfast sandwich wrapping.

Neither of us is making a first move in starting any conversation, so when I'm done with my breakfast sandwich, I brush my teeth and get dressed. Just as he finishes his food, I sit across from him, cross my legs and fold my arms, waiting. He notices with an amused smile.

"I believe you said you'd tell me your story first," he finally says.

Shit, I did say that.

"I did. You fell asleep," I fib with a joking tone.

"Sorry, I was tired," he says flatly, not wanting to play. "Look, I'm okay if you run into Mhairi and she tells you what happened, but I'm not going back."

"I don't think that's the way it works. You just fall asleep and then you travel to and fr..." I gasp sharply. "YOU SAW HER! You're HIDING from her! That run along Queen when you ducked into the menswear store!"

Jun steels his jaw and looks away. Then he says quietly, "There's nothing to go back to. The things that mean the most to me are all gone." He looks like he might cry, and he swiftly turns away from me. To give him some space, I leave him to take care of his garbage and dishes. But I readily hug him when he turns back my way. We stay like that for a while without saying anything.

"Let's go for that walk," he finally says. He brushes his teeth while I get my purse.

I want to wear my stilettos for a bit because they go super nicely with this outfit, so I put my ballet flats and a bottle of water in my purse in case we go too far. And napkins, because 40-year-old mom me would have wet wipes if they were available. I'll just make my own with the water and napkins. I make a mental note to try and restart the purse backpack as a fashion trend when I return to 40.

Sigh. It's Tuesday. I'd better think fast about what I want to do. As we get out of the dorm, I open the buttery bagel and the sesame seeds fall everywhere on the pavement. Jun sweetly takes my purse so I can just concentrate on the bagel with two hands.

What would it be like to forge that new path with you like you asked?

Stop it. This isn't real.

What do I do? Break this off now? Put a three or four-day time limit on it? Just enjoy until I travel back, then pine off the memories? Even if I look up Jun in the future, he'll still be in Vancouver living his life, and I'll be living mine with three kids including a newborn. I won't even have time for proper sleep.

While I'm enjoying the bagel, I resolve that I'm going to have to treat this as the line goes in the musical *Into the Woods* ... "this was just a moment in the woods." When the Baker's Wife has a romantic tryst with Cinderella's Prince.

I think we both know that this won't go anywhere. So, we're just not going to talk about it.

There are a few things left on my bucket list for this holiday:

- -- Go to the symphony
- -- Catch another opera
- -- Catch another ballet
- -- Eat tons of food I can't when I go back
- -- Go to restaurants that don't exist anymore
- -- Sex
- -- Find Conrad's friend (probably unnecessary now)

I'm trying to think of things I can do without the kids, but also with a 20-year-old body. And 20-year-old body discounts. I don't want to do family tourist attractions because I can bring the kids on a weekday. If I'm going to see any kids at all, I might as well spend time with my own. So that rules out the zoo, Casa Loma, the Science Centre, and Centreville. The aquarium hasn't been built yet.

"I think I want to go for a massage," I blurt.

"Okay," Jun says.

"And Indian food."

"Okay."

"And a dance class."

"Okay."

"And karaoke."

"Okay."

"You don't have to do all these things with me."

"But those things sound boring by yourself."

This is true.

"Finish your bagel," Jun says authoritatively as we get to a bench by the Royal Ontario Museum.

"Ooh, I wanna go in," I reply as I plop myself down. He sits down on the bench beside me and pulls out a Blackberry.

"Oh my God!" I exclaim, laughing. "Whoa! Dang, this is like the best 2005 has to offer?"

"I know," he says, rolling his eyes. "This was part of the stuff I had to do in Vancouver yesterday. It's a gift from my parents. I had to act really excited."

"I miss my iPhone," I say wistfully.

"Me too," Jun replies. "I was gonna get the new one too, I'm due for an upgrade. Aw shit, this fucking thing ..." Jun remembers that he has to use the scroll wheel to get through the apps and rolls his eyes again in frustration.

"You sure you want to stay here? I mean, modern medicine and better phones and, you know diversity initiatives have yet to come." I make jazz hands when I say "diversity initiatives."

"That's a loaded question right now, but the massage was a really good idea. Finish your bagel if you want to go to the museum. You can't take food in."

He finds what he's looking for and dials.

"Hello? Hello? ..." He walks off trying to find a better signal.

I finish my bagel and wipe my mouth and hands on napkins with water I spill out from the bottle. Wet wipes would do so much better here. I always have them in my purse as a mom.

When you're around your kids so much that you don't have time to miss them, it's damn well near impossible to forget that you have them. To not be with them for any extended period like this is half decompressing and remembering to be yourself as a person first, rather than giver-of-life, protector-of-small-people, constant-activity-director, snack-carrier, servant.

I throw away my garbage in the receptacle, slightly disappointed that it's still a few years before we'll get the kind that separates compost and recycling. I check myself in the small mirror from my purse to make sure I don't have sesame seeds in my teeth. Then I remember that I should reapply lip gloss. Jun comes back just as I put it all away.

"Okay, we're on for massages at 2."

"Oh, thank you. Somewhere close by?"

"Uh huh. Did you want to go into the museum now?"

I check my phone for the time. It's only 8 a.m.

"We can't. They're only open at 10. Boo."

Jun shrugs and takes my hand to pull me up. We walk to the front door. He peers in, then knocks with a wave. I expect nothing as I hang back, contemplating where to walk to next. And then a security guard with a turban opens the door, smiling.

"Mr. Sung!"

"Hey Rajeev!" They shake hands. "This is Claudia."

"Hello, miss!" Rajeev says with an even bigger smile. I wave hello.

"Hey Rajeev, sorry to impose, but we were just passing by, and I wondered if we could come in a little earlier if you don't mind please."

"No problem, no problem! Let me just radio the boss." He tells someone that Jun Sung and his guest would like early access. A crackle and voice comes back. "Sure, no problem. Hi Jun, it's Sadie."

Rajeev pulls his walkie toward Jun and presses the button to talk.

"Hey Sadie, thanks so much. We promise not to cause trouble," Jun says.

"I know you have no fear of 'you break it, you buy it'," Sadie says with a laugh.

Rajeev welcomes us in. "Enjoy, enjoy," he says happily.

We both murmur our thanks. It's crazy strange being in an empty museum but thrilling.

"How did you …"

"My family donates a lot to the museum," Jun says casually. Damn. Money does buy access. Literally.

"What do you want to see first?" he asks.

"Dinosaurs," we both say at the same time and laugh.

I change my shoes and we race upstairs. There's a feeling of eerie reverence in the hall. Things that came before us. Everything is quiet and not yet fully lit up. I study the apatosaurus, the pterodactyl hanging from the ceiling, the woolly mammoth replica behind glass. We walk through the exhibits – everything pristine and the plexiglass fingerprint-free. I have to pace myself because I want to enjoy as much as possible with this exclusive access, but I also don't have to crane around people to see things so I can read the descriptions for what's interesting.

We stroll through the knights' armor exhibit and the Egyptian galleries. We take our time through the Asian artifacts. I figure it's easier to end there because it's less crowded in this part even when the museum has peak traffic.

As we're looking at pottery from the Tang Dynasty, Jun comes up behind me and playfully puts his face next to mine over my shoulder. "What do you like better?" Jun asks. "The Met's Asia exhibit or the ROM's?"

"That's like asking which child you like better," I laugh. "The ROM has a bigger collection, but I feel like the Met has a better layout, so the stuff looks cooler. They're different, but outside of going to China itself, these are the best collections I've seen in North America."

"I could take you to New York, you know," Jun suggests. "We could go today … tomorrow …"

"Ciara's there!" I shoot back. I whisper, "That means no privacy to do naughty stuff."

"Then we won't tell her," he whispers back before bringing me in for a kiss.

"You are so hot right now," I whisper with a smile.

Jun looks into my eyes. His face gets serious – so serious that I was about to crack a joke to break the silence, but I dare not say anything.

Suddenly, the earth starts to rumble and shake like an earthquake. It should be strong enough that pottery around us should be smashing like crazy. Jun grabs me close and quickly shields me to protect me from falling debris and it feels as if the world could swallow us whole.

We lose our balance and sink to the floor. When the rumbling stops, it's Rajeev's voice that breaks the silence.

"Is everything okay, Mr. Sung?"

Jun uncovers my head and it's bewildering for both of us as to why there isn't tons of debris around us.

"Did you not feel that, Rajeev?" I ask gingerly.

"I'm sorry, feel what, Miss Claudia?"

I start to say "earthquake", but something tells me it's an "only-affects-time-travelers" thing.

"I guess I must have felt dizzy on my own. Thanks Jun," I say as he helps me up. "Everything's fine now, Rajeev. Thanks for checking on us."

When Rajeev walks off and seems out of earshot, I spin Jun toward me. "What do we do?"

"Do you know how to get a hold of Mhairi?"

"No … she doesn't have a phone. She has my phone number though. On a napkin. Which she might have lost."

"She thinks I'm in Vancouver."

"Oh shit."

We look at each other for a moment.

"She didn't tell you not to travel, right?"

"No rules."

"Yeah … I didn't really get rules either. She just said not to talk about the future. She should really hand out a pamphlet or something."

"So, what do you want to do?"

"I don't know that there's anything we can do. Even if we go find her at the Beaches, it's an hour to get there."

We look at each other, contemplating.

"Let's go to lunch and get the massages – that's two things off your list if we get sent back tonight," he decides.

"Are you sure?"

"Not really. But I also don't want to miss a 2 p.m. appointment for a 90-minute couple's massage."

"90 minutes?!" I shriek then lower my voice. "Neither 20-year-old me nor 40-year-old me can afford that or will offer to pay you back."

"It's okay. I didn't intend for you to pay for anything at all today."

The world might be ending but I'm going to die in bliss.

Chapter 22:

BLISS BEFORE THE WORLD ENDS

*W*e walk from the museum down Bloor and then through Yorkville. It's a little like when you have your first baby and the contractions start, but then they're so far apart and your water hasn't broken yet, so you've got time to get things done because you know your whole world is going to change.

We stop at a bench, and I change into my stilettos because I feel more like acting the part of Jun's girlfriend as we flit in and out of the swanky stores. I've never set foot in Hermès or Louis Vuitton or Bvlgari. I've just never had a need nor desire. But we go in just for fun and I look at things like $500 scarves, all while Jun is offering to buy me one. I decline because I'm not in a bracket to wear a $500 scarf and decide I'm done. I do want to stop at Tiffany & Co. though. There's lots to look at in there.

"Can we go?" I ask eagerly.

"Sure," says Jun.

In the first 30 seconds, I already see multiple things that I'd want to add to a personal collection.

"What's your style?" asks Jun.

"Silvers, blues, pearls, lightweight dangly earrings. Interesting designs in soft curves with a bit of detail," I say succinctly as I point to a blue ring with a floral motif. It's $17,000. I yelp and Jun laughs a tiny bit.

"Okay … let's go." I walk off quickly as if I might be

charged just for looking.

As we walk up to Yorkville Avenue, Jun casually takes my hand. I'm a little startled but I wonder why he hasn't been holding my hand all day. I instantly feel better, which is to be expected. Hand holding has been scientifically proven to lower blood pressure and decrease anxiety and stress levels.

I catch a reflection of Jun and me in a window. We look really good together, especially when we're both so happy. Damn, I left my camera in my dorm room. It's just not my habit to pack it since I've had an iPhone in my pocket for over a decade.

We carry on walking and find Utsav, the Indian restaurant I remember was here but couldn't remember the name of.

"Ah, here's where I was thinking of," I say, gently pulling his hand. We're seated quickly and I regretfully remember that I don't have Lactaid pills here.

"If you want to share, I can't do cream sauces," I tell Jun flatly. He nods, understanding what I mean without me having to say it. We order the Madrasi lamb (coconut curry with chilies, tomatoes, and onions) and aloo gobi to share. Each meal comes with a green salad, basmati rice, and naan. He gets a chai and I ask for a mango juice.

While we wait for our food, I lament that there's a restaurant in Old Montreal I used to love that had a coconut-based lamb curry with lychees in it. Now the place is a Lebanese kebab joint which I'm sure has delicious food, but I've never tried it.

"We could go," he says.

"It might not exist yet," I reply. Then after a pause, I get a brainwave. "You should think about a chai-based chocolate mousse for the shop," I suggest excitedly. "I make these awesome chai gingerbread cookies. You could put them on the top of the cup, like a cherry."

"Really?" he says, genuinely intrigued. "That's a fantastic idea." I smile broadly. I want to tell him that all these great ideas can be thanked with a sampler pack sent to my house in the future, but it pains me to think that I won't be able to eat chocolate mousse for a while because of the pregnancy, and also because I don't know if he'll remember me at all. It starts to make me a little teary, then I'm glad I get distracted by our server bringing drinks. The food arrives shortly after and we get into a conversation about TV series. I'm glad that Jun and I can talk freely about them without worrying if I'm telling him about one that doesn't even exist yet. We both gripe about the ending of *Game of Thrones*. I tell him the general gist of *Switched At Birth*. And *Cheer Squad* and *Home for Christmas*. I like that he listens to me with 100% undivided attention. We finish our food and check the time – it's 1:45 p.m.

"Perfect timing," he says. "The hotel is just right there." We get the bill quickly and I grab it before he can put his black card on it.

"Hey!" he says indignantly.

"I can manage this one," I tell him while flipping my hair.

"Thank you," he says graciously.

We head over to the Hoitview Hotel just two blocks away. The lobby features large chaise sofas and ornately carved walls and doorways like a modernized traditional Chinese-style, but I don't have much time to take it in. Jun leads me straight to the elevator and up to the 16th floor.

The spa has a big blue desk in the lobby with an ornate light fixture above it. I can see a pool off through glass doors and an outdoor terrace beyond that. The lady at the desk perks up when she sees Jun.

"Hello, Mr. Sung. How are you, today?"

"I'm great, how are you, Ursula?"

"I'm well, thank you."

"And your daughter?"

"She's doing fine, looking forward to graduating middle school. Thank you for asking."

"First stop high school, and soon she'll be one of Toronto's leading cardiologists." He winks at me. I smile. Sometimes it's fun knowing the future.

"Are there any enhancements you wanted to add to your 90-minute couple's massage today?" Ursula asks.

"Let's see … Clauds?" He hands me a menu of the spa services while he peruses his own.

I almost drop it when I see the price. It's $325 for a 90-minute message for one person. It's $25 each for a whipped shea butter enhancement and a coconut hair and scalp treatment.

"I'll say yes to the shea butter for both of us," he says half-consulting me, but I say nothing because I'm already floored by the price. "And then … I think Claudia will get the hair treatment. Not because she needs it, but I think she'll like the scalp massage." Before I can say anything, they're already agreeing to it and lining things up.

"Thank you," I stammer out. I don't remember ever spending $375 plus tax and tip on anything for myself that's over in 90 minutes.

"I'll prepay now so we're all taken care of when we leave," I hear Jun saying to Ursula.

I'm looking over the rest of the menu and there's a Mom-To-Be Massage, but there's no way Chad would let me justify spending this kind of money for 90 minutes in the future. Maybe I'll ask Ciara for a family-discounted gift card.

Ursula's gushing snaps me out of my daydream. "Thank you so much, Mr. Sung! We really appreciate it. You're always so generous!"

She's smiling broadly as she comes around the desk.

"Let me show you to your room," she says kindly and takes us to a brightly lit room with two extra wide massage tables and two armchairs. She opens the closets and two robes are hung up with slippers at the bottom. They look like the robes and slippers from Jun's condo.

"Enjoy," she says while leaving. She draws a curtain around the door, like a medical examination room but with luxurious fabric.

I wonder if this is like what Ciara said about getting everything at cost, but then leaving generous tips. It's probably that. I hope it's that.

Jun starts undressing and it makes me smile. I could watch him undress pretty much all day. We both put our clothing in the closet. I do a slow striptease for him and it makes him go hard. I laugh as he tries comically to get it down. He can't, so he gets on the massage table and lies on his side under the blanket. I climb under the blanket on my table as well. There's a knock at the door and a female massage therapist comes in without opening the curtain. Jun doesn't seem to recognize her voice so she must be new.

"Miss Claudia, I have a male massage therapist available, if you would like that?"

"No, no, we'll have two females please," Jun says quickly.

"Yes, sir," she acknowledges and leaves.

"That did it," says Jun as he rolls over onto his front. "There will be no ogling of my girl, no potential imagining of anything under the covers, other than by me."

My girl. Wow. I'm not even technically yours ... but I can't remember the last time Chad showed any sort of possessiveness.

I smile sweetly at him. I can only imagine separation being horribly painful on Sunday night. For now, I'll try to put it out of my mind.

The last time I had a massage was when I was pregnant for the first time. After that, I can't seem to turn my brain off for one, so it's been about 5 years. The 15-minute one at a work event doesn't count. I figure it's too much of a waste to have a thousand thoughts running through my head that I can't relax, so I don't even try to book appointments.

This massage (this very expensive massage) is delightful. The experience of the various scents, relaxing music and my (female) massage therapist's touch feels so wonderful that I can easily put all my worries on hold. She starts off chatty, but I politely say, "I'd really like to zone out, if you don't mind."

Jun volunteers, "I'm not sure that other clients would like it, but if you have iPods with headphones or something, totally feel free to use them during our session."

"Thank you," she nods. "You're the first person to offer that, and I'll take you up on it because I am learning Korean."

"That will be extremely useful in future," I pipe up, winking at Jun. His therapist doesn't say anything but just smiles and carries on. Maybe she knows who he is and would rather concentrate.

I don't ask about how my massage therapist is listening to Korean language learning tracks on her iPod because I can't remember if podcasts were big around now yet, and I don't want to start a big, long conversation.

Overall, she does an excellent job with my massage. Despite the feeling that the world might end for us, I'm completely able to zone out and focus on her touch. I choose unscented shea butter, but the coconut oil makes me think we're on an island somewhere. Halfway through, I get turned over onto my back, but I'm so relaxed that I don't feel like opening my eyes.

When we're finally finished, we both thank them pleasantly. Jun asks the ladies if they need the room after us.

"You're the only couple booked today, so we can use the individual rooms. Please take your time," is the response.

I'm so relaxed that I don't really want to move any part of my body. I stir the tiniest bit when Jun starts kissing my neck.

"Baby ... I'm gonna need to see your beautiful body under the covers," he whispers. I can hear his smile.

"You'd better make it worth my while," I say playfully begrudgingly.

He untucks one edge of the blanket and starts nibbling one nipple while rolling his fingers on the other side. Being around babies or being pregnant really makes any boob touch a total turn-off but right now, I feel like he could make me climax by doing just this. Under the covers, he uses his other hand to finger in between my legs and we both hear how wet it makes me. The massage table has long sheets draped down hiding the underside, but he finds and presses a button on a floor pedal to lower the table, then moves to hover by my head. He reaches down my body under the covers so that one hand is fingering my clitoris, and the other hand is gently pumping in and out with one, then two fingers. I get my climax and my whole body responds. Quickly, I take his penis in my mouth since it's right there, and it doesn't take me long to make him finish. He pulls out and comes on my chest. He takes a second to recover, then grabs a clean towel from a pile stacked up on a counter near the sink. He cleans us both off, then wraps the dirty towels in another clean one, placing it on his massage table linens.

"Whew, thank you. I snuck a couple of condoms in your purse this morning but that was a nice surprise."

I smile wearily. I wish I could be massaged right before bed, then fall asleep for the rest of the night. "I'm going to go shower – I'm sure the pool has showers, right?"

"Yeah, and they have extra robes in there too," he assures me.

We wash our hands in the sink together and it gives me another chance to have a naked feel up against him. I put on a robe and slippers, then grab my stuff for the pool change-room. He does the same. Holding my hand, we pass the men's changeroom first.

"There's the women's," he points down the hall. "I'll wait out here for you but take your time."

I turn to go as he lets the door close, but I hear, "Wait!" and he comes back out for a kiss.

Then he disappears back inside.

As I turn, I'm just in time to see Mhairi's stunned face. "Chocolate Mousse!" she says while pointing in Jun's direction. Then she points at me. "Frittata!"

Then she looks like she's putting two and two together. "That's why we're having earthquakes!"

Chapter 23:

JUN DESERVES A MAGICAL VACATION

"Oh my God, I'm Harry Potter," I say with this stark realization.

"What, dear?" Mhairi says cluelessly.

"Just that you happened to show up – I thought we'd have a difficult time finding you." Mhairi pulls me inside the changeroom. There's a plush sofa so we sit down together.

"He's fallen in love with you, Frittata. And he was never supposed to meet you again."

"Wow, it's earth-shattering love," I joke.

"It's not a time to be flippant," Mhairi says in all seriousness. "It's only a matter of time before you fall in love with him too. Then your whole future changes – for both of you. The earthquakes are a sign that the universe's events and timeline have changed."

"What are we supposed to do?"

"Break up. Go your separate ways."

"What happens if we don't?"

"Suffer the consequences then."

"What are the consequences?"

Mhairi sighs. "You get sent back to the future as if this was real."

"On Monday, you mean?"

"Correct. Sunday night. You go to sleep and your holiday is over. You wake up Monday morning and it's life as usual … but as if this relationship had carried on longer."

"Wait ... but that means not necessarily successfully ..."

"Right," she nods.

"And my kids could just be different kids altogether if Jun ended up being their dad."

"Ehm ... again, I don't have any control over biology. You could end up having all girls or only one child or none at all."

The gravity of the last part really hits me hard. "Have you ever had a case like this, Mhairi?"

"Nae. I suppose I should start handing out a pamphlet or something. I didn't expect in the least that he'd fly across the country. People don't usually waste their time on airplanes when given this experience."

I'm a little bit exasperated because this is really her fault and she should have given out rules, and I don't want to say it out loud because I've had an exceptional time except for this bit about my kids disappearing forever.

Buy time and ask questions, Claudia.

"Okay Mhairi, I'm supposed to go back Sunday night. When is Jun supposed to go back?"

"He doesn't have an end date. He needs to get a handle on what's happened to him before he can even process how to move forward."

"But he has to go back?"

She nods. "There's no changing that."

"Please tell me what happened to him," I beg her. "He said it was okay if I hear it from you, but he won't tell me anything himself."

Mhairi shifts uncomfortably. "I'll show you." She grabs both my hands and suddenly I'm transported to watching Jun at Fàn Times, his shop in Vancouver. I suddenly lurch forward and trip but I'm like a ghost, so my hands go through the display case and people walk through me. Jun looks like he does now – still athletic and well-built in tailored, collared shirts but wearing jeans and just slightly older. He's got the faintest hint of grey hair but he's aged really well. He walks from the front of the store where there are two responsible-looking, teenaged Asian girls with buns and hairnets and branded visor caps working capably in the front by the cash. It looks like a gelato shop, with all the offerings in refrigerated glass cases, but it's chocolate mousse and rice pudding. It's not a crazy big crowd, but it seems like a steady stream of customers that the seats are all taken and people are just taking their purchases outside. It's a warm day but cloudy. I follow Jun to the massive back kitchen where there's an older Asian woman with a hairnet, mask, apron, and gloves making a large batch of something. He puts on a branded baseball cap and a mask, then washes his hands before going to a different area of the kitchen where there's a clear door refrigerator. Inside, there are lots of small batch containers with labels of the many different flavors he let me try at his condo. The peanut butter chocolate pretzel; passionfruit; island breeze; dark chocolate raspberry; and dark chocolate apricot are on the top shelf, then he has other flavors below which I don't have time to read.

There are empty mini mason jars for the batch he's making now: sun gold kiwi chocolate bliss. He has a notepad for the ingredient measurements and labels for the flavor and date.

Wearing gloves, he fills jars, careful not to spill or waste any. A handsome Eurasian guy comes through the door from the storefront. He puts on a hat and a mask and washes his hands too. He's taller than Jun, with a partly-shaved head and a faux hawk. Cute smile too, but he's definitely less handsome than Jun because he's not giving me any of the feels in my loins.

"'Sup, bro?" Jun says to him.

"Declan," yells the older Asian lady. "Come here." I hear her scolding him for something in Korean. He looks like a teenager getting caught but apologizes sincerely.

Jun carries on with what he's doing without batting an eye. It must be a frequent occurrence for her to scold Declan. It gives me a chance to look around. Their walk-in fridge has huge commercial-sized cartons of whipped cream and coconut cream. Fruit purée comes in giant buckets. Chopped nuts are in humongous containers.

As if nothing just happened, Declan comes over soon enough with a clipboard and says, "Okay, time for that annual executives' meeting. Sign here for attendance." Jun signs the paper on the clipboard. Declan signs underneath. "Shareholders 50% each, check, check … date of annual meeting … items to discuss …" Jun gets the last container sorted out but leaves the lid off.

"Try this," Jun says. Even with a mask on, I can tell that he's proud of this batch.

Declan drops his mask, then grabs a tasting spoon and tries it. "Hmm … I dunno if I like the seeds in there."

Jun is a little taken aback. "Really? You can feel the seeds?" Jun briefly drops his own mask and takes a tasting spoonful from the same container. "I dunno, dude. If I get rid of the seeds, that's probably going to take more time and effort than it's worth."

Declan thinks about it. Then goes back for another spoon. He contemplates again. "Meh, people can get used to seeds." Declan finishes the whole container then puts his mask back on.

"Annual meeting completed. Back to business as usual. I'm gonna work from home for the rest of the afternoon if you don't need me here?"

"Yeah, I'm just gonna work here on new flavors."

"Sweet. See ya!" They fist bump and Declan leaves.

Jun fills out a branded form similar to the one he had with me with Declan's feedback, then carries on working for a while. He shifts around Post-Its with jotted notes and I can see he's trying to brainstorm flavors. I should tell him that you can do this in Miro … or in 2005, we'll just have to settle for PowerPoint.

I check out the rest of the flavors in the refrigerator. I

look around the shop. They have a display of merchandise like In-N-Out does: branded Fàn Times hoodies, umbrellas, t-shirts, and baby onesies. I bet Ciara suggested that when Timothy was born.

The crowd starts to build outside the store, and one of the teenaged girls from the front rings a bell which chimes in the back. The older lady scurries out to help when convenient. Jun grabs a branded Fàn Times cooler bag, two individually wrapped compostable spoons and an ice pack, then he puts in a bunch of the labeled containers and one from his newest batch. When we step outside, I realize his store is in Yaletown. We get to Pacific Boulevard and I can see the waterfront between buildings. Eventually he enters a residential tower – it's a set of two buildings with a swimming pool in the middle. We take the elevator through a boring lobby and upstairs to his place. He opens the door and calls out, "Babe, I got something for your sore throat …"

And there in the hallway, with panoramic views of the waterfront behind them, his business partner is standing 69ing a woman against the wall. They turn and see Jun. Declan almost drops her. But then he gently brings the woman down to the floor.

Jun looks like someone shot an arrow through his heart. To her, he says, "I thought you were home sick." To Declan, Jun says, "This is *my* home. And that's *my* wife."

And then he just walks back through the front door. Instead of waiting for the elevator, he takes the stairs. He's sweating then eventually crying. He wipes his sweat and tears on his shirt sleeve but just keeps running down the stairs. He gets down to the second floor, then still has to go through the lobby, avoiding people who see his distress. He runs out the front door, bashing the exit button to unlock it, and his phone rings. He ignores it and keeps running down Pacific toward the waterfront. The cooler bag becomes an annoyance on his arm, so he just holds it like a football. He lets his phone ring and ring. Finally, he gets to the waterfront and answers, catching his breath at the same time. It's his sister.

"Mei-mei, now's not a good time," he forces out.

As a ghostly bystander, I hear the whole conversation at the same volume he hears with the phone pressed to his ear.

While crying, she says, "Jun, Mama and Baba got into a car accident. They didn't make it. They passed away an hour ago."

Jun screams and collapses onto the grass.

I feel myself being yanked backwards and it forces my eyes closed. When I open them, I'm dizzy and disoriented for a second, then I'm back with Mhairi on the couch in the changeroom.

Mhairi lets go of my hands and carries on the story. "I found him a little while later. We sat down on a bench and shared the chocolate mousse he was carrying. He said he couldn't do anything about his parents, but wished he'd never met his wife or started his business with that partner."

I'm too stunned to speak.

Poor Jun. How awful for him. What pain he must be carrying. And he's so happy with me when it's just us.

I burst out with, "WHAT THE FUCK?! There's no way I can break up with him before Sunday night."

Mhairi doesn't speak for a while. She just stares at the floor. I leave her to think in silence. "It does seem quite cruel, doesn't it?"

I nod wholeheartedly.

"This is why I come for a massage once a week. This job is stressful." She goes back to thinking. "I don't like smelling like a cucumber, so I'll have a think while in the shower." She gets up. I give her a look like, "What the fuck?"

"You have a shower too, Frittata. See what you can come up with. I'll meet you back here."

See what I can come up with? I don't know the arbitrary rules of time traveling. In my daze, I still have enough sense to grab a clean towel from a pile. Ooh it's a bath sheet too! Focus, goddammit!

While showering, I use conditioner, then body wash instead of shampoo, and then shampoo my body. I've just wasted $25 on that leave-in coconut conditioner which I've now washed out. Shit. But that seems to be the least of my problems. I start crying thinking about what Jun has gone through.

I fumble with my clothing and get dressed without drying my hair. I don't see Mhairi at the sofa and I don't want Jun to worry, so I call him.

"Hi! You okay?" he answers.

"Um, I ran into Mhairi here. I'm going to be a while with her."

"Right, I'll be at the rooftop bar when you're done," and he swiftly hangs up on me as if she might try to catch him in the changeroom.

I catch a glimpse of myself in the mirror and see that my makeup is completely fucked. Luckily the sinks are just where I can still see the sofa in case Mhairi turns up. I use the very fancy disposable makeup remover sachets they have available. When my makeup is off, I start crying again. When I feel like I'm done, I reapply everything, but my face is still blotchy. This is really not the greatest way to end a $375 massage.

Mhairi finally makes her way back and catches me at the sinks. She's still in a towel.

She whispers, "Sorry, I'm hiding from someone, and I think I have to duck into the sauna until she's gone." She pulls me down below the counter level. "I don't have an answer for you yet, but I'll think of something and sleep on it. Can you meet me for lunch tomorrow? The Hot House Café?"

My eyes light up. "Oh, I love that place, yes. What time?"

"Noon. And don't bring Chocolate Mousse."

"Why would I bring chocolate mousse to a restaurant?"

"No, the person," she says, and I can tell she's holding back from calling me Dummy.

"Got it."

Mhairi grabs the towel just before it falls off her and sneaks away to the sauna. I guess I'd better go face Jun.

And try my hardest not to fall in love with him.

Chapter 24:

SUNSET AND LOBSTERS

I ride the elevator up to the top floor, all the while trying to think of what to say to Jun. When the doors open, the sun is just setting, and Toronto's skyline looks gorgeous through the floor-to-ceiling windows. The shades have been drawn just perfectly where the light hits at just the right angles without blinding anyone with brightness.

And there he is … at a table by himself … swearing at his "ancient" Blackberry. When he sees me, he instantly lights up and gives me the brightest smile, which I instinctively return. I hug him with all the strength I can muster, my arms wrapped tightly around him. He hugs me back and kisses me on the forehead.

"She told you, huh?"

"She showed me. I'm sorry. For all that happened to you."

"I don't want your pity," he murmurs while still holding on to me.

I move so we can see each other's faces. "It's not pity. So much happened to you in an hour, I think my brain would just go into emotional overdrive and shut down. It's okay to feel whatever you're feeling." I go back to hugging him like I was. "If you want to talk about it or not, that's up to you, but I'm here to listen if you need me. Although, I do recommend seeing a good therapist because I might not be as useful."

"I just want this right now," and he holds me a little tighter. We stay like this for a while until my stomach growls. It's fun to feel his whole body as he laughs.

"I felt that," he says, still laughing.

Jun orders us seared scallops with truffle carpaccio and oysters as appetizers.

"The chef just got in these gigantic lobsters. I'm gonna get one with truffle butter. Want one too?"

"Uh … yeah okay please," I fumble out. There are so many items on this menu that I don't actually recognize by name and normally I'd just discreetly Google it on my phone behind the menu, but I can't here in the land of Blackberry devices and landlines.

"Oh yeah, and I love this – it's spinach salad with pears, pecans, goat cheese and a dressing to die for. It has candied bacon and maple syrup in it."

My head cocks to the side. "How are you so equal opportunity when it comes to food?"

"What do you mean?"

"Like how do you bounce from food courts to … this," I gesture wildly at the exquisitely ornate light fixtures and sunset view.

"Good food is good food. But I will dress up my instant noodles though."

I laugh. I can't really imagine Jun with instant noodles. If anything, I feel like his family might have an organic kind shipped in from somewhere. Or maybe just hire a chef to make the best ramen as a guest in one of their home kitchens, then freeze containers of it in a massive freezer hidden behind custom cabinetry.

As I look around, there's maybe one other table with two people … and then I realize that it seems to be a staff meeting of some sort. "How come it's so quiet?" I ask Jun.

"They're probably doing a lot of room service. And it's generally slow around now because this kind of clientele isn't off work yet. We thrive on the late corporate business dinners… the law firm celebrations for big wins … it's not a bad scene for lunch but it's upscale and good for private conversations so people like that it doesn't get super busy. It hasn't been scouted as a tourist spot yet either."

"Only a matter of time before it gets into a New York Times '36 hours in' piece."

"Nah, I'll be putting a stop to that in about five years from now."

"Oh really?"

"Yeah, once the tourists get a whiff of your place, it becomes a different beast to manage. I'd rather have a phenomenal restaurant flying under the radar than have a blockbuster. It changes the dynamic ... traffic in the hotel ... it's just ... different. You know?"

I shrug. "Thanks for the schooling," I say and look away.

"I've got all this knowledge of said and unsaid things from my parents."

"Enough to fill a book?"

"It would take years for a cohesive knowledge dump." He looks at the floor. I let him ponder things in silence for a bit. Maybe he wants to open up about his parents?

Then he changes the subject completely. "What did Mhairi say?"

Oh right, her.

"Uhh ... she said you don't have to hide from her anymore. But you have to go back at some point."

He nods slowly.

"Did she tell you why the earthquakes are happening?"

Lie, just lie.

"She doesn't know. She'll find out options and get back to me," I hear myself saying.

The food arrives and while all the other meals I've had on this holiday were good, this is just superb. The scallops are humongous and seared perfectly so that the outside is slightly crispy and the inside just melts in my mouth. The carpaccio is not a tiny helping on a scallop – it's a legitimate plateful with a potato purée. The truffle sauce is buttery goodness, and I can see tiny people just eating this as an entire meal. I have one oyster, which is good, but I savor this dish and probably eat most of it.

"Should have ordered your own of that one," I say as politely as possible with my mouth full while physically hoarding the plate in my direction.

Jun laughs at me and leans in. "Maybe I will order my own for later," he fake whispers.

When they arrive, the lobsters are gigantic, and half-shelled in such a way that the meat can be easily pulled up with a fork. The truffle butter is as scrumptious as it sounded initially. They should package this and load popcorn with it. And while I don't usually go for salads, this one is superb.

"I think we're going to have to walk this off tonight with whatever we're doing," I tell him flatly.

He puts his cutlery down. "What are we doing tonight?"

"Really? You don't have plans already?" I'm genuinely surprised. "Aren't there people you wanted to see or things you wanted to do?" I wonder why he doesn't want to see his parents.

"I like your bucket list," he shrugs. "Are there people you wanted to see?"

I think about it. I saw Kyle already. I see Ciara all the time. My parents are on a cruise. Everybody I want to see ... I can see at 40.

"You know, I went to see *Tosca* the other night, but I don't remember anything about it."

I'll just leave out those details about being distracted by your voice-mail and wondering if I needed to get over you forever.

"Oh. Yeah, it's not for everyone. Hold on." Jun gets up and talks to someone by the bar. Then he disappears a little way down the hallway. He's left his Blackberry on the table, so I hope he doesn't get stuck in the bathroom.

He's gone for a while, and it gives me a chance to enjoy the sunset and my lobster which is downright fabulous. We will definitely have to walk this off later.

I finish my food and go back to our shared salad, dishing out more onto my plate. Why can't all vegetables be this nice?

Jun returns in a bit and says, "Ha, okay. Here's the plan: we're going to *La Bohème* at 7:30."

"How did you get tickets?"

"The concierge here is well-connected. Plus, you know, donor circle."

Man, I'd love to be in the donor circle tier of anything cool. Even if it was just for being able to park in an exclusive parking lot – a definite perk at the Natural Museum of History in Los Angeles when the nearby parking lots are crowded. But I wouldn't know about that. Sigh.

We finish our food and Jun pays with his black card. Again, he tips generously and knows the staff, fist bumping all over the place.

"Wait, how did you call the concierge?"

"There's a dedicated phone line down the hallway there by the bathrooms."

"Huh. Like an artifact."

"Shhhh," Jun whispers.

It's a good thing I dressed for an all-purpose kind of day. My dress has been great for the museum, lunch, dinner, and now the opera. I put the sweater on, and we walk to the Four Seasons Centre for the Performing Arts which is a real hike but the weather is nice. It's a clear night and a little chilly, but that makes it perfect for walking without getting sweaty on an upscale kind of night.

When we get to the theatre, I change into my stilettos and the outfit becomes just a little chicer. We go to Will Call where

Jun claims our tickets.

I didn't think much of our seats for *Tosca* because it didn't really matter to me at a discounted price. But when we go upstairs, Jun insists on checking my giant purse with the Grand Ring coat check.

"But if we check my bag here, then we'll have to come all the back here when our seats are … wait … where are our seats?"

Jun smiles and just checks it for me. Somehow, he scored Box Q tickets, row C in the Grand Ring. This is the balcony that overlooks the stage. Box N is in the center, then Box Q, from the stage view, is mid-left. There are only four seats in front of us. It's almost an unobstructed view of the stage. In the future (or Jun's and my present), these tickets are upwards of $374 each. I don't even know how much dinner was. This day has been like a $2000 date!

When the lights dim, I find myself mesmerized by everything happening on stage. Angel Blue is the soprano tonight and as a person of color, I just love seeing a Black female soprano.

When I was actually 20, an all-white cast in anything bothered me a bit, but not like today where I feel like it is truly unacceptable to lack diversity. For 2005, this is a decent mix, but of course no Asians unfortunately.

There's a scene in *Pretty Woman* where Richard Gere's character takes Julia Roberts' character to the opera and she falls in love with it such that, at the end, an old lady asks if she enjoyed it, and she says with tears, "It was so good I almost peed my pants!" I feel a little like that as I'm watching. This time, there are no distractions and Jun is sitting beside me, so my focus is completely on the experience, except for the times when I can feel Jun adoringly smiling at me (even in the dark) and shifting while holding my hand.

The two rows in front of us remain empty for a good while and every so often, Jun kisses me but I refuse to turn my face that way because this is a once-in-a-lifetime experience and I highly doubt anyone will get me these kinds of seats ever. And nobody goes to the opera to make out.

At the first intermission, Jun tells me he'll be right back and comes back with a very fancy glass bottle of water for each of us. I thank him and silently guess that it's at least $12. Still standing, Jun offers his hand and says that we should probably move up to Row A since the people in rows A and B aren't coming.

"If they do arrive for Act 3 ... that's weird since it's like past the halfway point ... meh, then we'll just move," he theorizes.

In Row C, we had a relatively unobstructed view except for the empty seats. In Row A, it's *completely* unobstructed and it's marvelous. Is this like traveling business class where I won't ever want to go back down? Oh my. But the next time I'll get to the opera is ... I have no idea.

I feel a sudden pang and miss my kids, but at the same time, this is totally a kid-free activity and I'm relishing the time to be myself, to be adored by this man who seems to be like a modern-day Asian prince without the politics of a royal family. As a mom, one can definitely miss one's children without actually wanting to be with them. A week away is hardly enough to recharge when in the throes of a daily grind of being a solo parent without being a solo parent – where you have another grownup there but it's not helpful in the least. In fact, that causes you more problems relying on him.

I'm glad I'm having these thoughts during intermission because when the lights dim again, I can focus on the opera and leave the world entirely behind. This totally makes up for the *Tosca* experience.

At the second intermission (which is a good two hours into the performance), Jun takes my hand and casually says, "Let's go to the lounge."

WOW. I got box seat tickets to the Toronto Raptors

once with a group and I loved the "buffet" of hot dogs and popcorn and non-alcoholic drinks, but this private VIP lounge has a plethora of fancy snacks!

"Why didn't you tell me this lounge existed in the last intermission?" I pout.

"I only discovered it at the end and then it was too late. Go use the bathroom here. There's no lineup."

I use it partly because I want to touch up my makeup, use the facilities, and wash my hands before partaking of the snacks, but I also love fancy bathrooms and am not disappointed in the least.

Jun is hobnobbing with some older white men when I come out and he's more than happy to accompany me to the food.

"Do you know them?" I ask while picking up smoked salmon and caviar and gourmet crackers.

"Nope. Just old rich white guy talk. The club … what properties you own … where you keep your yacht." He makes an exasperated bored face. I bet he does belong to some exclusive clubs though.

I wonder how that goes with Jun in the mix. Do they know who he is? Does Jun let on? What do they compare? Who owns which buildings?

"I really don't want to talk to strangers while I'm here," he laments as he falls into one of a plush pair of armchairs. "Nobody needs to know my business. And I don't want to think about anything." He turns to me. "Except right now, what's happening with you and me."

Oh shit, just stay quiet.

I smile and nod. And eat. Luckily, the lights soon start flashing to return to our seats in the theatre and I down some sort of delicious mocktail to get rid of my salmon breath.

The last act is just as wonderful and we give a standing ovation. Jun sits back down with me and we stay a while, waiting until the crowd clears out.

"Well, it's late," he starts. "But I have this mad hankering for karaoke and gamjatang in Koreatown. What do you want to do?"

My eyes light up. "All of the above!"

Damn. Jun gets pretty drunk off of soju. I haven't been drinking since I got here to 2005 because I remember that my face gets Asian-flush-red and it's not super flattering in any light. We're in a booth in a late-night Korean place, the name of which I didn't catch, and the place looks divey but the food is hella yummy. My gamjatang (pork bone soup) is the right amount of spicy with a huge potato and the banchan (side dishes) are all my favorites – sweet potato, kimchi, bean sprouts, fish cake. I hope this place still exists in the future because it's totally going to be worth the trek. Jun orders beef mandu and fried chicken, which I also wanted, but when it arrives, he goes back and forth over whether he wants it or not.

I resolve to finish my food because gamjatang is annoying to transport as leftovers. Plus, I think we're cabbing it since Jun is probably not going to be in good shape for a stroll back to either of our places.

With his slurred speech, Jun looks way less handsome and my instincts for having to take care of another grown-ass man are kind of worn down. But then he starts talking and I can't help but feel awful for him.

I'm really glad we didn't go to a place with a grill in the middle of the table.

"Why him? Why did she choose him because he's the same as me! It's not like he has way more money than me ... is he better at sex? It's his tongue, isn't it? I've seen him eat ice cream. I can imagine it …"

He goes on for ages. And doesn't even realize it's me he's talking to. He just slumps over and talks to himself. He talks so much that I finish my food without rushing. Then I move over to his side so that at least when he slumps over, I can rub his back and keep his head from hitting the wall.

"And why my place? He lives alone! They could have gone to his place. Now I can't go home. That's where all my consoles are and my big TV! But wait, I can't go to work either. He's there. Where do I go?"

I try to get him to eat a mandu so he can at least pass out on a full stomach. He pauses wallowing, eats three, and then slumps over again onto the table.

"When we arrange my parents' funeral, they'll both be there. I bet they'll be sitting together, and then holding hands in the back row. Because if they're not there, people will talk. 'What a bad daughter-in-law'. 'What a bad business partner'. Why did this happen now? Right when the business is the best it's ever been?"

He starts crying and looks so sad that I start crying too.

I'll have to plead my case for his sake. I don't think I can leave on Sunday night.

Chapter 25:

MHAIRI AT THE BUFFET

eople are surprisingly helpful when you announce that your dining companion's wife cheated on him with his business partner. Two young guys help me get Jun into a cab. One of the servers packs up our food, with a free container of hangover soup. I pay with my own credit card and tip extremely generously.

I waver for a bit and decide that Jun will be much more comfortable in his own home. I do two trips – out with the food first, pay the cab driver, then coax Jun out but find myself supporting most of his weight as he rolls out. Luckily for us, Jun's neighbor, a big tall handsome Black guy, uses his fob to get us into the building while my hands are full supporting Jun. He looks like someone I should recognize, but like many Canadian celebrities, I'll only figure it out once he's walked away. Plus, he's wearing a tuxedo.

"Need some help?"

"Uh ... yeah ... please," and this is a well-timed offer because right then and there, Jun curls into a ball on the floor. "I'm Claudia, this is Jun. He's going through a really bad time."

"I can see that. I won't hold it against him. I'm Charlie," he says, extending a hand for a handshake, which I take.

As if he were lifting a child, Charlie throws Jun over his shoulder and carries him into the elevator. I quickly gather up the food and find Jun's keys to fob us to his floor. I open Jun's door and Charlie comes in. He manages to effortlessly leave his shoes at the door and help me get Jun onto his bed.

"Thanks so much, Charlie. What unit are you in? We'll take you out for a meal and a better time to get acquainted with Jun when he's … better."

"I'd love that. Penthouse 2," Charlie says holding up two fingers. "I always like an Asian meal with Asian people, you know what I'm saying?"

"Oh, you look like a guy who loves upscale Chinese food," I guess.

"I'll go to a hole in the wall if you tell me it's the best."

"We could be best friends, Charlie." He laughs at this. "Wanna give me your number, so I don't have to bang on your door randomly?"

"Sure," he says, and hands me a card. "Have a good night, Claudia."

"You too, Charlie." As he leaves, I look down at the card. Charlie Prepill. Toronto Raptors.

Geez. This is a swanky building except for Jun's condo. Or maybe Charlie likes to slum it a little. Slum it to keep humble. Slumble.

I save Charlie's number in my ancient phone, then put the card in the little key basket by Jun's front door. Aha, there's the house key and fob that Jun uses when he goes running. I put the food in the fridge, cover Jun with a blanket, leave a detailed note that I've gone home and have lunch plans, and that I'm borrowing his house key and fob to lock the door. I call a cab before leaving so I'm not waiting outside by myself for ages.

I dream that my kids are soundly asleep with me and I marvel at how adorable they are. Then they wake up and start being boisterous. Timothy jumps on me and I freak out because he's bounced on his sister in my belly. But then my belly is flat and I'm not pregnant.

I wake up freaking out. I sincerely hope this doesn't mean that the future is already changing because that's just not fair. It's Wednesday.

I still have time!

My dorm room feels half familiar and half disorienting. I see the clock – it's 10 a.m. I haven't consistently slept in until this late in ages.

I spend the time getting ready to see Mhairi like a lawyer mentally preparing for a trial. But then I don't know what the options are, don't know what I can offer, don't know what the outcome could be. All I know is that Jun can't be left without a support person or network, neither here nor in the future. I opt for a simple black dress, blazer, and flats with my big purse and the stilettos inside. My days here seem to be eventful and if I land at the symphony or something, at least I'll be dressed properly.

I walk to Bay and Bloor and catch the Bay Street bus to King, then walk to where Hot House Café is. In the future, they drop "café" from the name but for now, it's the same place I remember. And now I know why Mhairi chose this place to meet – on Wednesdays, it's buffet day.

It's 11:50 a.m. and Mhairi shows up just moments after I do, wearing jeans and a flowing mid-calf purple blouse, with a thick brown cape/cloak on top. She acknowledges me, then spells her name for the hostess saying she has a reservation for two people at noon. The hostess leads us to a nice table near the back. We pass the buffet and it all looks as great as I remember. At first glance, I can see a selection of pizzas, pastas, salads, roast beef, various sides, breads, and then a separate dessert station with cakes, pies, dessert squares, and cookies. Mhairi leaves her big cloak on the chair, and I leave the bulk of my big bag, taking my wristlet with me to the buffet.

"Take two plates, lass. I have a feeling we're in for a long conversation."

I nod and do as she tells me. When we both sit down, there's just enough room on the table for our four plates.

"So um …" I start.

Mhairi cuts me off. "We don't need small talk. Let me finish one plate first, then I can talk."

We both dig in and even though this is uncomfortable silence for me, the food brings back great memories of family and friend gatherings here. The candles with the melted wax are still by the bar. The heavy use of purple everywhere makes me nostalgic. Halfway through my plate, I'm fine with the silence, peppered with, "Try the potatoes/mussels/curry, it's really good." Mhairi eventually looks me in the eye and says plainly, "You look like you wanted to speak first."

"You can't send me back on Sunday night," I blurt out. "Jun's life is tragedy upon tragedy. There's no way he can sort this out by himself."

"The deities have been considering that," she says thoughtfully. "And while it wasn't ideal, it was convenient for you to turn up when you did."

"So, we don't have to break up? Ugh, what am I saying? We're not actually together," I ponder aloud. "But my kids shouldn't have to suffer the consequences."

She nods slowly. "There's been a new development. There's the possibility that your children could be born with Chocolate Mousse as their father. You'd still have the two boys, but you might not have your girl."

Hunh. I slump backward in my seat. That's what the dream was about.

"Heavy news, I know," she sympathizes.

"Do I still have to go back on Sunday night?"

"For now. But then you both get sent back Sunday night to a different future."

"Can't we extend that? I married my husband after years together – how can we decide on being with each other after just a week?"

"If you stay longer than Sunday night, you become a student and there's too many circumstances and people you'll come in contact with to prevent divulging the future. And that's damage control we can't handle."

I want to scream that none of this was my doing in the first place and then I just … can't. I've had some amazing experiences and circumstances are what they are now, even if the original intent in sending us both back was to give us a break from our lives.

I stare at my food contemplating what to say next, but Mhairi beats me to it. "I'm going for dessert. Are you coming?"

I look down at my still-full plate number 2. "I'm going to finish this first."

While Mhairi is gone, I try to think of questions I should ask and my mind comes up blank. Wait – if Mhairi is as obsessed with food as I am, I need to schedule a lunch date, so I know she'll turn up. Yes! Clever.

When she returns to the table, Mhairi has two full plates of desserts, but they're *so* full that my eyes actually widen in shock. Then she pulls out a giant plastic container from the inside pocket of her cloak and brazenly empties the cake slices and squares into it. Wow, I guess when you're literally ancient, you don't have to give a fuck about anything. She stacks the container, then her empty plate, then her second plate, and carries on eating from the second plate as if nothing has happened.

I kind of expect other people to see what she's doing and be a little taken aback, but no one seems to have seen anything.

"Mhairi, can people see you?"

"Of course," she says incredulously.

Okay wait, I have to play the game where you have to coax the information out of her. She won't divulge anything readily.

"Do they see you like I see you?"

"Ah … no," she says flatly in between bites.

"How do they see you?"

Still eating, she latches on to my wrist. Like I did for seeing Jun's present/future, I see our table from the perspective of other diners. Mhairi looks like herself but she's not doing anything out of the ordinary. It's as if her container and two plate tower don't exist – she just has one plate on the table.

She lets go and I guess it's half the impact with one hand because I don't feel as dizzy and disoriented coming back.

There's something about Mhairi where I just accept what's happening and don't question it. Maybe, I realize, it's part of her powers to prevent being questioned.

"Mhairi, how would you like to meet me for lunch at Magic Oven on the Danforth tomorrow. Same time, noon?"

"I love that place. It closes in 2019, you know," she says after swallowing a mouthful of chocolate raspberry cake.

"Oh, was that when? I just remember feeling sad when I heard it closed. Too expensive for us to go frequently."

"I need to leave," Mhairi says abruptly. "I'll see you tomorrow. Thank you for lunch." And she just freaking walks off before I can say anything.

Well, I'm not about to leave, I'm having dessert before paying the bill. I take my time finishing lunch, pondering what I should do.

Having Jun as their father would mean that Timothy and Jeremy could live a luxurious life, and I'm sure with doting grandparents who would shower them with gifts. They could go to private schools, we'd have a nanny, be able to travel the globe, and put them in every extra-curricular activity possible. But at the expense of Baby Girl, and Chad, is it even an option? And would our future dry up to be sexless and day-to-day without romance? With only a week together and no lead-up to the future, we would have skipped all the in-between. I'd have no idea who he is in the future. And he'd have no idea who I am in the future.

But at the moment, I really have no desire to go back to

Chad. And every time I look at Jun, he gives me butterflies ... for now.

Regardless, I have to go back on Sunday night.

Just as I'm staring through the back window, lost in my thoughts ... I see Conrad's friend, Jordan ... the one who I should have met before Conrad. He's wearing a suit and looks good.

He's Eurasian and it's like he got the best of both worlds in terms of features. He's not tall, but he's taller than me, and with cool hair too. Without thinking, I race up and tap on the glass. He recognizes me with the biggest smile. I wave at him to come in and he nods. He's coming around through the front. I run up to meet him and we hug.

"Are you out for lunch?"

"Yeah, can I join you?"

"Sure! My lunch date just left so her seat is free."

"Great!"

Oh no, what did I get myself into ...

Chapter 26:

JORDAN

I don't really know why Jordan is saying yes, and I don't really know why I've invited him in either. Would this now be cheating on Jun when we're not in a relationship and I'm clearly a rebound for him too?

At the same time, I'm far too curious and the opportunity has presented itself so here we go.

As we take our seats, I ask the server for a new set of cutlery for Jordan and let them know I'll pay for my friend who just left.

I've always wondered what it would be like to spend time one-on-one with Jordan, because the only time I've ever talked to this guy is when we went to dinner as the three of us with Conrad.

There's the one time that Jordan and I ran into each other on the subway, but it was one stop before he had to get off, and because I think I had recently married Chad, there was no real reason to get together. Maybe if he were a different kind of friend, I would have followed him to chat on the platform for a bit.

Had it not been for the "bro code" and the idea of continuously running into Conrad forever after, I might have made a beeline for Jordan mere weeks after breaking up with Conrad.

I think they're best friends because they go to the same church and have grown up together since their parents are friends, but from the outset, these guys really had nothing in common. Their fields of study were completely opposite and by this time, Jordan has been working for two years and moving his way up for a major consulting firm with his own place downtown. Had I started dating him instead of Conrad, we would have at least had a great deal more privacy, homecooked dinners as opposed to constant fast-food dates, and no doubt, hooking up despite any Asian church or parental guilt trips. At least that's what I think without having spent time together with him alone.

"You hungry?" I ask him.

"Definitely," he replies. We get up together and go back to the buffet. I vaguely ponder having to do something athletic this afternoon but then I shrug off that thought because my 20-year-old body is getting enough sex and walking everywhere, whereas 40-year-old me would just be driving everywhere because it's too hard to walk long distances with small children, all while lamenting the foods I can't eat.

Jordan gestures that I should go in front of him and I do. I remember now that he's a gentlemanly type but that his casual fashion sense is a zero. Hunh. I might have changed that. And maybe he's letting me go first so he can check out my ass. Either way, my ass looks fantastic right now.

We lose each other while at the buffet but I find him at the end, and we sit down together.

"Can you take a long lunch, or do you have to rush back?" I ask.

"I've got some flexibility. I've been working a lot of overtime lately."

"Do you like your job?"

"It's busy, but I enjoy it," he says cautiously while looking around. Maybe he's scared people from work will overhear him.

I've spied on his LinkedIn profile in the future, so I know he stays there for nearly 20 years before moving on to something to do with solar technology.

"Do you find the work fulfilling?" I ask pointedly.

"For the most part, yeah."

"How long do you plan to stay there?"

"As long as I can, I guess."

"What's your ideal job?"

He explains what his current/future job is – basically arranging deals with major investors looking to fund clean energy. I half-jokingly tell him to make sure they're not backed by oil companies wanting to patent the technology to monopolize it. He gives me a sort-of half-glare, half look of realization that it might be true.

When the air clears a little, he tells me about wanting time on his own to do mission trips to developing countries.

Oh right ... he does mission trips ...

I brace myself for him to get into a whole pro-colonization-type spiel about spreading the Gospel and God's love and acknowledging Jesus and stuff ... but he doesn't. He tells me that it's just a faster way to summarize and justify it to his parents and friends. But really, he's going abroad to see how to implement micro-investment programs and sustainable economic resource pools.

Wow ... this guy.

Over dessert, we have a fantastic discussion about micro-investment in women's rights organizations and economically-viable small businesses in less fortunate countries. We talk about how church programs are often well-meaning but can sometimes have a toxic impact, especially when the leadership goes awry. He's surprisingly aware, especially given that his and Conrad's entire friend circle are church youth group kids who still say grace before meals together, even in public. I remember now that at this point in time, Jordan doesn't exactly fit in with his and Conrad's friend group, and his appearances are regular enough to warrant invitations but more because his sister is the frequent attendee, and he just tags along when convenient and it's not all couples. He's at a different place from them in life but he's still local as opposed to the professionals who have been scouted and moved away, so it's almost by default that he hangs out with them.

Jordan and I are getting along fabulously on a one-on-one level, but I'm not suprised, and I like that we're clicking intellectually. I always knew he was smarter than Conrad and way more sophisticated, except for being a fashion failure. I can guarantee that he'll grow into a dad who wears socks and Crocs and shpants and ill-fitting t-shirts.

We ask for the bills. I pay for Mhairi and myself; Jordan pays for himself. We're outside the restaurant and still talking as if the conversation could carry on for hours. But it does reach that lull where we can now part ways. I reach up to hug him goodbye. He hugs me back.

"You're brilliant," he says. "I can see why Conrad loves you."

Aw shit.

"Thanks, that's sweet of you to say." I shouldn't sound like I dumped his ass and good riddance because they're friends, but at the same time, I do want to sound like I've moved on, and I have since it's been a good 20 years.

"I have a question," he starts. "What do you see in him?"

"Um ..."

"You're way smarter than him. You're a lot more mature and sophisticated. I would have no problems taking you to a corporate party. That guy I don't even want to take for a tour around my cubicle."

Whoa.

"Um, I guess you haven't talked to him for a little while," I say cautiously.

"Why ... did something happen?"

"I dumped him," I say with a sheepish face. Jordan's jaw drops.

"This might be the last you talk to me for quite a long time. Or ... ever."

I quickly rationalize in my head that I have a total of

4.5 days left to have as much sex as possible and satiate the curiosities. For all I know, sex could also dry up with Jun.

Here we go, bucket list ...

"For what it's worth," I lean forward and say quietly, "I've always thought you were totally hot. If you want to take advantage of that, take me back to your place *right now*."

It turns out that his apartment is practically across the street, and still not the shoebox in the sky that I thought Jun's would be. It's a 1-bedroom, 2-bathroom with modern features and the layout is not bad for what I see of its open concept living room. His kitchen area is right by the door. I have a moment to notice as we take off our shoes, then it gets hot and heavy as we start making out.

I don't really understand how a guy can look this good and not have that much experience. He's a terrible kisser. His teeth keep hitting my teeth and it's starting to get on my nerves. He roughly grabs my boobs. And it bothers me that he's unzipping his pants without any consideration of getting me wet first. Or undressing his upper half. Oh no, he's a tighty-whities kind of guy and I'm immediately turned off because I know what that looks like when I have to do laundry. My hand reaches down to stop whatever madness is happening and ack! I move it away just in time because he's coming ... in his underwear.

There's a second where we both look at each other, mortified ... but weirdly, my 40-year-old mind kind of gets into sympathetic mom mode. I hand him the closest towel and start washing my hands as he inches around to the other side of the counter so I can't see his lower half.

"Well, sweetie, that's treatable and you should probably

get that looked at it because it'll affect your relationships down the line. In the meantime, make sure your lady gets her orgasm first. If you're looking at porn, invest the time in learning how to lick a pussy. And open your mouth more when you kiss so you're not bashing teeth."

I put my hand around my eyes like a blinder as I put on my shoes and grab my purse. "Bye!"

Well now we can check that off the bucket list.

Chapter 27:

INFORMATION I SHOULD HAVE KNOWN

I'm pondering what Mhairi said about a future with Jun but it's also making me feel hella guilty, so I'm going back and forth. I hate being pregnant with a third kid but at the same time, I love her sight unseen. I'm not particularly keen on returning to life with Chad. And I'm using maternity leave as an excuse to take a break from my job – a job that maybe I wouldn't even have to have because I'd be happy with Jun on his family's yacht somewhere. It would be a different set of life stresses, but the money cushion and wealthy lifestyle are incredibly tempting. Even if he wasn't as attentive a husband, he couldn't be as bad as Chad. And if I had access to things like $375 massages on a regular basis … I mean … that's a life upgrade right there.

Jun calls me as I'm wandering through St. Lawrence Market. "Hey!" I answer.

"Hey," he sounds hungover.

"Did you get my note?"

"Yeah, thanks. I'm just heating up the leftovers from last night. Was it bad? I can't really remember a whole lot."

I tell him about meeting Charlie and then pepper it with, "And you tried to make out with him!"

"What?!" he freaks out.

"Nah I'm just messing with you," I laugh.

Two hours later, I'm at his place with his roll-on that I picked up from the dorm. He greets me at the condo door with coconut-based rice pudding – dark cherries with a dark choco-late drizzle.

OMG … lifetime supply of rice pudding and chocolate mousse …

"Mmm … that's amazing," and I motion with gimme gimme hands for the rest of the container. "Are you working on new flavors?" I ask as I take off my shoes.

"Yeah … it's calming for me. I don't know what I'll do with the business though. I just like inventing the recipes. I don't like any of the other stuff."

"Sales, marketing, operations, logistics?"

"Yeah … that's what Declan enjoys." Jun sounds super sad.

If I wanted to problem solve, I'd suggest things like farmers markets and pop-ups but that might be out of his wheelhouse too. I settle on, "You're a smart guy. You'll figure it out. And you're the best dressed straight guy I know." I give him a wink and shooter fingers. He smirks.

Even though he's only dressed in jeans and a t-shirt, his fashion sense is probably the best of all the males I know. The shirt fits properly and hangs nicely on his super-built body. Where the sleeves cut off shows his sexy arms – the arms with which he can lift my whole body. Thinking of it stirs up the butterflies.

Unlimited access to that body …

I move to the kitchen sink with my dirty spoon and mason jar to wash them out. His kitchen is surprisingly clean.

"How come it's so sparkly here?"

"Told you, I like things neat. And I've missed having my own space to keep it that way."

A spouse who likes to keep things tidy …

"Should I go then?" I ask.

"No." He comes up behind me and puts his hands on my hips.

"Ack no," I dash away and giggle. "I'm all sweaty from the subway and I feel totally gross. I was actually planning on us going out."

I'm surprised at myself for turning down the sex because I'm definitely horny and want a redo of that failed make-out session from this afternoon.

Maybe it's that I've got too many thoughts swirling around in my head. What do I even say? Would you like a future with me? Is this dude worth risking Baby Girl for? Would we have a better life together? What are his parents like? What happens if we don't get along? Do his parents still die the same way?

"You're doing that stuck in your head thing," he smiles and leans with his forearms on the counter. "Let's stay in and relax."

He takes me by the hand and leads me to his ensuite bathroom with the bathtub. He starts filling the water and shows me the bottle of bubble bath. "See? Sensitive skin."

"Thanks," I smile.

While the tap is running and the suds are billowing into a soapy cloud, Jun takes off his shirt and massages my shoulders.

"Here, let's get unencumbered access," he suggests while slipping off my dress and my bra. He plants kisses along my neck and shoulder, then resumes the massage. I can feel his hairless chest when he brushes against my back. Everything about him is comforting and makes me happy. I wish he'd taken off his shirt in the future that I saw with Mhairi, just so I could check, but I'm pretty sure he keeps up this physique. I turn around to kiss him and yes, total redemption from the afternoon failure. I unzip his jeans, and he suavely steps out of them but keeps his focus on me, getting me to step out of my underwear, then he takes my hand, holding his out steady so I don't slip while getting into the bath. When the tub is full enough, he gets in behind me, positioning himself so I'm between his legs and we're both facing the faucets. He continues the shoulder massage and gently works his fingers up my scalp. It *is* relaxing. This was a great idea. When he eventually stops, he moves his body so I can lean back into him, and we stay soaking like this for a little while.

"Do you think we could do anything about future elections … or the pandemic … or preventing wars?" I wonder aloud.

"Nope," he says without hesitation. "There are too many chain events that happen because of those things, and we'd be a tiny cog in a gargantuan wheel. I don't know that we'd make even the slightest difference."

I turn to face him, squinting my eyes. Our conversation keeps flowing, but I turn the conversation so I get more pointed answers to my direct questions. I make sure we're on the same page with voting priorities. Vaccinations. Climate change being a definite problem. Gun control. Black Lives Matter. Social housing. Immigration. Refugee crises. LGBTQ rights. Science over belief.

Huh. It's surprising and yet not. Our values are very similar despite his wealthy background. Except that he has way more clout and wealth to be philanthropic with his causes. His parents play it safe publicly with arts and culture donations, while he's free to donate to the more political causes, just as long as they're anonymous. I can see Hoitview Group having many physical targets for anyone catching wind of their affiliations and punishing them for it.

Jun clears his throat. "This is my philosophy: everyone has a right to be a recognized human, afforded the things that let them live a decent life where they can contribute successfully to either bettering themselves, other people, and the planet."

I'm going to ignore that we're in a bathtub and wasting water, but right now, the words out of his mouth make him so sexy that yes, I will have my way with him now because I can. I pull the plug on the water and kiss him full on and passionately. He gives me a heads up about turning on the handheld faucet, and he rinses us both off, spending extra time on me and using his free hand to massage the parts that "need rinsing."

"Hold this," he says as he hands me the handheld faucet.

He quickly dries himself and puts on a condom, then carefully hops back into the tub with me. He gets me to face the faucet on my knees, then aims the handheld faucet at my clitoris before turning up the water pressure.

Oh ... wow ...

He inserts a finger, then two, all the while asking if I'm okay. Then he enters me while the faucet is going and it's phenomenal. He pumps in and out, and I can hear myself almost screaming in ecstasy because the bathroom acoustics are making my voice echo. It's not long before we both climax, and just in time because my knees are starting to hurt a little from the hard surface. I imagine his are too, but he doesn't say anything. He just smiles and kisses my shoulder before rinsing himself off and turning off the tap.

He disappears for a moment (I assume to dispose of the condom), then gets us warm towels. He wraps one around me, half using it to pull me closer to him. He spins me around to wrap it around me, then reaches over top of the towel to rub in between my legs.

"Want another one?"

"What are you gonna do?" I laugh.

He picks me up and carries me to the bed. He gets me to go on all fours, then slides under me upside down with the vibrator (as if to 69 me if he could) until climax number 2. By then he's ready again, so we do about three positions more and I climax in every single one. He has his shortly after my number 6.

He's exceptionally stealthy with the condom disposal, and I can hear him washing his hands before he comes back to me in clean boxer-briefs to snuggle with me.

Even more bonus points for being a post-sex cuddler.

"Come on," he says, catching me staring into his eyes. "Spit it out."

"If we were together in the future, would you be like this in our 40s?"

He looks a little hurt by the question and it makes me furrow my brow. "You enjoy the experience, right?" he says with an insecurity I haven't heard before.

"I've just had six orgasms ... you are definitely the best," I say while still luxuriating in aftershocks.

"I don't know where I'm falling short." He rolls from facing me to facing the ceiling.

He doesn't need to say it out loud – I can tell that he's wondering why his wife cheated on him. I have a vague guess that he's right about her missing the tongue action he can't provide, but I stay absolutely silent.

On the physical side, I am feeling incredibly satisfied. *Ours could be a good life. An exceptionally good life.*

If I had the luxury of time, we could draw this out, but I have neither that nor bandwidth for a long saga. I hesitate on what to ask specifically.

"Just say what you want to say," he coaxes.

So I do.

"Do you see kids in your future?"

"Oh, no," he says shaking his head. "No, no, no, no, no."

OH.

"Why's that?"

"I don't like kids. I would be a terrible father, and I'd rather just be free of dependents in my life."

Oh.

"Are you saying that because you have them?"

"Not that I know of!" he jokes. Upon seeing my stunned face not laughing at his joke, he continues. "I had a vasectomy two years ago."

Damn.

"That shuts things down entirely." I sit up, and I can't help but start crying.

"What was I thinking?" I mutter. "Of course it's too good to be true." I get dressed in a frenzy.

"Claudia, what's going on?" Jun says in bewilderment.

"Hey, hey! Talk to me." And he grabs my arms to hug me.

I push him away. "There's no point in wasting breath anymore. Or time. I'm mad at myself for even thinking of possibilities."

Of even thinking of sacrificing Baby Girl.

"You don't have kids in the future, do you?" he quickly asks. I can tell he's expecting me to say no.

"I have two adorable sons and a girl on the way," I scream at him. I can tell he's equally stunned at the volume of my voice and the news. "Mhairi told me they could be your biological kids if we go back to the future together – I was so stupid for even thinking of doing it."

"That was an option?!"

"Obviously not if she would have had all the information too!"

"What if we're together and we don't have kids?!"

I give him a bewildered but angry look because this is the stupidest thing he's ever said to me, even as a teenager.

Through gritted teeth, I tell him, "I'm not giving up my kids for you. I was meant to be a mother." In saying that, I have this profound and startling new empathy for women suffering with fertility issues. "Thank you. Goodbye."

"Wait! I'm sorry!" he calls out as I slam the door behind me.

I feel furious – mostly with myself. Guilty. Relieved not to have made a decision I might have regretted.

Oh no … now I just go back to life where nothing has changed. I'm stuck. I'm going to have Baby Girl and Chad will continue to be useless. I'll be completely dependent on him and that'll force me to be in charge of the kids and the entire house while I'm home. And then the pattern will never change because he'll always see me like that.

Weighed down by my thoughts, I slump down on the bench just outside Jun's building and put my face in my hands.

I knew that this was a holiday and I'd be returning to my

regular life. And I knew that Jun would be a one-night stand if anything.

Why do I feel so upset?

Chapter 28:

MHAIRI AT MAGIC OVEN

I don't know how long I spend crying, but waves of thoughts go through my head. When I finally have a handle on things, enough to know I have to get out of here and think, I uncover my face to search for a tissue in my purse.

Jun is there, in a towel and flip flops, covered by a coat. He startles me as if he were a flasher. I scream.

"Shh ... people will think I'm some kind of perv!" he whispers. "Tell me what happened."

I search for the words. "There's no future for us, Jun. I thought there could be and I was starting to look forward to it." I try to hold back the tears, but they just roll down my face.

"I'm sorry," he says quietly. He tries to hold me, but I gently push him away.

I get up to leave. "For what it's worth, I think you'd make a great dad," and I start to walk away.

"Wait - I don't want this to be our last memory together." He grabs my hand to stop me. "Let's have dinner. How about Huntingtonio?"

I'm frozen and can't move. Huntingtonio is a stupid name, but it was a partnership between a gay couple where the one partner was Canadian and the other Italian, so they smashed the name together as a big joke. It was one of my favorite restaurants before it closed down. They had the best veal chop I've ever eaten. It was so good that I once attended a wedding there and my date declined his because he was vegetarian ... so I ate his veal chop too. I went for a corporate dinner a few years later and got to order it. As an entrée, it came with a creamy, Parmesan mushroom risotto and roasted seasonal vegetables. And if you had lobster bisque to start and then their tiramisu ... you really could die happy.

"Um ..."

This is not fair. I would like to cut this man out of my life right now. Quit while you're ahead!

"Come on ... you know it closes in 2010."

"Okay fine."

"Great! I'll make a reservation for 7, okay?"

"Not tonight. I need time. And distance."

He looks so wounded.

"Clauds ... I ... need you. I've only been surviving the last few days because of you."

Girl, just take yourself to dinner! Oh wait ... that place is super expensive like $$$$$.

"Tomorrow. I'll be there."

Girl, what are you saying?!

"You promise?"

"Yeah."

I walk home. Slowly. Jun didn't offer to walk me home because he was cold. And that's fine. I don't want the company of a man in just a towel either. I'm glad I packed running shoes. My socks are comfy athletic ankle socks, so walking is fine. I grab samosas and a banh mi on my way back to the dorm. Maybe it'll tire me out so I can fall asleep quickly and dream of my kids. Maybe I'll be pregnant in my dream again.

I only dream of Timothy. I'm frantically asking him, "Where's Jeremy? Where's Jeremy?" but he's just a baby and he can't give me any answers. I wake up just as I remember that my kids have an age gap where Timothy was that young and I wasn't even pregnant with Jeremy. I have no idea what it means. If Jeremy didn't exist yet but Timothy was still so little, does that mean I'm back on track?

I get dressed in workout gear, even though it's only 7 a.m. But the glorious thing about my day of nothing (except for lunch and dinner plans) is that I am free to take a nap in the middle because there is no one small waking me up to make food for them. What can I do at 7 a.m.?

I stroll through the halls. Doors closed. No activity.

Aww.

I laboriously text Otis just in case. I don't want to call. Ugh. Maybe he can't even receive texts. Oh well. I think about taking a drop-in class at the Athletic Centre, but I don't want to risk running into people who know me, but I can't remember them. It's kind of smoggy but I decide to run toward Harbourfront and hang around there. I toast a Montreal-style bagel from the freezer, feeling a little sad that it reminds me of Jun. As I wait for it, I think about what we're going to talk about tonight.

I eat my bagel while walking so the seeds fall on the ground outside, toss my paper towel wrapper in a bin, then work up to running south at full speed. I'm amazed at how much energy I have, and how much things don't hurt or creak. With my iPod on and earbuds in, I try to keep up to the beat of my university days dance music playlist. I kind of wish I had my Amazon Music playlist, but ah well … this is a vacation. You can't have or pack everything.

I love running when a big city is just waking up, like in New York or Chicago. 7 a.m. is just before the commuters are coming in. Stores don't even open until 10 a.m. The morning light hits brightly and at some points, I have to squint until a tower blocks the sun. I run west along the pathways at Harbourfront. It's calming to see the water.

Part of me is worried about my kids. Another part is trying to figure out how I separate from Chad when we get back because by comparison to what I've had this week, I don't know how much longer I can hold out. I just can't really get my head around it. I don't think it would be an amicable split, not for getting full custody of the kids. I'd definitely win, but just having to disentangle assets and move three kids out … it's not really worth it. We wouldn't co-parent well – we don't even co-parent well right now and we live in the same house! I also have to get on hiring Mariana as a nanny.

I resolve that I'll feel better once I talk to Mhairi and find out where I stand. No use worrying about what I don't know … a lesson learnt by somewhat planning a future with Jun when it wasn't even an option.

I arrive back at the dorm just in time to see Otis packing up the cable company van. Like a flirty minx, I run into his line of sight and start doing sexy stretches. He notices.

Yeah …

"Well, well, well …" he says. "Aren't you a feast for the eyes …"

"Did you get my text?"

"Yeah, I can't text as well as you yet. I called you back."

"Oh, sorry, I was out running. Guess I didn't hear the phone vibrating."

"That sucks. I had a break that we could have done stuff in, but now I've gotta get going."

"Raincheck?"

"What happened to your dude?"

"It's complicated but I'm pretty much a free agent."

"Ah … I'm DJing tonight if you want."

On a weeknight?! Oh wait, it's Thursday. Practically the weekend.

"Cool. Same place?"

"Yeah. Tell the bouncer who you are. I'll put a Post-It on his list to let you come up."

"I have dinner plans, but I'll see how they go."

"Ooh ... noncommittal ... break my heart already," he jokes.

"All my meals are accounted for," I wink before running inside.

I shower and dress for the rest of the day, perfectly timed to arrive at Magic Oven for lunch with Mhairi at exactly 11:50 a.m. again. I choose a pretty formfitting pink pencil skirt dress with a pink sweater that has sparkly buttons and a pink satin ribbon around the waist. I have white tennis shoes for all the walking, and then if I happen to still be out around the time I meet Jun, I have stilettos and my makeup bag in my big purse to make this an evening outfit.

When I get to Greenwood station, I remember to look for hand sanitizer, wet wipes, and Lactaid pills at Shoppers Drug Mart and luckily, the extra strength are available. Phew! I also check out the condom aisle because I've got some time to kill, and Jun was right, he really did get just about everything that was available. I suppose it's considerate that he was using condoms – for one it keeps the mess contained, and two, if he's a fuckboy, they're essential for trying to stave off STIs.

Mhairi is already sitting at a table with kale-hummus dip and garlic wholegrain crisps (I know this because I pre-perused the menu).

"That looks good!"

"It is!" she happily munches.

We order a ton of food with intentions to take the leftovers home.

-- Gourmet Veggie Magic with tomato, grilled eggplant, garlic zucchini, roasted peppers, garlic spinach, goat cheese

-- Mushroom Melt Magic with garlic cream, portobellos, caramelized onions, asiago

-- Prana Magic with olive oil, garlic, parmesan, rosemary sweet potatoes, caramelized onions, figs, gorgonzola

-- Double Hawaiian Magic with tomato, bacon, parma prosciutto, roasted coconut, mozzarella, fresh pineapple

I get out the hand sanitizer for us both. Mhairi happily uses it too. I kind of thought she wouldn't, being mystical and ancient. She's full of surprises.

"So ..." Mhairi starts. "What's going on with Chocolate Mousse?" I catch her up on the vasectomy.

"Ooh ..." she makes an ouch face. "I'm sorry, lass, I didn't know that."

I regretfully tell her that I've agreed to dinner tonight as a last memory.

"I wouldn't advise that. Best to cut it off while you're ahead."

"That's what I said ... to myself. But he's taking me to Huntingtonio."

Mhairi literally does the freeze body thing that I did when Jun said it too. "Sweet Jesus ... is it as good as they say it is?"

"Better," I whisper.

"I can't say I'd have made a different choice," she says with obvious discomfort. "What will you do? Eat well then tell him thank you but you'll never see him again?"

"I dunno. Will we remember each other in the future? Like this?"

"My guess is yes, since he's fallen in love with you now. You made a big enough impact to disrupt your timelines. Is the feeling mutual?"

"I think I caught myself just before falling off the deep end. If he'd said yes to kids, as our kids, I would have fallen hard and gone all in."

"That's something," she offers hopefully.

I tell her about my dream. The one last night where I only have Timothy.

"See what you dream tonight. I can't tell from just that," she answers as comfortingly as she can.

"Even if I've got all three of my kids, I dread going back," I say quietly.

"Why?"

I remind her about Chad and rehash the whole thing about not picking up the kids from daycare, leaving my work event in a panic. The staff bring our pizzas to the table, and I see them gasping to each other as I recount the whole story to them.

When they leave us, Mhairi and I start talking quietly again. "Is he very secretive about his job?" she asks between bites.

"Yeah, he works as a Senior Engineer for Keeman Morleys in military-grade cyber information systems security. That's all I can say."

"Interesting ..." Mhairi nods, while thinking.

"What's interesting? What are you thinking?"

"I think you need to see it from his side."

"What do you mean?"

"Do you think he's telling you the truth when he gives you a roundabout story?"

"No," I say immediately. "I think a lot of that is bullshit and he's so used to not being questioned, he thinks he can get away with it."

"I know what might help ... put up your hand against mine."

I do as she says, and she flips around her hand so that we're connected where our pinkies and thumbs are intertwined, and we've got three fingers on the insides of each other's wrists. She presses down on my wrist, and I wince a little.

"Sorry." She readjusts, spreading those two fingers to grip around my wrist.

Suddenly I'm transported like she did with showing me Jun's future, but this is to Chad's workplace.

Chapter 29:

CHAD'S DAY FROM HELL

*H*e's wearing the same clothes as when I last saw him. It's as if I'm following him but I'm floating and I have no reflection in the silver elevator doors, nor the glassy-looking tiles in the hallway leading to them. We go up to his floor and there's Amanda sitting at the big reception desk. I've never been this far to his office – he's always met me in the first floor lobby. It looks like it could be a law firm, or tax firm, or anything other than people who work on highly sensitive information.

Everybody entering has a key card, but then I didn't realize that, once out of sight from the reception area, people go through a secondary door with a retinal scan. This is not … Keeman Morleys. This is something entirely different.

The second he opens the door, it looks like chaos. People are yelling and typing furiously at their computers. A white man with a Southern accent literally yells at him.

"PARKER! We needed you at 7:30, not 8:30!"

Chad is a night owl and a 7:30 start is a killer for him. Chad actually thinks better in the wee hours of the morning, and I've seen him come up with his best solutions around 2 a.m. His old boss was a lot more flexible, but this man must have been a former drill sergeant.

In this vision that Mhairi's giving me, I can simultaneously see and hear what Chad told me over the phone against what's happening here.

I had to go to work early because they said a VIP was coming.

The white man yells, "ETA 7 minutes!" When he turns to the side, I see an earpiece on him. It looks super high-tech. He looks like he's speaking into it.

Chad scurries into his office, closes the door, and powers up his desktop computer.

As soon as I get there, a bunch of US army guys came into my office and said they needed three of us to get on a military jet.

Just as he said, the white man bursts into his office followed by three men in military uniforms. One says, "Mr. Parker, we need you to board a military jet immediately, sir. Your presence is required at 0900 hours at an undisclosed location."

I was looking at my senior management the whole time and they're nodding like "yeah, yeah just go".

Sure enough, the white man is doing that and talking into the earpiece again. "He is en route, Captain."

Chad looks a little nervous as they escort him down the elevator. "Can you tell me where we're go-" Chad babbles.

"Negative, sir," says one of the military guys.

I was a little suspicious, then I saw this guy we worked with last month in the lobby ...

Chad meets a Black guy with glasses and a suit (who I'll call "The Nerd"). They fist bump, then the Black guy just starts giving instructions rapid-fire. He uses all kinds of terms I don't understand but it looks like Chad does because he's nodding and asking questions back.

... he's briefing me the whole time on stuff that sounds familiar ...

They head out to a big hangar and sure enough, there's the military jet.

Before we get on the jet, I ask this guy where we're going and he says, "Ya have your passport on you?"

Chad says, "Yeah, I got the card."

He says, "Good, we're going to Washington, DC."

"Okay but I need to be back by 5 p.m. I got kids to pick up from daycare."

The pilot says, "Roger that."

I tried texting you just before we took off but everyone is like, "Turn off your phone! Turn off your phone!"

Sure enough, this is true. And I see Chad secretly trying to text one more time:

Can't explain can't pick up ki...

The pilot makes an announcement. "Turn OFF ALL YOUR CELLULAR DEVICES IMMEDIATELY."

And Chad has to turn off his phone.

And when we land, I'm like, "I need to call my wife right now!" This huge dude who makes The Rock look small gets in my face and says, "This location is top secret. You are prohibited from disclosing any details."

All of this happens as he says, and the big man literally takes Chad's phone away from him like a schoolchild.

"You'll get this back later," he says with deadly seriousness.

Chad spends the entire flight anxiously fidgeting, putting his head in his hands.

When they land the jet, everybody rushes off. I have no idea where we are. It looks like the middle of nowhere with a very sophisticated building and a tarmac. It's a short walk from the jet into the building and right away, there's a guy with a New Jersey accent who meets Chad at the door. He talks so quickly about some code that Chad developed and that he needs to integrate it now because it's a Class J57 situation. Chad's eyes widen in shock and he quickens his pace. They set him up at a computer workstation and he starts typing furiously with a panicked face I've never seen before. It's worse than the time he forgot his mother's birthday ... it's worse than the time he accidentally called me the wrong name on one of our first dates.

Mhairi jolts me out of this vision.

"Don't worry, I'll put you back in, but he literally spends hours in the same position. I can't fast-forward through a vision, I can only jump back in."

I am hungry and the pizza is as delicious as I remember it. Mhairi and I stuff our faces. Neither of us can decide on a favorite, but we eat enough to take only one box home each, and we compile an assortment of slices from all four pizzas. I pull out the wet wipes which Mhairi is also happy to use. We link hands as before, and as she promised, we jump back into Chad's day.

Chad throws up his hands in victory. His shirt is soaked with sweat. "It's done! All systems are clear." There's a cheer around the place. What is this? A compound? It looks like NASA's Mission Control Center.

"What time is it? Can someone please give me my phone back?"

The man who looks like The Rock shakes his head.

Chad closes the windows he's working on and looks at the time. "It's 4 o'clock. I need to get back, my kids are waiting for me at daycare. Or can someone please call my wife?"

A bunch of old white guys laugh hard at him. Like stupid hard. Like a living meme of "this is what a fucking white patriarchy of old white men looks like."

"No, I'm serious, I need to call my wife, otherwise no one will pick up my kids from daycare," Chad pleads.

"You can't be serious. That's women's work!" The old white guys keep laughing.

Chad is obviously anxious again. "GIVE ME MY PHONE!" he yells at the big guy. The big guy hands him his phone begrudgingly then shrugs. "It won't work here anyway."

There's a "No Service" message on it, plus the battery power is down to 5%. He tries to resume his text to me, but the phone keeps going black then dies.

Chad tries to load up a web browser, but he can't – there's nothing that looks like anything resembling a web browser. He goes into some code source screen to get something that looks like it's downloading, and someone barks at him, "Civilian applications are prohibited in this facility, sir!" and they literally shut down his workstation.

"We'll need to undo that action," someone says threateningly.

The same three military guys from this morning approach Chad and one says, "You won't need this workstation anymore anyway, sir, we need you to come with us to another location."

Chad has barely enough time to make sure he has his dead phone in his suit jacket pocket.

Off they go, back to the jet. The Nerd is there too, looking equally exhausted, sweaty, and disheveled. The jet takes off.

Someone hands Chad a paper bag which he seems to recognize since he's grateful for it. He scarfs down a sandwich and bottle of water as if he hasn't eaten all day. He probably hasn't. The Nerd falls asleep. Chad asks for food for him for later too. Chad places it in a little mesh pocket attached to the seat since there are no folding tables due to the configuration of their seats.

Mhairi takes me out of the vision.

"They land somewhere, and he does the same thing. Do you want to keep going? It's pretty boring."

"Yes, yes, I need to. Please."

"Okay … I'm skipping ahead." Still holding on to my hand, Mhairi uses the other hand to eat a brownie with vanilla ice cream. She pushes mango sorbet toward me. It's a tasty break from the intensity of Chad's day.

"I'm ready," Mhairi says. I nod. We jump back in.

It's raining as the jet carrying Chad lands on an aircraft carrier. A speedboat brings them ashore, and they're shuttled into a building that looks like a normal office tower but it's not. There's a similar Mission Control Center feel to this place too.

A tall Asian man greets Chad, "It's a wave across the country – J57 dash 2b," he says grimly. We need you to do what you did in the last place."

"Please, I need a phone charger. I need to call my wife,

the kids are at daycare, she just needs a call."

A man appears out of nowhere and points a gun at Chad. "Your priority is national security, sir."

Chad puts his hands up in surrender, shocked.

WHAT THE ROYAL FUCKING FUCK?

No one can hear or see me, but I'm screaming, "THAT IS SO UNNECESSARY, YOU FUCKING ASSHOLE! IT'S JUST A PHONE CALL!"

Chad gets escorted to a workstation. "No funny business, sir." Chad starts typing as furiously as he did before.

A kind young woman comes by a few moments later and hands him a portable military phone. "I don't have a phone charger handy, sir. But in case you want to call your wife, here you go."

I see Chad looking at the numbers on the dial pad and just sweating. He can't remember my number. But things on his computer screen are popping up so rapidly that he has to jump in and keep typing to contain it. I have no idea what he's doing but a few people walk by approvingly and suddenly, the huge computer screen at the front of the room seems to come alive as if it's been offline all this time. There's cheering all around.

Chad slumps back in the chair and wipes his forehead with his arm. Then he literally passes out. And I watch as the three military guys scoop him into a wheelchair with his suit jacket (and luckily his phone in the inside pocket), then scurry him to a vehicle and ride through the city. I recognize it as Seattle. Taking him out of the vehicle, they go through a hotel lobby. One of the guys whistles sharply at a hotel front desk associate, who whips a small white box across the room which is expertly caught by the whistler. The guys eventually drop Chad onto a hotel bed, scribble a note, plug in his phone, and leave.

Mhairi brings me back.

"Oh my God … is that … how can that be real?!"

Mhairi gives me a look. "You're in your 20-year-old body, love. Anything's possible."

I need to catch my breath. Chad's work stress is on a completely different ... planet.

It's no wonder he can't handle anything at home.

I had no idea.

Chapter 30:

UNEXPECTED TURN OF EVENTS

"Do you still want to be married to him?" asks Mhairi.

I take a long pause. I don't know that Chad would have the bandwidth to handle a divorce. Unless I literally found him an apartment, set up the rent and utility payments on auto-pay, moved all his stuff in and then unpacked it in a livable way just so he could carry on as if nothing had happened to his life ... or his stuff.

If his job is this intense, he really just needs someone to make sure he always has clean clothes in his closet and an intact home to sleep in at night. I have a feeling that it wouldn't matter if his car was functional or not, they'd probably send a helicopter.

Surely he must be getting paid tons of money for that kind of stress? Why am I struggling with my job and working so hard to do what I think is keeping us financially afloat? Does he have secret accounts? Is there a mega life insurance policy on him if he seems that important that he's being flown to un-known, undisclosed, secret locations to save the day?

At the very least, we should have a conversation about his role in our lives. It's not fair to me to have someone who only lends his genes and then has no responsibility at home without providing a substitute. I might as well be a single parent for real.

"Mhairi, can I change his trajectory? Chad's I mean. So that he's in a different career field altogether?"

Mhairi looks like she's wracking her brain for an answer. "You'd have to meet him earlier than you did before. You'd have to make a big enough impression that he remembers you and has a reason for changing his life."

"Great!" My face goes from peppy to frowning. "That means I'll need to find him. Crap."

"At least you'll have pizza for the journey. Let me know how it goes."

Oh, I'm not searching for her in the Beaches AND Chad who knows where.

"Wait! Dumpling House on Spadina. Sunday, noon."

"Number 16 and number 34," we both say at the same time. Oh my goodness, somebody else who loves the pan-fried pork dumplings and beef stir-fried noodles to remember them by menu number.

"Yes," Mhairi says. "See you then. Thanks for lunch."

And there she goes, dining and dashing! Then again, if I were giving out magical vacations to the past, I wouldn't expect to be paying for any of my meals either. I put my pizza box in a giant paper bag.

I end up taking a long walk along Bloor all the way back to the dorm. I pass through Greektown, then East Chinatown, then the rest of Bloor. It's awkward carrying the pizza but it was expensive and delicious, and I burn off tons of calories walking and sweating (so I pick up a bottle of water from a convenience store). It's hard to keep smelling pizza in my hands and then having worked up an appetite again, I don't resist eating it. I put the remaining half in the fridge when I get back to the dorm. The whole way home, I was trying to think of all the locations that Chad might be at this point in our timelines. He's a few years older than me, but he could be doing one of his master's degrees, so I should go look for him in one of the labs. I'll do that thing that Ciara used to do – just hang around the medical buildings looking for a med student to marry.

I try searching for "Chad Parker grad student" but his

name is so generic that it brings up tons of search results.

I make a list for tomorrow based on how well I know him as his wife – I'll have to venture around the engineering buildings and see if I can spot him. At night. Ugh. Will I have to do that thing where I pretend I have an extra dirty chai on me? It's okay, I'll just ask for it with coconut milk in case he's not there. Oh no, can I do that here? Are places offering alternative milks yet? The list of my potential haunts tomorrow becomes an elaborate plan worthy of being called a stalker if anyone else saw it. Not really the way I wanted to blow a day of my holiday without children – I had planned a spa day, the kind where you get a massage and sit around in a jacuzzi and basically try to clear your mind and think of nothing. Because nobody will be calling me for any emergency whatsoever.

By the time I'm done with the plan, I'm mentally exhausted. I zone out with old Flash games until it's time to leave for dinner.

Huntingtonio is all the way at Yonge and Finch and though it's transit-accessible, it'll still take a while to get there. I'm sticking with my pink outfit but wear a lightweight black trench coat overtop because it gets windy at night in that area.

I arrive around 6:45. Jun isn't there yet, so I opt to wait in the lobby. At times like this, I wish I had my current/future phone because then I could just surf or play games. I'm not in the habit of packing a book because I've become used to having everything on my phone. In the future, I even carry a spare battery pack because I once went to the hospital after one of my crew members was in a car accident. I walk down the street to a convenience store for a magazine. I choose a Toronto Life just in case I'm missing out on cool stuff I don't know about.

At 7 p.m., Jun texts:

Srry, am late, b there soon

I let the hostess know and when I mention "Jun Sung", her

eyes bug out a little like she knows he's a big deal. "No problem, no problem," she says.

At 7:25 p.m., Jun arrives with a gigantic, gorgeous bouquet of peach ranunculus and roses.

"I'm so sorry, I got the flowers an hour ago and then stuff just … happened." He looks stressed out.

"What's wrong?" I ask, searching his face.

"It's … complicated," he answers quickly. "Hang on for one more second." He goes to the hostess and says something into her ear, covering his mouth. She nods, then talks back to him in his ear, covering her mouth. Then they wave me over to follow.

We get led to a large table for 2 in the middle of two long rows of similarly-sized tables. Across a narrow aisle from us is a long row of booths. Jun asks for the booth across from this table which is just clearing out. We wait for someone to clear the dishes and wipe down the table, then we take our seats. I'm glad for the booth because then I can prop up the bouquet without it getting damaged. Shortly after, a couple takes the table we were just at, choosing to rearrange the chairs so they sit at a perpendicular instead of facing each other. The white guy has a buzz cut, and I only see him from behind, then the Asian female with him sits in line with Jun. She's gorgeous, with long black highlight-streaked hair. Her makeup is perfect. She has large hoop earrings and a black sleeveless A-line dress that shows off her beautifully toned arms. She wears silver stilettos with a satin strap around the ankles. I find her mesmerizing.

When I look at the menu, I happily see that the veal chop is still there, and it's a $65 entrée. No wonder this is a special occasion place. Jun isn't interested when I rave about my memories of it and orders a truffle lobster pasta dish. That sounds good too … damn.

Jun and I look at each other a little blankly. I smile.

"Is there something you wanted to talk about?" I ask weakly, trying to fill the silence.

"Do you think we'll remember this when we go back to … you know?"

"I hope so. It would be a waste to forget it," I answer honestly.

"Would you answer if I call in future?" he asks.

"Yeah. I might not get to call you back for a few days. Or talk without being interrupted. Or keep awake," I tell him. "You can text me. You'll probably get faster responses."

"Why? Is your life that stressful?" He asks this completely naïvely. Right, he doesn't know what it's like to have kids.

I nod. "If you call me at work during work hours, you'll probably get more of my focus and attention but at home, anybody part of the procreation process has demands."

He laughs. "I know you're an awesome mom," he says sweetly.

"Thanks!" I laugh. "I'm glad you met me on my own though. It's different being in mom mode when…"

I lose my train of thought but it's fine because I don't know how much attention he's paying anyway. His eyes keep darting toward the couple who took our first table. They get their appetizers and are happily chatting away.

Our food arrives and I offer Jun some in exchange for his lobster pasta. He obliges and while I'm glad I got to try his pasta, I do love my veal chop, and it lives up to my memory's expectations.

"Mmm …" I melt with each bite but try not to make it sound like an orgasm.

Jun's phone buzzes on the seat beside him and I alert him to it.

"Please excuse me for a minute?" he says politely.

"Sure," I nod.

Jun disappears somewhere toward the front of the restaurant. If this is his idea of a last meal together, I'm not sure what he's doing and why we're not really spending the time together. He's gone long enough that I finish my food and feel much happier having experienced that. The couple at the other table has now pulled out a laptop and they're working on something together that gets them really excited. The more I watch them, the more I see that they're not a couple – they must be colleagues.

I stare at Jun's plate, mostly uneaten. I ask our server to pack it up for him because it's probably cold.

Jun returns from outside and says a polite thanks for the takeout container. He talks quietly. "Sorry about that. I had to arrange something."

"Arrange what?"

He nods toward the guy coming in through the door with a beautiful basket floral arrangement. He stops at the table with the gorgeous girl. "Maxine?" They both look up from their laptop.

She's stunned. "Uhh yes … thank you … but what's this for? How did you even know I was here?!"

The delivery guy shrugs, drops the flowers on the table, and disappears faster than I've ever seen someone run out of a restaurant.

"These are totally all my favorite flowers …" She silently reads the card and her head cocks to one side. She looks quizzically at her date/colleague.

Jun has an "oh shit" look on his face.

Maxine's date is speechless. "Um …"

"Thank you?" she says to him, definitely as a question. She reads the card and flips it toward him, "You're the most beautiful woman I know?"

The dinner date has a hand on his head, also trying to figure out what's going on. "Well, I mean, I do think that of you but the flowers aren't from me."

I look at Jun and he's turned beet red. He dashes up to them, quickly grabbing the basket from Maxine. "You know what, I'm so sorry, these are mine! Have a great evening," then he hurries back to our table.

"Here you go, babe!" and he hands them to me. I can feel so many eyes on me and I avoid making eye contact, but Jun is blocking the dude, so in my peripheral vision, I only see the woman staring at me in anticipation of my reaction. I act the part, cheerfully accepting the basket. When she goes back to her laptop screen, I hiss at Jun, "What is going on?"

We talk with the basket hiding our faces from the other table.

"I was trying something but it didn't go as I planned," he says, embarrassed.

"For me?"

"No, and I'm sorry that the timing worked out this way. I did want a nice dinner with you, but this is not about you at all."

Luckily the restaurant's music is a little loud so I don't think anybody can hear us.

"I wish that guy would just go to the bathroom, and we could talk wingman strategy," Jun mutters.

"Do you know them?"

It's clear Jun doesn't want to open up but I stare daggers at him until he relents.

"I recognized her car in the parking lot, and it started turning the gears – obviously for the worse. That's … my soon-to-be ex-wife. I thought she might be on a date. If she's hooking up with Declan … he's the type of guy that would …"

"Claim credit for the flowers?"

"Yeah. If she gets into a solid relationship that's not with me, we won't start dating. I'll get my wish – it'll be like I never met her."

I feel such sadness and pity for Jun in this moment. I move the basket and take his hand with both of mine.

"I want to hug you but I'm not squishing into the booth on your side," I tell him flatly.

"Nah, I'm fine," he says in a defeated way. "I just have to try something else."

Now that I've moved the basket, I sneak a glance at the

other table with a clearer view.

And then I'm sure it's obvious that all the blood is drain-
ing from my face.

"What? What happened?" Jun asks in a panic.

I struggle for the words. "She can't date that guy ... that's
my husband ..."

Chapter 31:

FIRE

*I*t's a little weird that I didn't recognize Chad's voice, but I've done it before on the phone ... once.

"Really? That's your husband?" Jun starts straining to look at Chad in the way that you'd tell your girlfriends not to look at the cute guy and they all bob their heads at him like a whack-a-mole game.

"*That's* your husband?" he says in disbelief.

I kind of get his point. Jun is like a 10 and by comparison, Chad is like ... a 4.

"Well, his babies with me are his sex trophies, so he has that," I say in some sort of weird defensive mode.

"I just don't see it," Jun says as he looks at me and then Chad, then me and Chad ...

"Could have been you but you had a vasectomy," I snap back.

"Touché," Jun says. "What are you gonna do?"

"I don't know," I reply.

Jun paying the bill gives me some time to think.

I really don't know what to do. I imagine going up to his table, making out with him, telling him I'm the woman of his dreams and his real life future, then we ride out happily into the starry night.

He'd get a little freaked out by that.

Or I could walk over, declare all the things I know about him, ruining any future relationship with Maxine ... and then that ends badly because he won't recover from it, and I'll look like a stalker.

Ah – wait, I'll ride the subway with them back to campus because I'm sure that's where they're headed and then even if I don't make direct contact, I'll semi-follow … like a stalker.

Okay, that's my plan. Right. After I go to the bathroom because you never know what could happen. You should always go to the bathroom before riding elevators or subways.

"I'll be right back," I tell Jun while grabbing my purse. "Before I forget, thank you for dinner." I say it genuinely and he smiles in acknowledgment.

The bathroom is swanky with blue and turquoise mosaic tiles up the walls and lots of tall mirrors around the sink areas. There's even a couch. As I'm washing my hands, Maxine walks out of a stall and smiles at me.

"Cute sweater! I have the same one in light green," she says warmly. "I'm glad you got your flowers in the end. Your name must also be Maxine?"

"Uh … that's my nickname," I lie. I can feel myself blushing because I'm a terrible liar, but she seems to buy it and/or not care about it being the truth. Or maybe she didn't hear me because she's washing her hands too.

"Oh, okay. You probably know, but your boyfriend is HOT. Good job," she says, pretend fanning herself.

"Interesting fact … he's actually not my boyfriend," I say rather smugly. I don't want to give away that he's had a vasectomy just in case that was a point of contention in their marriage.

"Have you hooked up?" she asks inquisitively.

"Totally!" I say, beaming. "He's not for me since I'm not one for a long-distance relationship, but if he were mine, I wouldn't give him up for anything or anyone."

I feel a little proud of myself for planting that seed with Maxine and I'm just about to tell her how to find Jun in 2005 without giving away his phone number (but I still don't have his email address, ugh), when suddenly, the fire alarm goes off.

Her eyes go wide and she screams, "The laptop!" and bolts from the bathroom.

I feel like I'm right behind her and in the next second, I don't see her anywhere. People are scrambling to leave with this blaring noise of an alarm. I can't see Jun anywhere in the crowd but there's a bottleneck and chaos as people can't get out fast enough. I'm a little trapped in the hallway leading to the bathrooms and then I see why. The fire is at the table closest to us.

I notice there's a fire extinguisher in a glass cabinet right next to me. As if on autopilot, I smash the cabinet and grab it. I yell at the people in the bathroom hallway to get out through the exit door.

"THAT WAY!" I point, and people follow like sheep to safety.

This clears the hallway, so I rush forward with the fire extinguisher. I did a fire safety product commercial once and the instructions kick in instinctively to P.A.S.S.

I *p*ull the pin, *a*im the nozzle at the base of the fire, *s*queeze the handle, and *s*weep the nozzle back and forth.

Even though the fire is put out relatively quickly, the alarm is still blaring. I can barely hear the people behind me clapping for my action. I smile, nod, then wave goodbye as I pass by our table and see Jun and all our stuff gone – including my coat and all the flowers.

Oh no, did it get stolen on the way out?

The whole restaurant is clearing out. It does smell weird and like burnt things, and as soon as I step outside, I see Jun. He hugs and kisses me with relief.

"It was just a tiny fire," I tell him reassuringly.

"I dunno, I just went to put our stuff in my car and when I came back, people were rushing out yelling about a fire and I heard the alarm. I figured you knew I wouldn't have left you even if I took your stuff."

Oh. Yeah. That is true.

"Where did Maxine and Chad go?"

He shrugs.

"Damn. There goes my plan," I sigh.

"What plan?"

"Never mind, I'll pick it back up tomorrow," I sigh again.

I'm frustrated. If I'd been able to leave with them as I wanted, it would have saved me a lot of time in my hunt for Chad tomorrow.

"Wait, I'm gonna run for the subway!" I say quickly.

Jun grabs my hand firmly. "No, I'll drive you."

"It's okay, it's right there," I protest.

"You won't catch them," Jun says emphatically.

I think you just want to spend more time with me.

Jun offers his hand, and I stupidly take it.

Just as we're about to leave, a manager grabs my arm to stop me.

"Hey Miss, as a thank you for putting out the fire, can we offer you some desserts on the house?"

Jun and I look at each other.

"Yes please," we say simultaneously.

After we're allowed back in once the alarm has been shut off, Jun and I settle into a different booth. I admit that this is what I wanted out of my few last hours with him. No Maxine, no Chad, no huge flowers getting in the way. We still want each other but it's okay being friends.

Sort of.

The restaurant staff are recovering from the fire chaos, and we overhear that there were a lot of dine and dashers. Still, they bring us a sampler of peaches and cream bread pudding, guava flan, tiramisu, and coconut layer cake that are all, simply put, divine.

Jun and I make small talk about how to channel these flavors into ones for his shop. "I'd ask you what you're doing this weekend, but I don't suppose you want to hang out with me," Jun says sadly.

"I'd love to hang out with you but I've got to take care of my life." I give him a small but sympathetic smile.

When the manager comes over to ask how things are, Jun offers to buy the staff a round of drinks and they happily accept.

"I'll follow you to the bar to pick up the tab if that's okay though," he says.

When he comes back, he tells me he's going to the bathroom. "If there's a natural disaster, just wait for me outside," he winks.

After a while, a server comes to clear away our dishes and ask how things were.

"The tiramisu was amazing as I expected, but the other desserts will leave an indelible mark on my brain forever," I laugh. "I was trying to make that sound poetic for how good they were."

The server laughs, probably out of politeness. "Thank you so much for being so kind to us!"

"For putting out the fire?" I ask.

"That too."

"What's the too for?"

"You don't know?" She looks at me quizzically, then leans in to tell me quietly, "Your man just tipped us $5000."

Aww ... what a guy.

If only we could have hooked up in my high school years.

If only he wanted kids.

I smile at him a little too long when he comes back, not wanting to confront him about doing such a generous good deed.

In the car, he offers to take me back to his place but I decline. We make small talk while driving and finally pull up to my residence building. I take a deep breath and I'm about to say goodbye, but he helps me bring the flowers up to my room. I kind of feel like crying but it's like I'm not quite there yet. I walk him back to his car.

"Thank you for the flowers ... and dinner. I had a great time with you – not just tonight."

"Do we have to say goodbye?" Jun asks earnestly.

Now I start crying. "Yeah," I mouth.

He clutches his chest as if his heart is breaking.

He holds both my hands and looks at me with watery eyes. "It should have been you," he says.

Then he gets into his car and drives off without looking back.

Chapter 32:

FINDING CHAD

*I*t takes me a long time to fall asleep. I have to put Jun out of my head because now I'm regretting not going home with him. Even though we would have been an emotional mess, it would have been a good time physically. A really good time. Damn.

I debate going to find Chad right now since he's probably in the lab, whichever one it is, but I'm exhausted both physically and mentally, so I'll take it easy and find him in the late morning/mid-afternoon.

I dream that I have all three kids with me in the bedroom. I can't see Baby Girl's face but I can feel her in my arms. The roof gets swept off the house in a tornado but I'm paralyzed.

Nothing bad happens past that but the sheer terror of being alone with three kids has me sweating when I wake up.

It's Friday. Three days left.

I'm not about to change my kids, I won't sacrifice their existences, and I also refuse to be a single parent. That leaves changing Chad.

I toast the last Montreal-style bagel from my freezer while I'm getting dressed. I choose a cute white blouse that shows off my boobs, a blazer to be "professional," then dark jeans, and flat-heeled boots. Shiny, dangling earrings. Great eye makeup but light on everything else. Honestly, I met Chad before I was wearing makeup, and I suppose I'm "competing" with Maxine, but she's also way out of his league. So, it's like I'm trying... but not trying too hard.

I just have to find the dude. I'm not concerned about what happens when we meet because honestly, at this stage of his life, he'd be inclined to date whatever woman gives him a blowjob.

I grab my now ultra-elaborate plan and a notebook since I probably should look like I'm taking notes when I talk to him about his work and walk toward King's College Circle where all the engineering buildings are. I have friends who did engineering but I never had reason to explore this part of campus, so this is all new to me.

Chad and I met through mutual friends who we haven't yet met in this timeline, so I'll have to come up with something else.

Computer engineering is mainly based out of two buildings: Sandford Fleming and Galbraith, and they're connected, so it's just a matter of searching one BIG building. I start with the top floor and wind my way down. I peek in lecture halls as unsuspiciously as possible. I knock on closed doors, apologizing for the disturbance and asking if they know a Chad Parker and where he might be. People are generally pleasant. Also, because there are so few female engineers in 2005, I'm probably something of a novelty. I work my way through the library, the store, the cafés, around the offices. I try computer labs, common rooms. All to no avail. I try the graduate studies office but it's closed for staff meetings. Classrooms are either full or empty. My elaborate plan was basically a list of all the places he might be. Now I've exhausted that.

Ugh. I need some air.

The Ken Ho's food truck is still there outside! I line up for it because by this time, I'm sweating and frustrated, the meals are only $4 and the options sound pretty good.

And then I see Chad! Wait – he's getting away! I run after him and grab his arm, but when he turns around … it's not him. "Sorry, I totally thought you were my husband," I say absent-mindedly.

Ugh. Now I've lost my place in line.

I take a break and walk to College and Spadina. There's a Thai place along here that closed down ages ago, but they had a delicious pumpkin and carrot soup as part of a combo meal. I'm so happy to find it that I don't even pay attention to the restaurant name. Doesn't matter anyway. I order a beef Pad Thai and spring rolls combo. It comes with the soup!

As I'm eating happily, it dawns on me that I should call Chad's mother. She'll tell me where he is.

I've never had a good relationship with Chad's parents but, in the future, they'll both end up in a nursing home (miraculously the same one where they can share a room) with differing forms of dementia. Chad has a hard time visiting because they don't even remember him and he finds it too painful. I don't go because aside from corralling two small children, they always think I'm one of the nurses and/or hurl racist remarks. I send the nurses a huge gift twice a year.

I once had a friend who made a rule about not dating guys who live at home with their parents. But while I regret not following her example, she did wait an exceptionally long time to find and marry her husband. I might have married Chad earlier, but he was definitely lacking in domestic skills I wish he'd developed while living by himself.

I dial the landline number from memory because it's made of 3s and 5s and ends in three 8s. When I joked to Chad's mother that some Chinese people would kill for that number because of the lucky 8s plus the combinations equaling 8, she literally thought I was talking about Chinese gangsters. Sometimes I think it's a miracle that Chad and I stayed together to procreate on purpose (and then by accident).

Chad's father answers.

"Good afternoon, Parker residence," he says with all formality.

"Good afternoon, I'm looking for Chad Parker please," I say with equal formality.

"Who may I say is calling?"

Oh shit, you didn't think of a cover story yet.

"My name is Claudia … and I'm a … student journalist for the Varsity," I quickly lie as I see a Varsity newspaper on the next table.

Ooh you are clever.

"One moment please."

Chad's father thinks he's covering the receiver but he's not, so I hear all the background chatter.

"Chad! Chad … Chad! There's a young lady on the telephone for you."

And then I hear Chad's mother, "He's not home! He's at school. Who is it?"

"I'm sorry, but he is at school at the moment. Is there a message?"

The thing about Chad's father is that he would always take the message but not deliver it.

"I don't need to leave a message, but would you know which professor he is paired with for his master's degree, please?"

Chad's father repeats a pared-down version for Chad's mother. "It's something Chinese," they come back with.

Facepalm.

"All right, thank you for your time. Goodbye."

Ah, so this professor is the secret bridge to Chad working with people of color.

Chad is from a small town so he would drive into Toronto every day despite a very long commute. Why he didn't just get an apartment here when he operates on such weird hours has always been beyond me, but he doesn't have student debt in the future, so whatever he did seems to have worked out for his and our finances.

I stake out an available computer at the library. I log in with my student number from memory because, like they say at UofT, you're not a number, you're a decimal (because there are so many students). And if you ask any UofT graduate, chances are that they still remember their student number decades later.

It takes me a while, but I find the website for the university's Computer Engineering Research Group. I painstakingly scroll through each Asian professor's name because "Chinese" to Chad's parents is just synonymous for Asian, and I finally find that Chad is listed as a graduate student under Professor Dan Nguyen.

Yeah . . . Chad's parents are not the greatest with details like someone being Vietnamese. Chad's mother once told me she had tried "Vietnam" food.

And it's not that I'm making the generalization that small-town people are like this ... it's that Chad's family is like this. No interest in exploring the world around them unless escorted or it's free (and it can only be a predominantly English-speaking place). No to trying new types of restaurants or watching anything with subtitles. I often see the same boring narrow-mindedness in Chad when he can't even fathom empathizing with immigrants, complains about the spiciness of the food at an Indian restaurant, repeatedly watches old series and movies starring only white people. It frustrates me to no end. I don't even try explaining racist incidents that happen to me because it doesn't compute when it never happens to him. The idea of being made to feel othered, or less than, or not wanted because of the unchangeable way you look, has never registered to him as something that would hurt in a deeply traumatizing way.

"People made fun of me for being tall," he once told me.

"Being tall isn't a cause for discrimination. It does not prevent you from getting a job. It is not the reason ordinary Black people are murdered while doing ordinary things like jogging."

I don't think he was even listening to me at that point.

I head to the room listed on Dr. Dan Nguyen's website and when I knock on the windowless door (which previously no one had answered), there's audible rustle, then finally ... Chad answers the door.

True to his oblivious nature, he doesn't recognize me from last night. "Hi. Can I help you?"

I pause in looking at him because he looks so much younger and thinner. He doesn't have a beard yet and still takes time to shave, probably because his mother has nagged him about finding a nice girl. He's not wearing glasses, but probably contact lenses because I know his glasses prescription. He's wearing an old orange sweater I managed to throw out and said good riddance to when he stopped wearing it in favor of hoodies.

This is the face I used to happily make out with.

I smile my biggest smile in hopes of dazzling him and it kind of works. "Hi. I'm looking for Chad Parker?"

"That's me," he says, surprised.

"My name is Claudia Lee and I'm with the Varsity newspaper. You've been selected for a random student bio. Would you happen to have a few minutes to spare?"

In true Chad form, he says, "Uh, one minute please." And then he closes the door in my face.

I can hear one of his male lab mates saying, "That girl is

HOT. Give her whatever she wants."

Another says, "Give her my number!"

Maxine is obviously not there.

When he opens the door, he has his stuff with him. The old backpack he used to take with us camping and the laptop bag that disappeared when we started living together.

"Should we get coffee or a more substantial meal?"

"Is the Varsity buying?" he asks.

"Sure," I lie.

"I didn't have lunch yet," he says.

I choose a nearby sushi place. At this point in time, Chad will eat about 12 salmon avocado rolls and struggle to finish any other food because he's unaccustomed to rice. (Jeremy can eat about 22 in one sitting!) But it means that he'll eat quickly then have lots of time to talk about his work.

My strategy here is to get him to talk, then pepper him with all kinds of questions about the practical world applicability, and then what kind of impact this will have if he wants a family. The pressure of his parents wanting grandchildren has never been an open conversation with the four of us, but maybe it's something they joked about out of my earshot. When they heard I was pregnant, they were as excited as I imagine emotionless people get.

I dunno. If kids aren't even on his mind at the moment, I guess I could always wow him with a blowjob to give myself a lasting impression.

This restaurant reminds me of one of our first non-date dates. One time, we thought we were going to an open mic night with the larger group of friends. When we were told we had to pay cover for a poetry slam night, we went for dinner instead - just the two of us.

Our first official date was at an Italian restaurant where he told me he couldn't figure out why I was still single, then proceeded to list why he thought I should have been snapped up.

I pretend to take notes but end up doodling while he tells me about his family and things I already know. Where I do take notes is on his specialty fields of study because I pass by his degrees on the wall every day, but they give no indication of those things. Then I pepper him with questions about his research project.

And Chad comes alive like I've never seen him with his limited scope of emotion. What he's talking about is so complicated that I nod and don't understand anything while I'm writing down random words in my notes, but it's genuinely lovely seeing Chad being this openly knowledgeable and sharing what he's working on.

He's ... brilliant. And not just in the stressed-out way I saw him working in Mhairi's vision, but knowing that his work could be revolutionary in systems and security functions for its applications before anyone else knows that there's a need for this. I can see why he'd be flown across the continent in a day to solve things – I am undoubtedly not the only one to see his skills. And I'm the only one right now who knows what becomes of his potential.

Then I make the non-life-altering decision to just ... leave him to do what he does.

Let's say it's for the sake of world peace.

When our meal feels like it's wrapping up and there's not much more to say, I pay the bill and thank him for his time. Since he's asked nothing about me, I don't know that we've made much of a connection other than what he thinks is for a fake newspaper article.

It's weird to be with my husband and yet we're strangers. And I feel ... ambivalent toward him. I'm not angry anymore about the daycare thing.

The kids are fine in my dreams despite me being a single parent, so I'll sort that out when I get back. I don't have any worries that I'll still meet-to-date him in our regular timeline.

I'm just not as in love with him as I used to be. And it's

bringing up a lot of feelings about whether or not I would have chosen him in the first place.

"Okay, thanks very much for your time, Chad. If you don't see the article, don't take offense. It could just be that the editor's cutting stuff because of the layout."

I go to shake his hand goodbye.

"Um, Claudia," he says in a small voice and looking at the floor before he looks into my eyes, "Would you like to have dinner with me tonight?"

Chapter 33:

FIRST DATE 2.0

*W*ell, this is nice. My husband wants a first date with me tonight. "I'd love to," I say with surprise evident on my face.

"Really?" *he* says with surprise. "Um, here, let me give you my numbers." He gives me two of them.

"416-978 means a UofT number, right?" I ask.

"Yeah, that's my lab number. The other one is my cell."

It's the old 905 area code number before he switched to a 416. "Do you have a Varsity business card?"

"Uh, no, budget cuts," I cough. I write down my number for him. "Do you want to choose a restaurant and I'll meet you there?"

"Sure. Sure. What kind of food do you like?"

"Everything except Italian and North American," I suggest. I'm challenging him on purpose. Because Chad in his 40s just lets me choose or votes for The Keg (which I don't mind). After I appear in his life, Chad in his 30s switches from chain restaurants (boring) to going along with the restaurants I choose and cycling through those. I want to know what Chad in his 20s chooses.

"Great. That's great. I have to set up an experiment that'll run for a couple of hours while we're out. I'll call you when I choose the place – for 7? Is that okay?"

"7 it is. I'm gonna go work out so if I don't answer, it's because I'm at the gym, okay? Just leave a message."

"Sure thing."

I smile and wave goodbye and it makes him smile back in a shy way. I turn back to see him victory pumping his fist in the air. It's sweet.

As much as I hate to say that I wasted time on my holiday working out, I really do go and work out. Plus, if one is eating at this many restaurants, it feels a little gluttonous not to balance it with physical activity. There's enough time that I do a few laps at the Athletic Centre pool. Wow, I used to have access to this every day, and I hardly used it. Shame on me.

When I check my phone back at the lockers, Chad has left me an adorably nervous message.

"Hi Claudia ... it's Chad. Please meet me at Hanoi 3 Seasons for 7 o'clock. The address is 1135 Queen Street East. I can pick you up if you want? I mean, just tell me where to ... um pick you up from. Or you could come to the lab and we can go together. Or if you want to meet me there, that's, um, cool too. Okay, thanks. Bye bye."

I can imagine him kicking himself a little for the way he says, "bye bye."

He must have had his professor help him choose a restaurant. It's a nice little place and I think he's chosen well.

I call him back after I've showered and changed and am at street level because the signal in the Athletic Centre has always been crappy.

"Hello?" he answers.

"Hey Chad, it's Claudia."

"Oh! Hey Claudia. How are you? I mean, I just saw you, but um --"

I laugh. "I'm fine thanks. I'll just meet you there – that's the location in Leslieville, right?"

"That's right. Um, I'm sorry, I'm just wearing what I wore when I met you this afternoon."

I laugh. "It's fine. I'll be wearing the same too. Did you set up your experiment okay?"

"We're just in the midst of it. Thank you."

"Okay, see you there."

"See you … see you there."

It's a little endearing to hear Chad nervous about our first date. I only vaguely remember him getting nervous about our relationship once. Maybe twice. Now I'm like a well-worn coat. No need to replace but no need to feel excitement toward it either.

I opted to meet him at the restaurant because I want to hang up my wet swim stuff in the dorm and redo my makeup first. I have wet hair, a look which I actually like, so I put up the hood on my jacket as I ride the subway down to Queen station, then catch the connecting Queen streetcar across to Leslieville. I notice I'm getting checked out by cute guys and if I was really 20 I wouldn't like the attention, but I don't mind it with my 40-year-old brain.

Chad is standing outside in the lineup but close to the door, in the same clothes as he said he would have on, and then a brown corduroy spring jacket that makes him look like he's from the 70s. I smile. He has zero fashion sense but I already know this because I married him and I see his pre-me clothes hanging up in our closet. And all the time, I wish we could just purge them.

"Hi!" I say brightly.

"Hi!" His face lights up when he sees me.

"Oh wow, I must have come here on a weekday afternoon. I didn't realize there'd be a lineup."

"Me neither. But that must mean it has good food!"

"It does! Great choice," I tell him sincerely.

He looks proud of himself.

The door opens and a Vietnamese man who I assume must be the owner says, "Chad, table for 2?"

We move together quickly, and I can hear Chad saying, "I'm Chad. Dan Nguyen is my professor?"

The man nods knowingly with a smile. "Ah yes, welcome,

welcome. We'll take good care of you like I promised him." He winks very obviously at Chad and it's the cutest thing ever!

While we're looking at the menu, the man brings us steamed mussels with ginger and lemongrass. "On the house," and he winks again at Chad. I can't help but laugh. It's SO CUTE!

I opt to forgo pho since it requires a lot of slurping and that's not great for a first date. Just when I wonder if Chad was ever good with chopsticks before meeting me, he shows off his skills with the mussels.

Hunh. So you just fell out of practice because at dim sum these days, you ask for a fork.

"I've been practicing with instant noodles in the office with the other guys."

"Ah, the staple of student life. I should pick up some for my dorm room."

He orders Ginger Chicken on Rice. I order Chicken with Lemongrass and Coconut Milk on Vermicelli. I ask if he's tried cold Vietnamese coffee and he hasn't, so we get two of those even though I know it'll keep us awake for ages. I down my dairy pills before the first sip. Vietnamese coffee is one of my all-time favorite beverages. I made Vietnamese coffee ice cream once and it was awesome.

We talk about me living on campus versus him commuting. He thinks he's too old to have roommates with this being his second master's degree and his parents pretty much leave him alone, so it's not that bad living at home. (Spoiler: his mother babies him and we have a lot of issues concerning boundaries later on.)

I tell him about Ciara and how much I enjoy living on campus – mainly because it's the opportunity to live downtown in Toronto with my best friend.

I plant seeds about how an apartment and time away from one's parents is good for building independence and one's own style for domestic skills. He says he'll think about it (but he won't).

In the future, Chad rarely concocts anything more than a sandwich, never meal plans, never does regular grocery shopping. He still doesn't think to take care of the laundry at home but at least he'll do it if I'm away or if it's a big enough load when he comes back from a trip.

Partway while he's talking about the commute home, which I know all about already so I tune out, I get this panicky feeling about whether or not I actually want to embark on this journey with him again. I mean, I don't want to relive the dating part – having to see his parents so often, the trouble with his family in which I endure years of bullying and frequent doses of microaggressions.

Do I want children at all with this man who will later just not be the person I want to be with? Maybe I've turned into a person he doesn't want to be with. Nah, I'm his personal chef and shopper, the person who maintains his tidy house, takes care of his children like the default parent, and magically ensures he always has clean clothes ready to go. And if he wants to go on a business trip, he doesn't even check whether I'll be okay managing the kids and house and my job on my own. He just fucking tells me his dates, whereas I orchestrate a production of childcare, frozen meals, and a fully stocked pantry of convenience foods if I'm ever away.

He asks about me and my degree.

I tell him my dream about becoming a nonprofit spot producer.

"That's so cool," he replies. "I bet you have a lot of transferrable skills."

"I do," I acknowledge. "I have the potential for a long and incredibly successful career track. But do you know what I'm concerned about for my future? That having kids will force unnecessary pauses and being saddled with all the responsibility if my spouse is too into their career."

"Do you want kids?" he asks.

"Yeah." I hold back on saying any more in case this all seems off-putting to 28-year-old Chad.

Our food arrives and I think he's going to change the subject. He doesn't.

"You seem bothered," he says quietly.

I am bothered. One would think that this is a great time to have a romantic date with my spouse, but the thing is that it's not like the old days. There's a world of difference between me at 40 and me at 20. Knowing what I know now, I would have demanded that he learn a series of domestic skills before we moved in together. I would not have put up with his family's ill treatment. I would have done a year abroad program to gain experiences before committing to a relationship where we just don't travel as a family because it's too hard with the kids and being pregnant. When he travels on his own in the future, he has no desire to bring us along because it's inconvenient.

I wish I could be one of those people who is so blissfully at peace with the life they lead that they can and say emphatically that they wouldn't change anything for the world, not even their spouse.

I can't stop my mouth. "It's a pattern I see far too often in heteronormative relationships – women who carry the household's mental load, so guys just show up asking when dinner is. Or if the guy is supposed to barbecue the meat, it's the woman who went grocery shopping, found the meat on sale, scheduled the meal, got the accompaniments, and coordinated the plan. He just stands by the barbecue with a beer, and not even with a thought because he's in screensaver mode."

I concentrate on my food. So does he. We both just eat in silence for an uncomfortably long time. Such a long time in fact, that we both finish our food.

"How does one break that pattern?"

I stop eating because I'm surprised that he's asking at all.

"It would help if both spouses knew how to cook entire meals from scratch independently. And if one spouse does the grocery shopping, the other spouse helps carry them into the house and puts them away in the proper places, not just into an empty space because it's convenient to shove them there."

And then my brain suddenly just disconnects from my mouth, and I start rattling on as if he's Chad from the future.

"In the mornings if we're getting ready to take the kids to school, I don't want to see you standing around with your hands on your hips, staring out the window. Do that when the kids are actually ready, then you can stand around all you want. Or go shovel the driveway instead of parking way back near the garage and then driving over the snow so it's harder for me to shovel later, especially while the kids are waiting in the car, and I have to shovel the sidewalk or else get another ticket from the city."

It doesn't even matter that it's 2005 Chad in front of me. I don't actually have the face time with him in person to do this at *any* point in time because I've become his last priority.

"If we have to go somewhere important, prioritize getting gas if it's low the night before instead of when you get in the car. And fuck also stopping for your coffee and chocolate milk because 'you're late anyway' - there's no time for that. It's rude to keep people waiting because you couldn't get your shit together."

I'm nearly crying now but I can't stop talking. It's all my pent-up frustration and suppressed anger pouring out like a waterfall of words.

"And when somebody insults the person you love and makes her feel like shit with these awful words that you've tuned out because you physically cannot hear your mother's voice anymore, you need to tune back in and believe her before you spend weeks in therapy together so you can actually get married."

I look at Chad with tears in my eyes.

"And even if you're not close to her, you go to your mother-in-law's funeral without using work as an excuse because your wife needs you there!"

I open my wallet, throw cash on the table.

"You know what? Your work will always come first. And I don't want to be a single mom to three kids. I'm sorry, I don't want any of this life."

I grab my coffee and purse, and leave.

I've left my husband before the end of our first date.

Well, shit.

Chapter 34:

HOW DID YOU KNOW

People in the street are staring at me crying. But Toronto can be like mini-New York – people cry for all kinds of reasons, and you can offer tissues but you leave them alone.

Chad catches up to me.

"What did you mean about the coffee?"

"That's what you got out of that whole thing?"

"No, I mean how did you know I get the coffee and chocolate milk?"

I heave a big sigh just to get myself to stop crying.

I open my mouth. "You know what? It doesn't even matter." And I keep walking.

He catches up to me but keeps walking backward so he can try to maintain eye contact. "Please tell me. Claudia, please."

"I'm done with you. I'm not giving you any more of my life."

"For the sake of our kids."

That stops me. And him.

I have no idea how much damage control Mhairi will have to do, but I'm stuck in this proverbial mud puddle now.

"What's my favorite color?" he asks.

"Blue."

"What's my secret favorite color?"

"Brown."

"What car am I driving now?"

"A green Beetle your grandmother left you when she died."

"What's my tattoo of?"

"What? You don't have any, you're too scared of needles."

His face is aghast.

"I know you, I know you better than you know yourself," I tell him with my finger pointing in his face.

"Please talk to me. Let's go somewhere private though," he says cautiously while looking around.

"Buy me ice cream first, a dairy-free kind," I pout through gritted teeth.

We walk to Ed's Real Scoop. I get mango and lemon sorbet. He gets strawberry ice cream. While he's paying, I down a dairy pill and take a giant bite out of his ice cream, just because that's the kind of mood I'm in.

The explaining to your husband why he's a shithead in the future kind of mood.

"Let's go to your car," I say, handing him his bitten ice cream. He reacts for a second but has his "I deserved that" face. "You hate parallel parking, so I bet you've chosen a lot somewhere close by."

His eyes widen.

"Don't even think for a second that I'm your stalker. There's no financial gain and you're not a celebrity."

He stops to take stock of this. We stroll and eat in silence. My sorbet is refreshing for its flavor and something to do other than talk.

"How many kids do we have?" he asks quietly.

"Two. A third on the way." I'm having trouble keeping eye contact with him. I'm just mad.

"How do you know this?"

"You wouldn't believe me if I told you."

You can tell that Chad is figuring out in his head the statistical likelihood of me telling the truth. And he's gambling whether or not to believe me at all.

"What do you have to lose by listening to me, Chad?" I snap impatiently.

He takes a deep breath. "What are they like?"

"The kids?"

"Yeah."

I wax poetically for ages about Timothy and Jeremy's beautiful faces, their long eyelashes, their adorable smiles. The funny things they say, especially when they can't pronounce certain letter sounds. How they make me laugh with the "stories" they tell us about daycare and other kids. How they help each other when I least expect it. The way they can entertain each other in silly but endearing ways. How they draw us funny pictures and how it's a big deal that anything for Daddy is subpar, but everything for Mommy gets framed immediately. How they make up silly dances and we have dance parties all the time. How we like to recreate photos from Chad's childhood with certain outfits and post them side-by-side for our friends and for holiday gifts for his parents. As I describe the outfits, his eyes go wide in recognition – he knows … they're absolutely real.

"I sound like a shitty husband," Chad says as he finishes his ice cream.

"You are," I reply flatly.

"Not even a second of hesitation?"

"Nope."

"It could be worse, right?"

"If it was worse, I would have left you a long time ago. The thing is that you're not there. You're not a partner, you're just like an absentee roommate. But instead of just leaving me dirty dishes, you've also left me with three kids and all the responsibilities of running a household and carrying a full-time job. And then I still have to pick up after you."

"I'm sorry."

I shrug. "Chad, you absolutely excel at what you do," I

say with a sigh. "You might be the best in the English-speaking world. They call you a Senior Engineer in military-grade cyber information systems security, but I think that's just because you hate the idea of managing other people that you don't want a promotion or better title. Maybe just focus on that. The rest seems like a distraction."

We get to the parking lot and I can see his car. Chad is processing all this new information, plus the likelihood of it being probable and true.

"I'll let you process in peace," I say. "I'll see you if it's meant to be."

"No wait," he grabs my hand. "I'll take you home. I have to go back to campus anyway. And ... I'll know you're safe."

"Okay. Thanks," I shrug. I throw away my garbage in a bin. Chad's car is notoriously dirty for garbage on the floor. It's not like he keeps a bag for garbage.

UGH. Chad's 20s car is even worse.

"I'll get the streetcar. Thanks for the ice cream," and I wave goodbye.

"Wait! I'll clean it up. Please just – just wait."

I nod my acknowledgement. He probably wants to know more about the kids. I guess I would want to know the inklings of my future too if I could. Even if just to get my hopes up.

"Please," and he motions for me to get in. "And thank you for dinner."

He's a bit disoriented in this part of town so I direct him pretty much all the way to the dorm. "Do you know where you go from here?" I ask.

"Yeah, now I do." He takes a big pause. "What do I need to do to change the future? If I want to be with my family."

"Prioritize us. That's all. Maybe you sacrifice job opportunities if you know it'll take you away too much."

He's thinking about it as he looks down. "Did you ever love me?"

"Of course. I still do, even though I'm always mad at

you."

We look at each other for a moment, then we both lean in for a kiss.

Oh … he used to be a good kisser until we stopped making out as much and he fell out of practice.

We're interrupted by a beeping device. "What is that?"

"Uhh … the experiment I'm running – I have to get back to it, I'm sorry."

"No problem," and I'm already halfway out of the car.

And then I feel someone grab my hand in a semi-supportive way. It's Jun. With a bouquet of flowers.

Chad's eyes go wide. "You were at the restaurant last night."

You can tell Jun is drunk because he's slurring. Jun points at Chad. "She might become your wife but right now, she's mine."

Chad gets out of the car, fists all clenched, and is about to say something but his cell phone rings. He's torn in answering but he does.

"I can't talk right now, I'll call you back. What?"

Whatever is happening on the other end sounds catastrophic. "Fucking hell! Okay, I'll be there in 5."

He looks at me. "I'm sorry …"

"Just go," I say. "There's nothing you can do about this."

"I'm coming back," Chad says defiantly.

I look at Jun, definitely drunk but now smug. Oh boy.

Chapter 35:

BOARD GAME CAFÉ

This guy is just not going away.

I park Jun on the bench and thank him for the flowers. The bouquet is something you'd get as a quick pick-me-up from the grocery store, so I don't feel bad about giving it to the front desk staff. Besides, I still have the basket and the bouquet upstairs in my room and they're top notch. Jun does have impeccable taste – probably a result of his upbringing and the variety of options available to him.

"Let's go for a walk," I tell Jun as I try to get him to his feet. He doesn't get up and pulls me in for a hug. Then he starts crying. I genuinely hug him back.

"Bad day?"

"Yeah."

Jun has spent all day sending eligible bachelors to Maxine's office. Maybe that's why I didn't see her at the lab. I don't know how, and he's too drunk to answer questions, but from what I gather, he's either catfished them or literally went up to guys to ask them to ask her out.

"I chose nice guys too. If they were creepy, I said 'shop's closed.'"

"That's not cool that you sent any guys to her at all, Jun," I say sternly.

"I know … I know."

"Especially at her workplace."

"I know … I know."

"You're gonna stop, right?"

"Only if you help me think of something else."

I sigh. I honestly don't know how to help Jun. I have no idea what happens if he doesn't meet her, or marry her, or start his business. Or even in the future, what happens if he closes his business?

"I don't know, dude. Maybe you're just meant to be with her until the shit happens, you know?"

"Why would I waste all of my time with her when I can just avoid it altogether?"

I sigh again.

"You're spending so much energy trying to avoid her. Why don't you try meeting someone else?"

"I did meet someone else. You."

"But you can't have me."

"Yes, I can. You just don't have to choose that nerd."

"Come on, we're going around in conversation circles." I pull him up to his feet.

"Let's go for that walk," I say more firmly.

He holds my hand, and I let him because otherwise he'll stagger off or not pay attention to the lights for when to cross. Jun leans on me and hugs me every few feet.

Goddammit, he's so hot.

The aim is to walk him back to his place. We'll stop for whatever tasty things are along the way and open late, so he'll sober up.

By the time we get to Snakes & Lattes in the Annex, I'm tired. It'll be a good place to hang out since you can order food and for a small nominal fee (which goes up to $8/person in the future), you can play as many board games as you want while you're there. I choose Scrabble because it's a game I can't play with anybody in my immediate family. Chad hates it and refuses and the kids can't read.

"Why do they have so much handsy food when people are getting grease all over the board games? They should be serving things with chopsticks and little tongs, so you don't get your hands dirty."

This is a fair point which I'm surprised Jun is making while still kind of tipsy. He gets mac and cheese so he can just eat it with a spoon.

I order an apple cider because I'm still full and super caffeinated from the Vietnamese coffee. I think I'll be up all night.

He gets a bit better while playing Scrabble. I win one and he wins the next game. He goes to choose a new game and comes back with Upwords. It's like Scrabble but you can stack letter tiles.

"I used to play this as a kid!" I tell him.

We play for a while but because it's Friday night, it's busy. I feel bad taking up the table without ordering more food. Jun sees it too.

"Let's get out of here," he says. We clean up the game to return it. Playing (word) board games was a nice way for us to spend time together without having to talk.

I don't know what to say to him once we're outside.

We walk in silence for a while.

"I'm taking you home. You know that, right?" I look at his face as I say this, and he nods with a smug smile.

"I'm gonna have to see Chad later."

Jun shrugs nonchalantly. "I'm apparently winning the battle because who's got the girl right now."

"You're impossible," I sigh.

We finally arrive at his building.

"I'm sober now. I can drive you back," says Jun.

"Nah, I'll be okay," I tell him half-heartedly. I actually don't want to walk back. My body is tired but I'm still wide awake.

"Are we doing the Chinese thing where you say no, no, no, and I have to insist?"

"Aiya, I guess," I say, and he laughs.

"Oh no!"

"What's wrong?" he asks.

"I have to use the bathroom," I squeak out.

He laughs. "You can have anything you want," he says while hugging me.

"Don't squeeze me!" I yelp.

He takes me upstairs to his place and I run to the bathroom. His whole place brings back a flood of memories and I try not to think about it.

Get in, get out.

I open the door and there's Jun with his shirt off.

Goddammit.

I slam the door closed. I can hear him laughing on the other side of the door, and that makes me laugh. "I can't sleep with you anymore!"

"We can just talk," he calls through the door.

"I can't talk to you while you're trying to seduce me," I call back.

"Okay, I'll put my shirt back on," he laughs.

When I open the door, he beckons me to the living room area and gestures for me to sit down on the opposite end of the couch. "I have a proposition for you."

Skeptically, I take a seat. I cross my arms and my legs defensively.

"Are you cold?" he asks.

"Actually yes, I am," I reply. He gets a blanket for me and drapes it around my shoulders. "Thank you," I wrap it around tightly. Then he sits back in his spot.

"What if we go back to the future … I move to Toronto … you divorce that nerd and come live with me?"

My face scrunches up. "With my three kids?" His face changes as if he didn't think about them.

"Well, no, see, you have them at home for your days and then when it's his turn for the kids, they stay with him and you come to my place?"

"Are you …?" I stare at him in disbelief. And then I'm just so disgusted by the plan that I turn speechless. And then I throw the blanket off and get up to leave.

He runs in front of me.

"Okay, wait, tell me what's wrong with that plan. I can see it in your face, but please, tell me out loud," he pleads.

"How are you so thoughtful in other cases but you come up with this stupid-ass plan? Kids need you all the goddamn time. Especially when they're little, I will literally be the food source for the first six months. People might do it because they have to, but I'm not about to struggle over pumping breast milk to spend time with a boyfriend who doesn't want anything to do with small people I grew inside of me. Did I assume right? You don't want kids and so you won't be a part of my kids' lives?"

He looks like I caught him in a lie.

"Future me is a package deal, dude. I come with two little boys. My body is out to here with a girl," I mime the big belly, "And all this is just a mess," I gesture to my lower half.

I can tell he's trying to imagine it, but he can't.

"Just before this time traveling happened, a girl in her 20s asked me what advice I'd give her as a young person. I said all this bullshit about traveling and meeting people. I really wanted to tell her, 'fuck everyone you can while your body looks amazing'."

"Wow, you really have body issues," he says almost laughably.

"Well, yeah, man. I look cute in a maternity dress but naked pregnant me just doesn't make me feel good. Ugh."

And I spring up to leave.

"Where are you going?" asks Jun.

"To fuck a no-strings-attached DJ," I answer. "Solve your own problems."

Chapter 36:

CHALKBOARDING

"*P*LEASE," he begs. "I don't know what to do. You're the only one who understands what I'm going through."

This is true. And why I've felt so guilty about leaving him on his own.

"I think we need to whiteboard this," I suggest. "This is beyond either of us."

"Should we find Mhairi?" he asks.

I shake my head. "Even if we start in the Beaches, we won't find her since she doesn't have a phone. She could be anywhere."

And then it dawns on me. A person good at problem solving. I call the lab. Chad answers on the first ring.

"Hi. How far are you into your experiment?" I pounce.

"Crisis seems to have been contained but I'll be here overnight. Turns out Vietnamese coffee is my new favorite thing. I'm alert."

"Good, because we need an empty classroom with a chalkboard."

Jun is resistant at first, but I manage to convince him to get Chad's help. Besides, Chad is the only other person that we don't have to talk in hypotheticals with, and that shorthand alone is worth cutting through the frustration for a solution. Even having another mind is helpful. And although Chad doesn't have a lot of common sense, he is brilliant when it comes to theoretical things. Like a friend of mine later says, "Ain't enough space in that boy's brain drawers."

We stop for Korean food from the same place Jun and I went to that gave us hangover soup. I get stir-fried beef with vegetables for Chad because I know he can't tolerate spiciness.

I think out of competitiveness, Jun gets himself the spicy version.

I get pan-fried beef mandu and gamjatang but, because it's messy and will take time to debone, I get potato pancakes and kimchi pancakes too.

Jun pays with his black card like it's no big deal and I let him. After all, this get-together is to solve *his* problems.

Street parking is no big deal by campus at this time of night, so Jun easily finds a spot.

Chad is waiting for us at the main door to the Galbraith building. The guys don't really acknowledge each other so it's a bit awkward. Chad leads us to an empty classroom.

"I'm going to the bathroom," Jun tells us. "You can use the time to get him up to speed while I'm not here."

I nod. I wouldn't want to relive telling my painful history either if someone else could do that for me.

I close the door to make sure Jun is out of earshot. We unpack the food and I fill Chad in on the details that he needs to know, all the while assuming he's not questioning the fact that we're from the future. I explain Fàn Times being in jeopardy if Maxine and Declan hook up and cheat on Jun. Jun's plan to not meet Maxine at all. How he thinks I might be an option –

"Oh no, that's not happening at all," Chad resolves without hesitation.

"Thanks for your input," I laugh nervously. I'm startled by Chad's possessiveness. In the future, I think he'd find it amusing but not in the least bit threatening. "His first failed plan was to try and get you and Maxine together."

Chad sighs and shakes his head when I tell him about the flowers at the restaurant. "What, like *The Parent Trap* style?" he says in disbelief.

"The man is clearly desperate. And it's a long story as to how I saw it, but I totally understand his heartbreak and shock. It's broken him."

"So, I'm helping to fix him to keep him away from my wife, is that it?"

" ... uh ... if that's what motivates you, sure."

"Fine," Chad nods. He makes his "get to work" face.

"Also ... there's one other thing." I explain Jun finding out about his parents' tragic death mere minutes after discovering his wife and business partner cheating. Chad's face changes.

"Damn," he says sympathetically.

Jun knocks at the door and I let him in. Chad takes a potato pancake and mulls at the chalkboard.

"Should we worry about Maxine barging in on us?" Jun asks.

"Not at this time of night," he reassures us.

But just in case, he writes "Declan" and "M," looking to me for approval. I give the thumbs up with my mouth full. He goes back to staring. The silence is deafening and frankly, I'm not a fan of the chewing sounds. This is also the weirdest thing that has ever happened to me – my husband and my high school crush/pseudo-ex-boyfriend trying to figure out a workable future to lessen spousal anguish.

I want to joke about how this is like that logic puzzle where you have to get a goat, farmer, and cabbage across the river, but you can't leave the goat and cabbage alone, but this is dire in the sense that Jun's future is at stake, so I keep my mouth shut.

"To recap, the scenario when you go back is that you'll have to live with them both, correct? If you see Declan at work all day and they're now together, then chances are you'll still run into Maxine," Chad summarizes.

Jun nods.

Chad continues, "If you close the business then you see neither of them again!"

"Right, but if I don't meet her, the business continues, and she doesn't factor into the equation at all. I'll feel bad about people losing their jobs at Fàn Times if we close. And it's a successful business. I don't want to close it."

"What does Declan do?" Chad asks rapid-fire style.

"He does operations and business affairs. I come up with new recipes. He doesn't handle anything to do with food."

"Who's your backup business partner?"

"Don't have one," he says remorsefully. "The other people are marketing and biz dev but not the same skillset."

I suggest Jun comes up with a bunch of new recipes, get them up to producible quality and then release them once a month for a while.

He entertains the idea for a minute until Chad pipes up with, "What if you sell your half of the business to him and then take on a consultancy role for new recipes?"

"I'd still need access to the physical location for that, so I might as well keep it in the current structure."

"Will you have to take care of your parents' estate or does someone else do that?" I ask.

"My siblings will do that. I'll help out but they're the ones in the day-to-day. I could jump in at any time if I wanted to though."

Chad starts scribbling notes on the board.

"What happens if Declan marries her before you start the business?" asks Chad.

Jun puts his head in his hands at the thought. "Depends on

if I keep my memories from all time frames. Ugh, yeah, for now I don't want her in his life sphere either."

I pipe up. "Yeah, it'll fuck with his head to see them all the time. You'll still know what they did."

We go back to mulling.

"Did she know you had a vasectomy before you met her?" I ask. Chad does a doubletake with this information and raises his eyebrows.

Jun nods. "She would have asked for it if it wasn't already done."

"Okay, she doesn't want children either," I conclude.

Chad goes back to mulling. He hovers on Maxine's "M". He gets super quiet and pensive.

"Clauds, can you remember any awards I might have won?"

Jun rolls his eyes. "Seriously?"

"There's a point to this. Really," Chad argues.

I strain. "It sounds like chicken. The Albert Chicken Award."

He looks at me with this "oh you poor thing" face.

"The Albert Spicken Award."

"I dunno, man. You couldn't name the awards in my industry."

Jun grunts in agreement with a full mouth.

Chad looks deep in thought. "What year was the award for?"

I strain again. "2006?" He has the statuette displayed in our living room. Every once in a while, I get a stepladder and vacuum it. He squawks at me for vacuuming it, and then I squawk back that he should be dusting it himself. It's one of our stupidest repetitive arguments.

Chad is calculating in his head. He puts his hands to his temples while thinking deeply. Then with the utmost clarity, he starts erasing the board.

"We choose to do nothing," Chad announces. "We're

going to have the most relaxing weekend, do our best not to worry, and see how it pans out."

He sees our stunned faces.

"Maxine's reaction could be that she moves out, makes herself scarce realizing what she's done, and files for divorce from you. Because you don't have kids, you never have to see her again."

He circles Declan's name. "Declan begs your forgiveness, makes plans to follow Maxine which include finding a suitable replacement for himself, then you never have to see him again either. If the business closes, you use your extensive network to help find new jobs for your employees. You carry on making chocolate mousse and rice pudding for your friends so it's still a hobby unless it's too painful."

Wow, my husband with his limited scope of emotion just used it to pragmatically shut down Jun's thought spiraling.

"The ball was never in your court," he summarizes. "Do nothing."

This seems like a very un-Chad-like answer to the problem though. It lacks his usual theoretical problem-solving creativity.

But since I'm out of suggestions, this is it. For now.

And Jun seems good with someone else just telling him to relax. Something just doesn't sit right though.

Chapter 37:

DOING NOTHING

*I*t's around 3 a.m. and the Vietnamese coffee is wearing off.

We send Jun straight home and Chad offers to walk me back to the dorm. "You're not really telling him to do nothing, are you?"

"I'm percolating on a theory, but I didn't want to offer it to him in case things are too out of our control."

"There it is," I say knowingly.

"There's what?" he asks.

"I know you're smarter than what you were giving out. You just need more time and complete silence, right?"

"Who are you?" He physically stops me.

I tell him. About the failed daycare pickup. The day after. The weird call from him. Waking up in my dorm room. Mhairi. Trying to find him on Friday. I leave out the parts about being together with Jun and the threat of our children not existing. The story seems broken without that, but I think what he's hearing is wacky and nonsensical anyway.

Chad goes silent. Processing. Processing.

"Can I meet her? Mhairi?" he asks ever so timidly.

"I dunno," I hesitate. "It's like we're in two spheres that aren't supposed to meet," I mime with my hands. "And she might erase your memory."

"I think that would be okay," he says surprisingly calmly. "If she's had such a profound impact on our lives, I'd like to say thank you."

Chad is certainly full of surprises sometimes.

We get to the front door and I ask if he wants to come up.

"No thanks, there's some things I need take care of for my experiment, but would you like to do nothing with me later today?"

"Nothing, as in we just sit around and watch TV all day?"

"If that's what you want to do."

"Your future self forgot about my 40th birthday."

"Call me when you're awake. I'll make up for it."

I nod. I've learned to lower my expectations to zero with Chad, so it could just be a box of donuts.

I wake up without remembering my dreams. Maybe this really means things will be okay. It's Saturday. Tomorrow night I go home.

I keep my promise and call Chad when I wake up around noon. He answers on the first ring again and asks me for my email address. I give it to him. Immediately, he emails me a questionnaire asking about my allergies, when my next planned event is (I say lunch at noon Sunday), and if I own the items on a packing list for today's activities.

Okay …

I email him back and he calls me a minute later. "I'll pick you up in 30 minutes. Is that okay?"

"Uh, yes, thank you."

"Have you had lunch?"

"No."

"I'll bring it."

I get my stuff together in a bag and as usual, I overpack for the "just in case" cases. Luckily, it all fits into a big backpack. I'm wearing jeans, cute boots, and a cozy-looking sweater that fits me just right. I choose a trench coat I like that'll double for the evening if need be.

Chad picks me up with a classic cold cut banh mi, Vietnamese coffee, and Chinese pastries from Chinatown. There's nothing I dislike in Chinese pastries, per se, but I tell him out loud that I love his choice of majority char siu bao (barbecued pork buns) and curry beef buns in proportion to his other choices.

He smiles proudly.

I want to tell him that the kids really like them too, but I feel like it's a bit overkill.

Thinking of them makes me smile though. "Where are we going?" I ask.

"It's a surprise," he tells me while beaming. "But you packed the things from the list?"

"Yes," I nod.

We drive in silence for a while because I don't want to distract him while navigating city streets. When it seems fine to talk, I ask Chad how his family is doing.

"My brother is going for an interview at a company our Dad's friend owns. We'll see how he does."

"Bob's? He didn't get the job." Chad gives me a look.

I have to ask. "Is that a how did you know look or a how can you remember look?"

"Both," he says.

"Bob gave me a ride from a bus stop while I was waiting once. I asked him to explain his side. You wanna know the full story?"

"Yes."

"Bob is your Dad's best friend. They've known each other since elementary school."

He nods in agreement. "Correct."

"Your Dad expects that Bob will give Isaac the job because they're best friends, but your brother showed up 45 minutes late to the interview. Bob can't hire him because that'll look like super nepotism to his existing employees. But Bob didn't even hear the reason why your brother was late because he had just fired his secretary. Isaac was helping car accident victims."

Chad gasps. "Is he okay?"

"He's fine. He couldn't call the company because his phone fell out of his pocket as he was doing CPR, and it smashed even harder because the paramedics rolled over it with the stretcher by accident. By the time Isaac got to the company, Bob had needed to move on to another meeting. He didn't think Isaac would be a good fit anyway, but your Dad just wants him to have a job, any job, so it was a good out for both Isaac and Bob."

Suddenly, Chad exits the highway and pulls into a parking lot.

I just keep rambling. "This is good if we're stopping anyway. You should call your Dad before he calls Bob. Otherwise, they'll argue about a bunch of things that have nothing to do with the interview. And also, tell him why Isaac's phone is broken, otherwise your Dad will think that Isaac is lying about losing 'yet another thing'." I air quote and mimic.

Chad stares at me in disbelief. "That's exactly the way my Dad says it."

"Call," I urge.

Chad gets out of the car and makes the call. He's gone for a little while so I can finish my banh mi and rapidly eat two bao without judgment. I'm sipping on my Vietnamese coffee when he suddenly opens my door. He takes my hand holding the drink and kisses me!

"You just prevented a massive family crisis." When he gets back in the driver's seat, Chad recaps putting both his Dad and brother on speaker phone together and asking pointed questions that lead to verifying this story. He's acting like I've just performed the world's greatest magic trick.

"Oh good," I smile. "It would have caused a rift between your Dad and Bob for two years." I sip my drink. "And by the way, your brother becomes a paramedic because of this very event. He's fantastic in an emergency."

"You know, he really is. He's so absentminded though."

"I know. For Christmas, you and I are teaming up with a bunch of family members to buy him an Apple Watch since he forgets his phone all the time."

"A what?"

"Never mind."

Chad is so happy driving the rest of the way that he doesn't mind playing whatever CDs I choose.

Finally, we get to the surprise. It's an outdoor spa.

"I've totally been wanting a spa day!" I exclaim. "This was my Friday plan until I got wrapped up in trying to find you."

We get checked in and change into our swimsuits, then spend an amazing afternoon lounging around, reading magazines, talking, dipping in and out of cold and hot pools. When it's just us, he kisses me whenever he can. It's such a change from our future where he doesn't even want to hold my hand. It makes me a little sad to think of the future, but his smile right now makes me hopeful that this experience changes things for us later.

I notice that Chad has had to buy a spa robe, but his swimsuit and flip flops are his own.

How did that happen when he didn't go home?

"I keep a gym bag in my car for times I can swim at Hart House or the Athletic Centre."

"We could have run into each other a thousand times but never have? Whoa … you really are just a decimal at UofT," I laugh.

"Are you hungry?" he asks.

"Always," I laugh.

We go to the spa restaurant and he tells me to wait at a table for two. He talks to the hostess who nods. Then at our table, a server brings two slices of chocolate cake. The restaurant is proud to say it's dairy-free. Mine has a huge chocolate decoration that says, "Happy Birthday, Claudia."

I beam. I love this version of Chad. I kiss him thank you. The cake has layers of chocolate ganache, coconut cream-based mousse, and a tropical fruit coulis. It's phenomenal.

After the cake, we keep alternating between the hot springs, cold pool, and the whirlpool. We stay until it starts to feel like there are too many people and the sun is setting. The shower is refreshing and I feel like I'm ready for bed.

The drive back to the dorm feels faster and shorter than the trip to get to the spa.

"Thank you for an amazing afternoon," I tell Chad. "I've been wanting to do this with you in the future, but I'm always afraid of being away from a phone in case the kids have an emergency. Plus, you can't sit in a hot tub when you're pregnant."

Chad smiles at me. I wonder if I'm just talking and it sounds like Charlie Brown teacher talk sometimes, or whether he's just taking it all in and parsing through which details are nuggets to mentally file away. But his smile is genuine. It's his giddy face.

I invite him up to the dorm room, but he has to get back to the lab again to check in. He's been incommunicado all day.

"We're meeting Mhairi at noon at the Dumpling House on Spadina tomorrow," I remind him.

"I'll be there," he says.

I lean in for one more kiss, then send him off with both of us smiling. My body is too relaxed to do anything except fall asleep while watching TV.

But a few hours later, I wake up with a start. It's my last day. Now I'm panicking.

Chapter 38:

LAST DAY

*I*t's a good thing I have this lunch plan with Mhairi and no way to cancel it because it keeps me on track for getting out of the dorm.

Are there other things I should do before this trip ends? I'm never coming back to this body, this lack of responsibility, this freedom.

I check my bank account because I haven't all week. That'll tell me the options. After I pay off my credit card, the balance is $400. Oh shit, did I blow off a part-time job this week without realizing it? I check my planner. Nope, I was responsible and took a two-week break. I'm supposed to go back tomorrow, doing a bunch of odd jobs like tutoring high school kids and data entry.

If there's one thing I appreciate about getting older is that we do have savings and there's a financial cushion. It's not "we don't have the money", it's "we prefer not to spend it now in case we have to spend massive chunks of it later." But especially after his work ordeal, I'll ask Chad to take a vacation. Even if it's diapers in different scenery, different scenery is what we need as a family. And our workplaces will just have to deal with it.

And another thing I've learnt in getting to 40: there's no sense in burning out at a company you don't own.

I realize my phone has been in my purse and off since yesterday. I can't even remember the last time I had my phone

off for more than overnight while I was sleeping.
There's a voicemail from Jun.

"Hey Claudia ... I guess it's good that I'm getting the voicemail. You don't have to call back. I just wanted to say ... I'm sorry. I don't know quite for what but I feel like I should say it. Okay ... bye."

If anything, his message is strangely calming. It's been a wild ride of a week and a weekend. I finally scored with my high school crush, put a bunch of looming what-if relationship questions to rest, experienced some amazing things, and ate some incredibly delicious food. And I connected with my Mom - that's probably the most important thing I can take away from this whole trip.

I know that going back, it'll be a hard change with my diet and work not being great, to say the least. But I'm hopeful that my marriage will be better. At least I've seen sides of Chad that I haven't for a long time, and it reminded me of who he is despite the years together and the change we've both seen in ourselves.

I get dressed for lunch with Mhairi. The idea suddenly dawns on me that I should try to get rush tickets for something. So I dress nicely but multifunctionally – black pants, cute light blue top, white blazer, boots, trench coat, big purse.

Even though they're away on their cruise, I call my parents and leave a message on their answering machine to tell them I love them and hope they enjoyed their trip. I can imagine my Mom playing it back and smiling, so it's one thing I want to leave for her while I still can. It's a little thing but it's hard knowing I can't do that in the future.

I take a slow walk so I can think about what I want to do this afternoon and evening.

Chad calls me to tell me he's running late.

I'm about to cross the street at Bloor and Spadina when I see a mom struggling with her two kids. The walking kid (probably 3) is crying about her turn in the stroller and her shoe falling off, all while the mom is trying to get her baby into a baby carrier. I help with the toddler's shoe, strap her into her stroller seat, and open her yogurt pouch. The mom is struggling to hold wet wipes and wipe the baby's face, so I hold the wet wipes for her. The pouch looks like a wristlet, so I use the strap to attach them to the stroller like I have on my own in the future.

"That's brilliant," the mom gasps. "Thank you so much!"

"No problem," I say. And I continue on my merry way.

It's weird. I've spent all week just not seeing kids at all except my own in my dreams and now I feel like I'm ready to go back. I miss them and I'm ready to claim my snuggles.

I hear a familiar voice coming up beside me. "You really are a mom." It's Jun. After all that's happened, he feels like a friend. Maybe a good friend. "Did you get my message?" he asks.

"Yeah. Apology accepted." I smile. "What are you up to?"

"Just had brunch with a Vancouver acquaintance who's graduating with an MBA from Rotman. I planted some seeds so maybe he'll be a good contact for when I go back."

"When are you going back?"

"Funny you should say that. I was thinking of trying to find Mhairi."

"Interesting. Maybe you should come with me to lunch."

Our timing is just right that I open the door to the Dumpling House. "Surprise." Mhairi sees us both.

"Chocolate Mousse and Frittata together!" she exclaims.

"Not as a couple though," I smile. She's sitting at a table for four, with her facing the door. I take the seat against the wall, Jun takes the seat next to me.

"You've been avoiding me," she playfully scolds Jun.

"I have. I'm sorry," Jun replies sheepishly.

"It's fine. At least I can give you notice that both of you go back tonight."

There's a pang of sadness in Jun's eyes. "Do you know if we'll remember this? Each other?" Jun asks her.

"I don't know, love. It's different for everyone. You'll have to find me and let me know. If you remember me."

"If it's in my powers, I could never forget you, Mhairi. But you might have to call me a different nickname depending on how my business pans out. Thank you for everything." He gets her to stand up so he can hug her. She hugs him warmly, like I would have expected her to.

"I've already eaten so I'm going to get out of here and leave you to catch up." He turns to me and holds both my hands in his. "Claudia, I want to hear from you in the future. Please call me. You can get my number from Ciara."

I stand to hug him. I make no promises. "Bye Jun."

He waves goodbye and leaves us to it. I feel okay.

"Will I remember all this ... with him?" I ask Mhairi.

Mhairi smiles. "It sounds like it was intense enough to leave a lasting impression."

We order our food - the pan-fried pork dumplings, stir-fried beef noodles with vegetables I've been craving for, eggplant in garlic sauce, and beef brisket noodle soup.

I ask Mhairi what she's been up to for the last few days.

"Oh, this and that," she says. I don't pry because who am I to interrogate a fairy godmother?

"Tell me all about what's happened to you," she says.

I catch her up on the last dinner with Jun, the flowers, the fire, Maxine, and finding Chad. Our first date 2.0. Helping Jun figure out his situation. Roping in Chad to help.

Mhairi's face changes when I mention this. "How much does he know?"

"Almost everything? Sorry, it was a case of having to ask for forgiveness rather than permission."

"I see ..." Mhairi says thoughtfully.

"He's supposed to come here so he can meet you!" I tell her quickly.

"Ah. And there he is."

I turn around and Chad is there. He's spiked up his hair so at least it looks styled. He kisses me when he reaches me and shakes Mhairi's hand, introducing himself.

"I don't want to interrupt, I just wanted to thank you. I think you've changed both our lives for the better," he says.

"You might as well stay, lad," Mhairi responds without a beat. "I know a great deal about you already."

He sits rather obediently and I dish up food for him. His presence absolutely changes the dynamic for us. Mhairi eats, then stares at him like she's trying to read him. He tries awkwardly to make small talk but she shuts him down.

"You want to know if I'm real," she says bluntly.

"Um ..." Chad starts.

"Don't talk," Mhairi snaps. She keeps eating and it looks like she is really enjoying the food. I know I am.

She stops eating and looks at Chad. "Your wife prevented a family crisis yesterday."

My eyes go wide. "Whoa! How did you - oh, never mind." Of course she knows.

When she looks like she's finished, she sits back in her chair. "I'm taking all the leftovers," she tells us flatly.

I nod. Chad gives me a look like, "She does this?" and I give him the nod that says, "Just go with it."

Chad pays. I help pack up the food for her. The whole time, she's staring at Chad as if she's reading him.

Finally, she speaks. "I think you know that I'll purposely have to erase some of your memory. But there are parts you would benefit from keeping. May I?"

Chad nods solemnly.

She does that wrist hand hold she did to me when showing me the vision of Chad's workday. It lasts for about 10 seconds. Nobody seems to be paying attention to us as I look around.

They separate hands and Chad looks like he's just come

off a rollercoaster.

Mhairi tells him pointedly, "You won't see the results of your actions for months, but it was a noble deed I think deserves the reward you intended."

Something about how she says it makes me shut down all my curiosity. It feels like a very private moment I won't ask him questions about.

Mhairi gets up and we stand too. Chad hugs her as awkwardly as he hugs everyone. She thanks him for lunch. I give her a full squeeze, as hard as I can. "Thank you for everything," and I start to cry.

She looks into my eyes and says, "Things will be all right. Your life choices, your relationships, everything that happens to you make you who you are. But sometimes it's good when I can help course correct," she winks.

Mhairi leaves and since we still have food in our individual bowls and plates, we stay to finish it.

I walk him back to the lab.

"I go back tonight," I tell Chad. "I don't know when you'll meet me again, but I know you will. We'll see what happens."

He looks like he might cry. "I hope I don't have to wait too long."

Chapter 39:

LAST NIGHT

Ciara calls as I'm walking to the dorm. She's back and managed to get free tickets to *Evita* at the Princess of Wales theatre this afternoon through a friend who ushers. I've never seen it but I like the music, so I jump at the chance.

"My tickets are at will call! I'll meet you there!"

I take the subway and the King streetcar. She arrives in a cab almost at the same time. We hug. It feels marvelous to hug my best friend after being apart for a few days.

I'm glad we can watch the musical and not have to talk. Otherwise, I'd be rambling and trying not to tell her everything that's happened since she's been gone. At intermission, we both run for the bathroom and don't get to talk then either. After the show, she suggests an early dinner at an Ethiopian restaurant. It's not that I'm not a fan of Ethiopian, it's just that I recently shared an injera with someone who refused to wash her hands or use hand sanitizer before diving in with only her hands and I thought that was straight-up rude. I always liked her husband more and when I heard they divorced, I thought of this incident and told him he was better off without her.

Ciara has yet to hear this story because to her it hasn't happened yet, so I just say, "Uh … do you mind if we go to Kama because it's right there?"

"Oh, sure!"

This Indian buffet restaurant is another of Toronto's

classics that closed a few years ago, but it was one of my favorites. Ciara and I used to go every few months right up until we got married.

When we have our plates of food, Ciara tells me all about her New York City getaway. The museum exhibits she got to see. Some cool parties she went to with some of her cousins.

"What happened to that DJ?" she asks suddenly.

"Oh ... it didn't work out. It was just a fling," I say casually.

"Bummer," she sighs.

"How's it going with Jason?" I ask.

Her face lights up. They've been messaging every day. She's excited to see him tomorrow for a date.

"That'll be awesome!" I smile. I'm so happy for her – her young love stage is beautiful but, at the same time, their love has aged differently and is still wholly intact.

I choose not to tell her about Jun because I don't want to complicate things. Maybe she'll remember this nugget in the future? I don't know. And I don't want to find out.

"I heard the DanceSport Club is having a mixer Latin ballroom event tonight. Wanna go?"

"YEAH!"

Ciara and I once took a Latin ballroom dance class and thought it was the best thing ever.

That's actually one of the things I would have loved to have kept up with, but Chad isn't into dancing of any kind, so it fizzled.

"It's my treat tonight," Ciara says as she grabs the bill. "I feel badly for abandoning you on your holiday week."

"Oh no ... I was totally fine," I reassure her. "But thank you."

We race back to the dorm to change into better outfits. The event is from 7 to 10 p.m., so I can be back with enough time to (supposedly) gear up to start classes tomorrow. Ciara admits she just came back early because she missed Jason. It's sweet.

I pay our $5 covers and we get to the dance floor right away. Two guys immediately come up to us and ask to dance – to my surprise, my partner is Otis! The music is too loud to talk but he gives me that dazzling smile. I mouth to Ciara, "he's the DJ!" and she's such a terrible lip reader that I just say, "Forget it." He's an amazing dancer and exactly who I would have wanted to be there for my last night at 20. He flits between dancing with me and running the DJ booth, so it's not like we get to spend huge amounts of time together. It's fun to flirt and feel that energy while getting my groove on though. Can't do that as a pregnant lady. At least this pregnant lady can't. Ciara dances with an acquaintance who I'm pretty sure is gay, so Jason is definitely safe there if fearing that someone else is hitting on his lady.

When the event feels like it's wrapping up, Ciara and I just ghost when I don't see Otis anywhere.

Since Ciara has to do laundry anyway, I do mine at the same time so we can bond. I think of saying something as I'm changing my bedsheets, but I don't have to because she notices her sheets smell funky and puts on a load of those too. While we're waiting, we watch Korean movies Ciara borrowed from her cousins. It's fun seeing familiar actors but so much younger.

Ciara and I help each other put on our clean bedsheets. We sort our laundry and put it away. This building gets weekly housekeeping so someone will be by tomorrow to clean the bathroom and floors and kitchenette. It feels like tidying up after staying at an Airbnb, before hosts went all rigid on cleaning fees and rules.

When we're all ready for bed, Ciara suggests I finish the movie with her in her room. We dim the lights and carry on, but I can't keep my eyes open.

Goodbye, 2005.

Chapter 40:

THE END

*W*hen I wake up, I'm back in my bedroom in the correct time. I'm pregnant and feel Baby Girl kicking. I hear the boys' voices downstairs.

I hear Chad's voice. "You did it, buddy, you went potty!"

Jeremy cheers back. "I did it!" I can hear the flush and them washing their hands together.

"Hello?" I call out.

"Mommy's awake!" Chad yells and he bounds up the stairs with Timothy and Jeremy. The boys jump on the bed and I grab them both to snuggle. I've missed them so much, I didn't realize how much until now. I give them endless kisses and tickles until they squeal for me to stop.

The kids look the same as I left them, and Chad is … thinner. Wow. And he's clean-shaven. He doesn't look as haggard as he did when I last saw him (in the future).

"Are we late?" I ask him, putting on my glasses. It's 7:15 a.m. I slept in.

"No, remember? You checked your email at 5, and nothing had been sorted out at work, so you called in sick. You texted me."

"Oh, good for me."

"I called in sick today too," Chad says with a smile. "But let's still take the kids to daycare," he mouths.

Yeah, we pay for it even when they're not there.

When we all go downstairs, Chad has already microwaved steamed beef bao for the kids and he's serving them their juice. I help pack their lunches. Chad gets them to choose their snacks and he prepares their snack containers. This is way more than I usually see Chad doing, so it's a bewildering but pleasant change.

I get out my ingredients for cheesy scrambled eggs and berries for breakfast. Chad tells me, "It's okay, I'll do that for you. You get dressed and we can drop the kids off at daycare together."

"Thanks!" I say, delighted. He kisses me. I lean in to kiss him again.

Chad announces to the kids, "When you've finished brushing your teeth, you can watch ONE episode of *Pocoyo*."

Wow. The former version of Chad wouldn't have known what *Pocoyo* is.

I help the kids brush their teeth, then dress quickly in a floral maternity dress with pockets and black leggings underneath. I choose a light green sweater I've had for a while, which goes nicely with the dress. I'll wear a jacket when we go out.

I quickly put in my contact lenses and do my makeup as fast as possible. My face is definitely chubbier with more lines around my eyes than I was getting used to yesterday. I have to rest my big belly on the bathroom counter as I strain to get closer to the mirror, and then I remember we installed the wall mirror that you can pull toward you for this very reason. I grab my phone from the charging station.

My phone! I've missed you!

There's a message from Ciara telling me to call her later for my baby sprinkle plans.

When I go downstairs, Chad is putting breakfast on the table for me. "We're now out of eggs. Let's go grocery shopping together later."

Wow, what else has changed?

Chad's eggs are perfect. They're amazingly creamy with the cheese blended in. They might be the best homemade eggs

I've ever eaten.

And suddenly, I have this déjà vu feeling. "Do you remember our first date?" I ask him.

"Yeah, brunch."

I close my eyes. Yes, I remember this! But I also remember meeting him while pretending to work for the Varsity. Does he remember that? I'll ask some other time.

I brush my own teeth, use the bathroom for the ten thousandth time before leaving, then we drop the kids off at daycare together by 8 a.m. I dare not bring up the late pickup to Sherry – maybe it hasn't happened. The kids are happy to have us both send them off and we cheer them on for a good day.

Chad holds my hand going back to the car.

This is a nice surprise too.

"Let's go to the beach," he says.

He drives us to the same point where I usually park – the one where I parked on the day we met Mhairi. I'm hopeful we can see her.

But there's no café whatsoever. It's as if it never existed.

"That's nuts!" I say aloud.

"What's nuts?" Chad asks.

"Oh … I could have sworn there used to be a building there."

"You know how it is. Things go up and down in Toronto all the time," Chad says reassuringly.

We spend some time walking along the boardwalk. I ask Chad about his work. "It's fine. Takes time to get used to a new job but it'll be okay."

New job?

I try not to act surprised because this is information I'm supposed to know. "What title are they putting on your business cards?"

"Oh, they're already done." And he pulls one out of his wallet for me.

It says "Director, Software Engineering." The company

is an up-and-coming start-up that's been in the news lately. It's for 3D printing technology, but their big thing is philanthropic efforts in less fortunate countries. They're trying to 3D print schools, homes, and medical facilities.

"That's amazing! I'm so proud of you."

"Thanks," he says as he leans forward to kiss me. "Are you getting tired? Should we head back to the car?"

I nod. We talk about the Apple Watch we're getting for his brother for Christmas. Chad doesn't seem to remember anything about that conversation on the way to the spa. I dare not bring up the spa day either, just in case.

"Let's go home. We can do grocery shopping after lunch," Chad suggests.

When we arrive, Chad tells me that he has to check on some things for work. I do too, I tell him. But really, I scurry online. There's an email from Jun to call him and I do.

"Hey," I say when he answers. "It's Claudia."

"You remember me!"

"Of course I do."

"What's the last thing you remember us doing?"

"Dumpling House."

"YES. Now we can have a real conversation."

He tells me he woke up to his place not having any traces of Maxine but, instead, there's another woman there and it's as if she's been there all along and he remembers everything about their experiences together. They aren't married but they've been together for a long time, living separately since she's an actress. Her name is Amaliya Shui. (I'll have to look out for her.) She splits her time between Vancouver and Beijing. Fàn Times is still doing well. Declan is still a single guy, but Jun keeps referring Amaliya's friends to him just in case he finds The One.

But he wants to talk because he's been doing research all morning.

It turns out that Chad's mantra of "do nothing" was to purposely, literally do nothing. The spa day he spent with me meant that he was incommunicado, so it was Maxine, as his graduate research supervisor, who picked up the fallout and discoveries from the experiment he set up. He must have spent the time preparing her beforehand, whatever it was. But she ran with it, expanding the ideas, and it became so radically different as *her* groundbreaking work. In turn, that Albert Chicken, I mean Spicken, Award went to her. And instead of it catapulting Chad's career into military technology, it did that for hers. Now she's a VP at the company Chad used to work for. As far as Jun can tell, he and Maxine have never met.

I run to the living room. Instead of the statuette, in its place is a set of cool Japanese whiskey glasses.

"That's why he was asking about the award," I gasp.

There's an iMessage tone as we're talking, and I see it's from Ciara. "Jun's parents died in car accident. Flying to Vancouver tonight."

I tell him about the message. "Ah, you called Ciara for help. That's good. How are you coping?"

"Surprisingly better than if I had to deal with Maxine as well. I'm just glad she'll be a non-memory in a while. I have Chad to thank for that, but I don't know that I'll ever say it to his face."

"I know what you mean."

"I gotta run. Literally. Liya's up. We run along the waterfront."

"Call if you need to talk," I urge him.

"Will do."

I barge into Chad's office and kiss him deeply, passionately, appreciatively. We'll be okay.

The End

Acknowledgments

To my editor and publisher, Elizabeth Riley, thank you for being the one to say "yes" to my first novel and inspiring such a fitting title. Calling my manuscript "exceptionally well-written and very clean" gave me such a writer high – who knew that your words would be printed and framed as encouragement to keep writing.

Thank you to Connie Choi and Keika Lee for being my cheerleaders through writing the manuscript. Your sweet messages, reactions to each chapter, and keeping up in real time were such a blessing in motivating me to get it done – and here we are with the final product.

To Gurita, Orlie, Anna, Tiffany – thank you for also being my literary guinea pigs, lovingly catching the typos.

To Sydnia, for being Ciara-like in that I would want you in my return to the past.

To Nattasha, for inspiring it all.

To my Dad – I love you. Sorry you don't feature as much as Mom in this one. Thanks for being my Dad.

And most of all, to my little family – my husband and my two boys, I love you to the moon and back and beyond.

About the Author

Photography: Alice Xue
Makeup: Rhia Amio
Hair: Hollie Kendall
Courtesy of Sticky Brain Studios

Identifying as Canadian-South African-Chinese-American, Deborah Chantson is the Writer/Narrative Designer on the video game, *Rooster*, and the newest unannounced title at Sticky Brain Studios. Her career in games and television spans over 17 years, specializing in preschool and educational projects. She was also a Community Manager for 9 years. Deborah has written for several games in development, blogs for Sony PlayStation, and several featured blogs on GameDeveloper. com. She is a Writers Guild of Canada member and a Certified Accessible Player Experiences® Practitioner. She lives with her husband and their two boys near Vancouver, Canada. She originally wrote the manuscript for *Past Perfect Vacation* in three months.